NIBIRU RISING

Planet X

Ken Womelsdorf

Order this book online at www.trafford.com
or email orders@trafford.com

Most Trafford titles are also available at major online book retailers.

Printed in the United States of America.

ISBN: 978-1-4269-8242-2 (sc)
ISBN: 978-1-4269-8243-9 (hc)
ISBN: 978-1-4269-8244-6 (e)

Library of Congress Control Number: 2011913068

Trafford rev. 07/27/2011

 www.trafford.com

North America & international
toll-free: 1 888 232 4444 (USA & Canada)
phone: 250 383 6864 ♦ fax: 812 355 4082

PROLOGUE

Katie Curic sat facing the cameras smiling broadly, "Thank you for joining us this evening. We all live our daily lives in relative security relying on our government and local authorities to keep us safe from harm. We have heroic fire departments that come to our rescue when needed, and a broad and extensive medical profession that steps into our lives in times of stress to relieve our pain and make us whole. Tornado and tsunami warning systems around the world tell us when to take shelter and move out of harm's way."

She smiled broadly then wrinkled her brow, "You get the picture, but what happens when a threat, greater than the sum of all those protective measures, enters the world we live in?

Dr. Ian MacGown's latest book is non-fiction, but reads like science fiction in portraying just such a threat.

*

Katie reached over and gently touched the wrist of her guest, "Welcome to Sixty Minutes Dr. MacGown, it's a pleasure to have you here."

"Thank you Katie, it's a pleasure to be here among friends."

Katie laughed, "I don't understand, you must have many friends."

"Yes, I do, but not as many as I used to, not since my last book came out."

"You mean "Nibiru Rising," that's why Sixty Minutes asked you to join us this evening. You said in your book that our Earth is going to be hit by another planet," Katie laughed, "you can understand that might make you a little less popular than you were before."

She paused and pursed her lips, "Do you feel that may have been the reason you were recently skipped over for Chairman of the Department of History at Northwestern University."

Dr. MacGown grimaced at the quick change of subject, "The University and I had more differences than my book. Unfortunately academia is uncomfortable with people who stray too far off the beaten path."

"If I may elaborate, historians like me in attempting to study the past, has been focused on the Middle-East and particularly Egypt. However, that body of academia, which we refer to as Egyptologists, have had their heads buried in the sand; if you'll pardon the pun. For instance they refuse to consider the possibility that some alien presence at some time in history may have been a factor in the development of civilization as we know it today; and have steadfastly ignored any attempts to delve into and develop information at their disposal, that could enlighten us in what could be an important area of study. That being said, there is information scattered around the country of Egypt on walls of old temples and steles that may be very important not only for what it tells us about the past, but what it may have to tell us about our future."

"Pardon me for interrupting Doctor, but what does that have to do with your book?"

Dr.MacGown looked intently at Katie before answering, "It may well be that there is more information waiting to be discovered and understood that could help us through the very difficult situation I described in my book. My book is derived from assimilating and understanding that kind of information left by the ancients in a variety of forms, much of which is located in Egypt."

Katie smiled touching him again on the wrist regaining control of the interview, "Let's get back to the book and its message. Many are beginning to call you the ultimate Dooms Day Prophet in the sense that you are effectively declaring the end of the world. What do you say to that?"

"I would say you have to study your history books. I'm small potatoes compared to a much more famous man. Sir Isaac Newton, one of the world's greatest scientists calculated the end of times as 2060AD. He believed Armageddon would come at that time, but kept the papers explaining his ideas in hiding, and asked that they not be read until the time of his death. Pertinent to our discussion is the fact that he derived his information from texts he found in the Bible, texts which he thought had encoded information in them. I don't pretend to be on a par with Sir Isaac, but believe there is important information encoded in many of the ancient texts that exist in the middle-east. My book simply delves into that kind of information and offers some uncomfortable conclusions."

Katie sat back away from Dr. MacGown as if the distance would make his suggestions less real, "Are you saying you agree with Isaac Newton and the end of the world is coming in 2060. That's only forty-one years from now.

"That's not what I meant. I only meant to use the analogy of encoded information existing in old, ancient documents."

"Katie, recently many new authors, who have not built a career or reputation in academia, but have ventured out into a new world of research and writing, have spent long hours reading and deciphering much of the old literature that exists, particularly from the middle-east. They're beginning to offer different conclusions about what those old documents really say, not necessarily what the establishment has been telling us for many years. They're beginning to put meaning to important evidence left by the ancients."

"Are you one of those writers Dr. MacGown? Is that what you're here to tell us?"

"Well yes, that and actually a little more."

"What about this planet you say is coming our way? What can you tell us about it? Do you think it may actually hit us?

"It's been called Planet-X and has been much discussed on the internet among other places, and is also identified in much of the ancient literature; and yes, as I said in my book, I believe it may actually hit us."

"Let's cut to the nub of it Dr. MacGown, what is your estimate for the date this awful event you say in your book is going to happen? Is it 2060 like Sir Isaac Newton predicted? I have to be honest with you and say that's why we all wanted you on the show, to tell us if and when this awful thing may actually happen"

"That's the point Katie, I don't have an exact date, but need help in finding one. That's why I agreed to your interview, I thought..."

Katie raised her eyebrows and sat up straight, "I'm so sorry, but we're out of time. She reached over touching him on the wrist as she had when the interview began, "I'm sorry Dr. MacGown, but we need to take a commercial break now, thank you so much for being on our show."

Chapter 1: Old Friends

Dateline 2019

Ian MacGown stood outside of the entrance of his favorite restaurant studying the tree lined street with its old fashioned street lights and quaint little shops scattered randomly about like old memories. He remembered his high school days when he bussed at The Montgomery Inn on weekend days trying to make enough money to pay for gas for the old jalopy he shared with his best friend and Soccer adversary, Bob Schmidt. Bob called a week ago when he heard Ian was going to be in Cincinnati.

Ian thought to himself, "How odd that Schmidt would call when, he had been thinking of calling him. It was an unusual circumstance that, if he got lucky could pay big dividends. Smitty was a crafty guy, however, and it would be a mistake to sell him short in any kind of negotiation."

His thoughts ironically went back again to the old jalopy. Here he was worrying about a negotiation with an old buddy and he's thinking about something that happened in high school, "I really wasn't fair, we owned equal shares in that old jalopy, but I drove it seventy percent of the time. I hope Smitty doesn't hold a grudge."

"Hey you, what are you doing hanging around my favorite restaurant? Causing trouble?" The familiar voice came from behind him, and Ian without turning around shouted back, "It's my favorite restaurant not yours, everyone knows that."

Large powerful arms wrapped around him lifting his six foot three frame easily off the ground.

"Yeah, but I can still have lunch here if I want to." Ian endured the taunt and several hard shakings to his dangling body, "Just like high school," he thought, "the guy will never change, he's just a big kid."

"Smitty, how the hell are you?" He asked shaking himself loose from Schmidt's grip.

"How'd you know it was me?" Schmidt asked with presumed innocence.

"Well it wasn't easy, but the only other person who bear hugs me like that is back in Chicago, and she has a much softer touch."

"It's great to see you Ian, it's been a long time, at least three years," Schmidt said emphatically.

"It's great to see you, you old dog, although I never really did like you. How could I like anyone who was always standing between me and the goal every time I had a decent shot."

"You probably would have missed anyway. The fact that you made All City first team was a fluke, just like me only making second team was unfair."

"You are one crazy son of a gun but it doesn't matter we were still the two best soccer players in the city, right?" Ian said with a huge grin, "Come on Smitty, I'm buying at your favorite restaurant."

Ian pulled open the large oaken door with a huge brass handle that had suffered from the ravages of both weather and age. As you enter the Montgomery Inn sports memorabilia including both professional and college teams that played in the Cincinnati area fill the walls around a large impressive bar which stretches out into the foyer. You are initially left with the impression you may have missed the entrance to the restaurant until the hustle and bustle of clanging trays and dishes sing out from an adjacent room carrying the enticing aroma of ribs and a pungent sauce.

Ian noting the absence of soccer teams in any of the memorabilia looked around and in a loud voice directed to Schmidt and the bartender quipped, "I guess they haven't gotten around to soccer yet. I don't see my number anywhere Smitty. Do you see yours?"

The bartender offered a thin smile, continued wiping glasses and waved Ian down a hallway to his right, "You might want to check in the John."

"They will if Cincy ever gets a pro team," Smitty joined in half heartedly. He seemed more interested in where they should sit than pursuing the memorabilia. "Let's sit over here it's a little more private. We've got a few things to talk about Ian." Smitty pointed to a table in a corner of the bar.

Ian slumped rather than sat in a chair that appeared to have been designed to be uncomfortable, "What's up Smitty?" He asked brusquely, "What do we need privacy for? Are we going to have a beer before you start to grill me?"

"Who said I was going to grill you? Of course you can have a beer. I could probably do a better job of grilling you, if that was my intention, if you had several beers."

Schmidt's banter didn't in any way disguise his intentions, so Ian just sat back and waited. Schmidt was on cue and offered a sly grin, "Come on Ian you know who I work for, besides I saw you on "Sixty Minutes" with your dooms day prophecy. What's that all about?"

"It wasn't a dooms day anything and I'm not talking until I get my beer, they simply interviewed me about some of the books I've written and I answered candidly."

"And who do you work for Smitty? I'm not sure I know?" Ian was ready to dodge anything Schmidt had in mind, but prepared to keep the conversation open.

"I think you know damn well that I work for Senator Rosenthal. He's the guy heading up a commission to investigate "The occurrence of celestial bodies impacting Earth," that must sound pretty cool for a guy like you Ian?" Schmidt said probing for a response that would allow him to make a point.

Ian sat unresponsive and grinning at Schmidt all the while he continued his probe. Schmidt recognized where the conversation was going, shook his head, grinned back at Ian and said, "Rosenthal saw you on television and, when he found out you and I knew each other, asked if I would extend an invitation to you to be questioned by his commission. It would be an honor for you," Schmidt said emphatically not allowing any room for a retort before making his point.

"Whatever happened to foreplay Smitty?" Ian said dryly, "We've been here less than two minutes, I still don't have my beer and you have me in front of some commission just because I was on television. I thought you were a guy who basically played defense. We should put a sign on you warning people about the change, and besides, I didn't know that," Ian hesitated then continued reflecting inwardly as he spoke, "I didn't know you worked for Rosenthal."

Schmidt started to answer than just sat back grinning and listened as his old friend, who he knew basically played offensive, continued his line of thought. "Rosenthal wrote to me a few weeks ago. I just never got around to answering him. Am I being subpoenaed? Do you guys have that kind of clout?"

"No, no, nothing, like that Ian. This commission is run as a closed session. The Senator seems to think your input could be important." Schmidt wriggled in his chair, trying to keep a friend calm that he remembered could be volatile in his responses, "Like I said, I think this would be an honor for you," Schmidt repeated, thinking as he spoke, "That's dumb, he hates flattery." He sat up straight in his chair trying to be more assertive and positive, "I think they, the commission, believe you may be able to help them in offering some definition to a very unwieldy problem they're dealing with."

"Is that why I got fired?" Because someone thought my input might be important?" Ian fired back cynically and out of context.

Schmidt felt like he was about to lose control of the conversation and said softly and forgiving as though he had been involved in the firing, "I didn't know you had been fired. What's that got to do with this?" Schmidt said very carefully not wanting to ignite whatever fire might be burning underneath Ian's terse response.

"Well to be honest it's more like I quit," Ian retorted ignoring the lack of continuity in his thinking, "Those old farts in the academic world don't want independent points of view wandering around in their hallways, and certainly not in the media."

Schmidt's brow wrinkled and he asked with honest concern, "Are you all right Ian? I mean money wise. When did you lose your…, quit being a professor?" He wasn't doing a very good job of handling this negotiation and he was beginning to realize it.

Ian in turn picked up on Schmidt's concern and suddenly became more magnanimous. He had his own vested interest in the conversation and didn't want to over play his hand and scare away the opportunity with the commission.

"Hey don't worry about me. I've got royalty checks piling up in a drawer. In fact I'm going to pay for lunch. Are you ready to order? Isn't that why we came here?"

Schmidt fell back in his chair a little more relaxed and grinned at his old friend thinking to himself that he had come on too strongly after three years apart, in what was a more sensitive area than he realized, and tried a more friendly approach. "Yeah, I'm going to have the ribs. It's the only intelligent thing to do in a place like this."

Ian turned to the waiter at the bar and signaled they were ready and offered a huge smile, "Let's have the beer we should have had before we started this damn conversation."

Schmidt nodded yes to the beer and the ribs to the waiter, who was standing ready with a small pad no bigger than his hand and thought sarcastically to himself, "I hope he doesn't forget such a large order. It's a good thing he has that pad."

He looked up to see Ian staring intently at him.

Schmidt acknowledged the stare with a smile, remained relaxed and confident, and attempted to restart their conversation at a different level, "You know we must be a little bit crazy. We haven't seen each other for three years and I drag you into a conversation about this damn commission," Schmidt looked genuinely apologetic.

"How are your kids dealing with your split from Sarah?" Schmidt continued, incongruously, trying to show honest concern.

Ian picked up on the shift in conversation, sat back in his chair and with a slight shake of his head replied, "Not good, at least not for me. They both think their father is an awful kook who let their mother down. Neither one is at all comfortable with the books I write or my willingness to express my particular point of view to the world, let alone to their mother. On the bright side," he sat up briskly in his chair to continue, "they're both doing very well and Julie is planning to get married as soon as she graduates this fall. I'm not sure if you were aware but Scotty has been part of an astronaut program with NASA for the last two years," Ian paused a little awkwardly for no apparent reason, "I'm not sure how I feel about that but I guess it'll be okay."

"What's your concern, that's a pretty prestigious program?" Schmidt gave a shrug showing a positive response to what he knew of the program.

"I guess I'm just struggling trying to figure out how it factors in with my wild ideas and our relationship."

Schmidt tried to help, "Don't sweat it, one of my guys joined the Marines right out of high school. He's in some sort of officers training group and doing well, but I had presumed he would have done the college bit first."

Schmidt knew the conversation was drifting, but couldn't shake loose from family, "How about your folks Ian, how are they doing? Did your Dad handle the situation with his prostate okay?"

Ian answered within the boundaries of the conversation that Schmidt had established, but he was obviously distracted, "He's fine. He came through the whole thing with flying colors. Mom's fine too. They're both a lot happier with that behind them. What about you Smitty? How is everyone?" Ian asked politely.

Schmidt replied in turn on his family fortunes, "Nothing much has changed. I'm still married to the same old gal with the same old kids all doing well even the guy in the marines." Schmidt couldn't help but think to himself, "I'm losing him."

The conversation nonetheless continued back to family and the good old times carefully avoiding the subject of the commission and Ian's potential role in meeting with them.

Then Schmidt without any transition abruptly came back to the real subject at hand. He looked squarely at Ian, "Ian, the success or failure of this commission could have very long term ramifications for a lot of people, for all of us," he added emphatically, "for our kids, yours and mine."

He started to continue then looked at his watch, jumped up and said, "Oops I haven't been watching my time." He extended his hand towards Ian's grasping it firmly, "Ian, you have to meet with this commission! It could be very important. Please think about it. I have your number in Chicago, if we have to talk some more, I'll call you Monday, okay? Think about it please." He started to leave then looked quizzically at Ian, "Who does the bear hugs in Chicago you mentioned? Anything I need to know?"

Ian grinned, "She goes with me everywhere I go, that might be important if I'm going to meet with your commission."

Schmidt smiled knowingly, released his grip on Ian and darted toward the door waving his right hand over his head without looking back.

Ian sat forward and picked up the bill that sat on Schmidt's side of the table. He motioned to the waiter he was ready to pay and broke into a grin. He couldn't wait to get back to Chicago and tell Sadie the good news. They wanted him to meet with the commission, he would definitely go. They would both go. It's what they both wanted.

As Schmidt moved to the large oaken door he thought to himself. "That was easier than I thought it would be." Then he saw Ian's reflection in one of the glass memorabilia cases. Ian was smiling from ear to ear.

Chapter 2: Sadie

Ian watched the oncoming traffic as his father darted the Chevy into the inside lane of the bridge spanning across the Ohio River from Cincinnati to Covington in Kentucky. The traffic on US-75 is competitive and unforgiving; and Ian would have preferred to have taken a limo to the airport rather than endure the traffic with his father at the wheel and his mother in the back seat. His mother insisted they drive him since they hadn't seen that much of him. Beside that she didn't understand why he had spent all afternoon with Bob Schmidt. Why couldn't Bob have just come to the house for lunch like he used to? Ian could hear the wheels spinning in her head as they sped up Dead Man's Hill on the Kentucky side of the river.

"I'll never understand why they put the Cincinnati Airport in Kentucky," he thought to himself.

"Do you still see Sarah? Do you ever talk to each other?" a somewhat hostile inquiry came from the back seat.

"No Mom, it's difficult with her in California and me in Chicago. Besides she doesn't seem to like me anymore. Not since my last book came out," Ian said a little on the defensive and trying to inject humor into a subject he would have rather avoided.

"I didn't like your book either, and I didn't think much of your interview on television," came, the terse reply, her tone growing more hostile.

"Why do family meetings always end like this? Ian thought to himself, "Why now?"

He took the plunge anyway, "That's why we split Mom because she couldn't get comfortable with who I am and what I believe," he tried to continue but she interrupted.

"Who is that woman who answers your phone sometimes?" She persisted she was not going to leave any stone unturned.

"My housekeeper," Ian replied sarcastically.

The inquiry continued with Mom probing endlessly and Ian dodging every thrust until Mr. MacGown, who had remained silent for the whole trip announced, "We're here. Do you want me to park or should we just let you out?" knowing full well what the best answer was for his son in light of the conversation with his mother.

"No, no don't park. Just let me out at the Delta Terminal. I'll be okay," Ian ran for the escape hatch before his mother could argue the point. He thought to himself, "I'll be sixty-five and they'll still be driving me to the airport, chewing me out all the way there."

With the car parked at the curb Ian's Mom was out of the back seat giving him a hug, "Please do a better job of calling, not just on my birthday and mother's day."

"I will, I promise. I'm sorry, but I really have been busy. I'll do a better job of calling," he assured her as she slipped into the front seat of the car.

She held the car door slightly ajar, looked out at him, wrinkled her brow and said wisely, "You don't believe all that stuff you said on TV do you?"

Ian hesitated, than replied with a knowing smile, "No Mom, not all of it." Then his smile broadened and he winked at her, "Maybe some of it. See you guys. Thanks for driving me."

The car door closed and after a brief pause pulled out into an oncoming line of traffic headed for the terminal exit.

Guilt swept over him as they drove away. He knew with all that was waiting for him it was more likely things were going to get worse, as his books implied, before they got better; and he had avoided saying anything about it to them.

"Maybe not in their lifetime," he thought to himself, "Some things are better left unsaid."

He walked into the terminal thinking again of Sadie and what they had to.

*

Ian looked down from his Delta flight to the shimmering, sprawling lights of Chicago, which stretched endlessly to the horizon and faded into the glare of Sunday's sinking sun. Ian caught up in the broad expanse of the Chicago skyline drifted into a reverie of thought.

"After the economic downturn in the early part of the century things returned to an expansion mode that looked like it would never end, just like it looked before the downturn," He thought to himself. "But this expansion is pure vanilla with no driving force behind it. It's only a simple accommodation to a burgeoning population, guess we'll never learn," he muttered aloud, "At any rate it allowed him and Sadie to buy a nice downtown condo near the lake that was convenient for both of them."

"The economic rebirth, which hit early in 2015, was tied directly to the Western world coming to peaceful terms with the middle-eastern countries. It had benefits for writers like him in the last four years in that it allowed them to revisit many of the old ruins of civilizations lost in antiquity, and sift through secrets written on old temple walls, steles and old clay cylinders.

All except Egypt, they had tightened up more than ever to the western world when it came to research of historical sites. "Egypt, that's where we need to go, I wonder if they'll allow us access?"

His musing was interrupted by the address system imploring the passengers to, "Please fasten your seat belts and bring your seatbacks and trays into a full upright position. The plane will be landing in approximately ten minutes."

*

Ian nudged past two people at the baggage turnstile to grab a bag that was almost past him. "This airport has to change. Those damn terrorist have certainly left their mark on us," he thought to himself. "I remember when I could take an overnight trip and not have to check one silly bag."

He continued to think about how things had changed, "After the initial terrorist attacks the demand for resources, particularly oil exploded. The ultimate result was a peculiar stagnation that set in on economies around the world. Businesses couldn't get what they needed to expand their operations and services, so they just sort of stopped in their tracks offering the same old stuff with less and less quality."

"Whoa Ian," he pulled himself up short, "you're rambling all over the place. Even I don't know what your point is or where you're going." He smiled broadly at this interplay of words and humor with himself.

As he walked to the exit he stopped short and mused out loud, "There are too many of us. If they only knew what danger they're in. What a mess!"

A young girl, who had been walking on his heels, bumped into him after his abrupt stop, brushed by him and shouted back over her shoulder, "Oh, excuse me sir."

The "sir" had an inflection he wasn't sure of and didn't like, "Sir," he said aloud. "Sir, hell I'm only forty-five not sixty-five. That young chick has no idea how dependent she may be on this old body." Then he shook his head, picked up his pace and moved rapidly towards the exit and parking garage.

"I've got to see Sadie. I wonder if she's home," He mumbled to himself still deep in thought.

*

"Sadie, you home? I'm home, "Ian called out as he entered their downtown Chicago condo.

"Yes dear, yes I'm home. Don't shout please. Did you see your folks? Are they okay?" Sadie asked in staccato fashion firing her questions like bullets.

"Folks are okay, they asked me to say hello to my favorite girl."

"I better be your favorite girl and there better not be too many other candidates," Sadie paused and straightened up taut in front of Ian. "Did you get a chance to see Schmidt? Did you talk to him? Does he know about us?" She asked a little apprehensively.

"No, no my love he does not, but..."

Sadie interrupted, "Are we going to get a chance to talk to the senator?"

Ian replied, "Whoa! Hang on just a second, too many questions all at once." He took her by the shoulders and looked into her eyes with a gentle smile," Schmidt's going to check and give me a call on Monday. It looks promising."

"Did he say anything else?" She was becoming a little demanding.

"Yes, he did."

"What?" Sadie barked at him.

"He said, if it does work out, I would not be allowed to bring any pretty, mid-eastern women with me."

Dr. Sadie Haddad smiled demurely, "But you need me."

"I know," he grinned, "but not just for that," he said and pulled her towards the bedroom.

"No, no," she giggled, "I'm a complete package, it's all or nothing."

Ian grinned, "You know I wouldn't go without you."

She abruptly pulled away from him, "Ian I saw two of those men yesterday across the street, just standing there." Her concern written across her face made it apparent she was no longer kidding.

Ian reflected her concern, "How do you…"

"I know," She said cutting him off.

"Okay, I hear you. I believe you, but we can't do anything about it right now. You've got to stop fretting about something that may be nothing at all; and we've given this plenty of conversation. Come on give me a smile and a kiss."

He nudged her once again towards the bed room.

*

It was morning and bright sunlight, unusual for Chicago filled their condo. Ian gently opened the bedroom door as he always did trying not to waken Sadie, then he thought to himself, "Why?" He wanted her awake.

"Sadie, Sadie," He called from the doorway increasing his volume in direct proportion to her lack of response. "Come on get up, we're on."

"On what," She asked with eyes still closed.

"Do you want to go to Washington with me or not?" He asked dryly.

"Oh yes, yes," She quickly sat up in bed, "that's great. This is important Ian." Her response was affected, intended to be grave, but excited, than her humor came back to her as she grinned at him, "Are you going like that?"

Ian stood in the doorway in his skivvies and a cup of coffee in his hand leaning on the doorknob. He was a solidly built man of Scottish heritage and looked like those old Scots who tossed the Caber. Whenever his Scottishness, as he called it came up, it was important to him to point out that MacGown was Scottish not Irish. "Look it up," he would say.

Sadie didn't wait for an answer but grinned at him, "Do we have to go right now? Do we have time for…?"

Ian sat the coffee down and stomped toward her, "Come on you little vixen get out of bed, yes, we do have to go right now. We've got someone's attention. Smitty called early this morning while you were sleeping. Get this," he emphasized, "he's wiring tickets for both of us for pickup at O'Hare. They want us to leave today for a meeting with Senator Rosenthal in the morning then on to the Commission. Better get dressed we don't have a lot of time."

CHAPTER 3: OFF TO WASHINGTON

It was early Monday afternoon and O'Hare Airport was packed. Ian walked briskly along deep in thought, Sadie at his side. He thought to himself, "Smitty must have gone right back to Washington on Saturday to see Rosenthal."

"Ian, be careful," Sadie grabbed his arm to steady the luggage he was pulling, that was weaving erratically.

"I was just thinking," his only explanation for the wandering bag, "Smitty must have hustled back to Washington, right after our conversation, and he left in a hurry on Saturday. He told me earlier he intended to be in Cincy until the middle of the week."

Sadie gave him a worried glance maintaining her focus on the errant bag, "Well, that's good isn't it, I mean good for us, Right?"

"Yeah, someone is definitely showing us some interest, and it can't just be Smitty. He doesn't have that much clout," He added distractedly, "let's hope they listen."

As they approached the Delta ticket counter a young man stepped up to Ian touching him on the arm to get his attention. Ian drew back unsure of the approach. There were still religious groups that operated in airports that would try to detain you, although the airport had put a stop to the practice years ago; and there were also Sadie's phantom strangers that could prove to be real.

"What?" Ian demanded abruptly.

"Dr. MacGown? The young man asked politely.

Ian nodded, "Yes," and accepted an oversize envelope thrust into his hand.

"These tickets are for you sir. They're From Mr. Schmidt," The young man explained and was gone as quickly as he had appeared.

Ian mused aloud looking quizzically at Sadie, "How the hell did he do that?" referring to Schmidt, then he shook his head and said, "It doesn't matter, let's go." He took off toward the Delta Concourse.

Sadie never smiled, frowned or said a word. Just shook her head slightly and fell in beside him.

*

The plane ride to Reagan International Airport was quiet with Sadie working crossword puzzles as a distraction to her dislike of flying. She wasn't fearful. She just didn't like flying. It was boring and a great waste of her time.

Ian kept thumbing through notes in his laptop. He had presentation material in his suitcase, but reviewing notes would keep him fresh. The familiar "fasten your seat belts" brought him back from the notes to Sadie's side. "Get it all done?" he asked, "Do you need my help?"

"It's done the minute we land," she smirked, "whether I finish it or not, it has served its purpose. No I don't need your help. Not on this, maybe later," She grinned at him.

"Come my lovely, there is work to be done. Later may be quite a while later." Ian took her by the arm and nudged her toward the exit of the plane.

"Good pilot," Ian thought to himself, "the plane landed without a bounce, a lot different from some of his trips around the world, particularly the middle-east."

Sadie interrupted his thinking, "Ian, do you think we brought enough clothes?"

"I have no idea, and Schmidt probably didn't know what direction to give us. In fact, I doubt if this commission knows at this point how long they may want us involved. Don't worry about it. We'll buy clothes if we run out." He paused and added as an afterthought, "Besides there's always the launder-mat or the wash tubs in the basement of the hotel."

Ian didn't wait for a reply but, walked quickly in the direction of the baggage pickup area.

"You're not funny Ian, you had better have your wallet ready, if we stay longer than two or three days," Sadie called after him following a few steps behind him.

"You know the best thing, that could happen to us, would be if they kept us here for a week to listen to what we have to say; and what we feel needs to be done," Ian said very soberly.

"Ian, look," Sadie stopped walking and put her hand on his wrist, "That man over there has our bags and a sign with your name on it. Your friend Schmidt is pulling out all the stops for us."

Ian waved to the man, who approached with a smile and said," I have a car outside for you and your lady Dr. MacGown. Please come with me, your bags will be taken care of."

They followed him outside to a waiting stretch limo. He politely held the door for them and with a slight bow closed the door behind them.

"Hell, we could be being kidnapped for all we know about this. We didn't ask for credentials or anything," Ian grinned at Sadie.

"Who would want to kidnap us?" She asked grinning back at him.

"How about your phantom friends who stand outside of our condo?" he asked rhetorically.

Sadie leaned forward and took a hard look at the driver through the glass panel dividing them from the front seat of the limo, then leaned back and with a glare at Ian, snapped, "Stop it Ian. They could be real. Talk to him. Ask him where he's going. The sheet with the tickets said we're staying at the Hyatt."

She nodded in the direction of the driver as she spitted out directions to Ian in her staccato fashion. A pattern of speech she adopted when she was nervous about something.

Ian leaned forward, pushed the glass panel between them and the driver to one side and asked loudly, "What's our destination?"

"Where to?" the driver replied in a heavy mid-eastern accent that was barely understandable.

Ian fell back against the seat, grinned at Sadie and said. "You tell him."

Sadie leaned forward and snapped, "Hyatt Regency"

"Where to?" the same heavy accent replied.

Ian broke up in laughter.

Sadie repeated Hyatt Regency to the driver again in what seemed like a different language to Ian. Sadie knew so many different languages. Her tone was not polite. "But the Hyatt Regency is the Hyatt Regency in any language," he thought to himself with the same self assured grin he had started with.

A sharp look from Sadie spoiled the grin and the driver pulled away without another word.

Sadie then slid over on the seat closer to Ian and snuggled up next to him. "Ian I'm afraid. Who are those men?"

Ian pulled back a little impatiently, "Sadie, we have got to focus. We can't be distracted by shadows."

"They are not shadows," Sadie insisted, "You saw them."

"I know, I know, we'll have to deal with it at the appropriate time."

The rest of the drive to the hotel was quiet.

It was after six in the evening when the limo pulled up in front of the Hyatt Regency hotel. Ian gave the driver a nice tip, although he wasn't sure who he was tipping, the limo company employee or the government, and grabbed both his and Sadie's bags. He knew from his travels that Hyatt hotels had instituted express check-in kiosks and there would be no need for a bellman. Never the less an older, grizzly looking man ran up to him ready to take the bags.

"Yer all checked in. There's a message for you at the desk," the grizzled one sang out in a raspy voice.

"Why am I not surprised at that voice?" Ian thought to himself, than called to Sadie, who had moved out of his way as he grappled with the bags from the limo, "Sadie, can you get that message please?"

There was a brief pause and Sadie called back to him. "Sorry, the message must be received only by Dr. MacGown, who must have picture identification."

Ian successfully retrieved the message and read it aloud to Sadie, "Bob says he'll pick us up at 9:00 sharp in the morning. We're meeting alone with Senator Rosenthal." He added his own thought, "Apparently, we are to be vetted by the senator before we get in front of the commission." Then after a brief pause, lost in his thoughts, he added, "That's great we can have a nice quiet evening to collect ourselves."

"Good," Sadie volunteered enthusiastically, "Let's start that nice quiet evening with something to eat, I'm hungry. It looks like there's a nice restaurant in the hotel. We can make a quick check on the room, have our dinner, and then maybe take a walk."

"That sounds good to me," Ian nodded affirmatively.

Dinner was quiet as advertised at Hyatt's American Grille. "Upscale, but not posh or pretentious," Sadie thought to herself, "Besides, they weren't dressed for much else."

"Come on Sweetheart," Ian said in his best Humphrey Bogart imitation, "Let's go, it's time for a walk."

"I don't think that was Bogart, who said Sweetheart," She said as she got up and pushed her chair back to the table.

"Who did you think it was Sweetheart?" Ian continued relentlessly.

"I don't know, but it wasn't Bogart," She countered, "And that was not a very good imitation. I hope you do better tomorrow."

He ignored the reference to the morning meeting, "How would you know about old Humphrey? Your mom was too young to know who he was, how could you know?"

"I like old movies, and old guys, lucky for you. Are you taking me for a walk, or are we going to stand here and argue?" She said taking his arm and pulling him towards the door of the hotel.

The banter continued as they walked to their right from the hotel towards the capitol building which was only a few blocks away from the hotel.

Ian didn't see the two men standing a few steps down the street from them until the larger of the two ran and hit him broadside, while the other smaller man grabbed Sadie around her shoulders from the back pinning her arms to her side. The first man miscalculated Ian's size and strength and bounced back from him, then swung at him with something Ian couldn't see, but managed to duck away from. He rose back up and dropped the man in his tracks with one punch, then spun around to help Sadie, who was screaming at the top of her lungs.

Sadie, who was almost as big as the man, who was pinning her arms, bent strongly forward with the assailant draped over her back. Her right foot kicked deftly backwards and upwards like it had a homing device attached to it into an exposed groin area as the man struggled for balance. A heavy groan announced the arrival of Sadie's foot and the assailant's arrival on one knee on the ground, vulnerable to Sadie's follow-up kick to the middle of his chest.

The first man ran past Ian leaving the second man withering in pain on the ground, as two more men moved towards them from a van parked across the street.

"Sadie run, inside," Ian pulled her back to the entrance of the hotel as the sound of a siren split the silence that ensued after the scuffle. All four men with two of them carrying the injured man ran, jumped into the van and with tires screaming sped away.

Miraculously, but late, a police car appeared, tires echoing the scream of the van's tires as it lurched to a stop in front of Ian and Sadie. "Are you all right? Did they hurt you?" A tall, burly looking policeman asked as he exited the patrol car.

"I'm okay, you okay Sadie?" Ian asked gently holding her against his chest.

"Yes!" came the exasperated reply, "Who were those men?" She demanded.

The policeman reached forward toward Sadie in an attempt to brush her back off, immediately thought better of it and stepped back.

"We're sorry madam, we don't know, they've been sitting there all day. We moved them three different times since it's a no parking zone. One of Senator Rosenthal's men came by earlier and noticed them, and asked us to keep an eye on them, but we had another call. Are you sure you're alright?" He asked again nervously entwining his fingers together as he talked.

"It must have been Schmidt," Ian interjected, "Was he a big guy?" Ian started to ask then raised his hand to wave off anything further by the policeman. "We're fine," Ian said emphatically.

"Are you sure? Do you want us to call it in and ask the night shift to keep an eye out for you? We're off in about an hour," The policeman asked looking for further assurance or direction.

"Thanks officer, I think we're okay for now, you okay Sadie?" Ian's hesitant speech showed he was not quite sure how she felt.

After a pause long enough to taunt both Ian and the officer she said somewhat sullenly, "Yes, I'm okay, can we go now?"

"Yes madam, I'm sorry we weren't faster to the scene," the policeman said.

"It's okay," Ian said pulling Sadie towards the hotel entrance.

The policeman took one last shot at it, "Did you get a good look at them?"

"They looked like mid-easterners all wearing black jump suits," Ian said over his shoulder disappearing into the lobby of the hotel.

Sadie was exasperated, "Why did you let the police go? We apparently need their help. Who were those men? Do you believe me now? Why are we being followed and attacked? How do they always know where we are?" She looked at him despairingly.

"I don't know, I just don't know," Ian said shaking his head, "Maybe we'll find out tomorrow. Come on it's getting late. We need to get some rest."

CHAPTER 4: THE VETTING

Bob Schmidt pulled out of the driveway of a modest home in Derwood, Maryland and headed for the Metro Red line that would take him to downtown Washington to pick up an old friend from his high school soccer days. He smiled at the thought that he could never think of Ian without remembering him as a rival in soccer, although Ian had attained so much other notoriety recently based on some very unorthodox views about the future. Although, they played for different schools he had gotten to know Ian very well. He was an excellent athlete and a regular guy, but was considered by most to be somewhat of an egghead who would rather talk about Star Wars then the Cincinnati Reds.

Schmidt slipped into a parking spot at the Metro station, grabbed his brief case and ran for the train that he could hear in the distance clattering down the tracks. His timing was perfect as he glided through the open doors of the train and slid easily into an open seat. "This is going to be an interesting day," he thought to himself.

"Did you read this?" The man in the seat next to him announced himself to Schimdt by pointing to a small article in the morning paper. "Two tourists got roughed up out in front of the Hyatt Regency. This town is getting worse every day. I stayed there when I first moved to town," His seatmate continued without interruption.

Without realizing what he was doing Schmidt grabbed the paper from his train mate, "Anybody hurt?" There was urgency in his voice, "Who were they?"

"Nah, it says here the man was a pretty big guy and gave them a run for their money, kind of like you." The train mate made a though review of Schmidt's size and girth. "I still don't like to read stuff like that," he said taking the paper back more politely than Schmidt had taken it from him and continued to read his paper.

Schmidt spent the rest of the train ride trying to get his thoughts together. Rosenthal had asked him if he thought there might be any reason for concern about Ian and his lady friend. Schmidt assured him Ian could take care of himself and did nothing more about it except to ask the local police to keep an eye on a funny looking van hanging around the Hyatt. Then it hit him, "What if that damn, van was the problem? Apparently I was right though," he thought to himself, "Ian can be pretty tough for an egghead according to the paper."

The train lurched to a halt at Schmidt's stop and he bounded out the car breaking into a run as he exited to the street. It was a short distance to the Hyatt and he pulled up short from his run as the Hyatt came into view. Ian was standing at the entrance giving him a high five. Schmidt was close enough to see that he was smiling broadly.

Ian called out loudly enough to bridge the distance between them, "Hey, slow down old man, you'll hurt yourself running like that."

"I'm not worried about me getting hurt, I'm worried about you," Schmidt shouted, "I thought you stopped starting fights with people when you got out of school. Are you guys okay?" His query was sincere and in earnest, although he realized he was still shouting even though they were closing ranks rapidly.

"We're alright," Ian said with a smile in a more even tone, "You should have been here, I could have used some help and you were always pretty good on defense," he continued on a high note. "Of course, once Sadie got into it, two of them had to carry the third guy off."

"How many were there?" Schmidt asked a little incredulously.

"Oh, only about nine or ten," Ian kept smiling then said, "Honestly, only four, but the police broke it up just when we were getting on top of them."

"Okay, I'm glad to hear you're alright, I was worried. I read about the whole thing in the paper on the way in. I knew it was probably you, unfortunately, Rosenthal is going to want a little more information than that."

Then Schmidt slowed his walk, relaxed, and seemed comfortable with the fact that Ian was standing in front of him apparently unharmed.

Ian picked up the change in mood and asked, "Where's your car Smitty? Are you going to make us walk? Did you run all the way here?"

Schmidt content with the change of subject answered, "The Senate Building is right down the street. It's an easy walk unless you're too tired from all of that fighting."

Schmidt wasn't ready to let go completely, "Besides nobody drives in this town, if they don't have to. I take the train every day but Friday when the trains stop running at three."

Ian looked at him and grinned as if to say, "So what."

Schmidt in turn threw up his arms with palms open and abruptly demanded, "Where's Sadie? I want to meet her. Is she alright?" There was concern in his voice, "Maybe he had misread the situation because Ian seemed alright."

"Sadie's fine," Ian's tone was self assured, "You should see the other guy, who was dumb enough to tangle with my body guard." Ian grinned through his words.

"I'm not your body guard, nor your handmaiden, nor any of those things," The lilting tone of the beautiful woman standing behind Ian made Schmidt think she was probably right. He was eager to hear more from her.

"Hi, I'm Sadie," She extended her hand graciously towards Bob Schmidt.

He pulled back a little awkwardly impressed with her presence in the moment, "Dr. Haddad, it's a pleasure to meet you. I afraid Ian has been a little selfish in sharing much about you with me."

"Sadie, I prefer Sadie unless there is a point to be made, than it better be Dr. Haddad," She smiled easily at Schmidt.

Ian looked at Sadie with raised eyebrows he was impressed at how confidently she moved through new situations. Was this the same woman who saw phantoms outside her condominium? But then again he always underestimated her. "Don't be taken in by those flirty eyes Smitty, the guy from last night is probably still paying for that mistake," Ian raised a finger as a warning to Schmidt.

"Really, he was even easier than you," Sadie retorted.

"Okay, what's our agenda for today?" Ian came back in a more serious tone without even a wink at Sadie, "Do we get to meet Senator Rosenthal?"

"We're all set, but not until 10:30, so we have an hour to kill," Schmidt answered, and continued, "We're meeting at the Hart Senate Office Building, which is just down the street. Have you ever been to the Senate Building before?" He asked than continued without a response, "Perhaps you would like a short tour or I could buy us all a cup of coffee."

Ian piped in disclosing he knew a little bit about the terrain, "How about if we take a quick look at the Library of Congress. I've never seen it and there could be a day in the future when we may want to spend some time there. Okay with you Sadie?" He shifted his gaze to Sadie.

"It sounds good to me. I'm sure there's something in there that I haven't read," Sadie quipped.

Schmidt couldn't help but grin. He hadn't expected humor from this seemingly sophisticated lady. "I wonder what their relationship is really like," He thought to himself.

*

The visit to the Library of Congress was short and uneventful, and they entered Senator Rosenthal's conference room at exactly 10:30. The senator was waiting sitting alone around a large circular table. He rose graciously extending his hand to greet them.

"Good morning. Thank you for coming. I'm Senator David Rosenthal."

Ian stood with his hand extended as the senator slipped by him, took Sadie's hand and bowed slightly. "Dr. Haddad, it's a pleasure to meet you. I am somewhat aware of your work from my association with Senator Blessing from Illinois."

Schmidt held back his surprise, "How could his boss know more about Dr. Haddad then he did, when he had just met her. He glanced at Ian as the Senator turned and grasped Ian's outstretched hand clasping it between his own two hands, "And Dr. MacGown, I've read some, not all, but a fair representation of your work."

Ian nodded acknowledging the Senator's awareness of his books, which he reminded himself mentally were focused primarily on historical research. Since the plot to any of his books, if there was one, would have centered around life at least five thousand years ago, he wondered why the Senator would have picked his particular genre to read. "The answer should be forthcoming soon," he thought to himself.

"Please sit down." The Senator motioned them to the chairs surrounding the large circular table. "Tell me first about your unfortunate experience last night. The police reported in to my office after I was gone for the evening. I actually read about it in the paper on the way in and was worried it might be you. One of my staff confirmed it to me this morning. I thought we had something like that covered," the Senator glared in Schmidt's direction, "What do you know about this Bob?"

Schmidt shuffled a little awkwardly in his chair before answering, "I asked the police to keep an eye out for anything unusual and was assured that they would. Apparently they were on the job, but just a little late."

Schmidt sounded both assured and a little defensive. He felt within himself that he may not have done enough to handle his assignment.

Ian came to his defense, "Part of this is my fault, Dr. Haddad has told me several times recently she felt we were being watched or stalked. I'm afraid I just ignored her. This may have been their first encounter past stalking, whoever they are."

Sadie started to say something, but the Senator, who leaned back pensively in his chair, directed his question to Ian.

"You think it may happen again? Do you have any idea who your assailants might be?" he asked.

Ian hesitated, glanced at Sadie and sat forward with his arms on the table as if ready to make a confession. "There is no reason to believe that if it happened once, it wouldn't happen again." After a pause and rubbing his hand on his chin Ian volunteered, "Yeah, I have an idea about who may be involved."

Everyone including Sadie sat up straight to listen to Ian's next input. He paused and continued reflectively, "For the last five years I've headed up a group of writers and researchers that effectively operated as a Think Tank. Dr. Haddad has been a part of that group. We called ourselves, "Protect and Preserve," we were attempting to collate our respective research efforts into one cohesive conclusion about events that may have happened thousands of years ago."

He continued. "The title of the group is indicative of the focus of our research. We were attempting to rationalize the behavior of an ancient group of people, who we thought were both trying to protect civilization on one hand and on the other hand worried about preserving it, if their initial efforts failed."

He sat up straight and paused, "This isn't going to make any sense to you until you've heard the whole story we've come to present to the Commission and that may take a while." He paused again and continued in a different vein, "It may be relevant to last night's incident, however."

"As far as the identity of the assailants there was extreme disagreement that developed within the group as to how we should proceed with our conclusions. The "Preservation" thinking was strongly opposed to the "Protect" thinking. One man, in particular, who represented the "Preservation" side of the equation, confided his feelings to me as the head of the group, that he was extremely upset. He felt the two ideas of "Protect and Preserve" were not in sync from his particular perspective and eventually left the group."

Senator Rosenthal stepped in to rescue Ian from what appeared to him to be tangential reasoning for the assault on him and Sadie, "So you think someone from your group may be in a strong enough dissenting position to have assaulted you, and at a time when you've come to testify in front of our commission."

"I'm not sure, but it seems like the only reasonable conclusion for now," Ian replied.

"Do you have a name you want to volunteer?" The Senator asked.

"I'm not sure it would be prudent at this time. It's basically supposition on my part. Maybe it's my ex-wife." Ian injected humor into the query attempting to douse the fuse he had ignited. Nobody laughed.

The Senator scratched his head and gave a slight shrug, "Well, in a way that may answer some of the questions I've been concerned with." He didn't elaborate, but simply sat back in his chair.

He shrugged his shoulders, looked at Schmidt and said, "Maybe the best way to handle this for now is to make sure we offer a little better security and get on with the commission's hearing. Bob, will you see to that. Can you stay in town this evening?"

Schmidt gave the Senator a big high five and said, "I'll take a little stronger lead to make sure they're covered this time."

The Senator than assumed a more official tone in his manner, "Before proceeding with the commission tomorrow I would like to spend some time with you explaining where we are currently as a commission and what our procedures are. I can also fill you in on the members of the commission and what their respective roles are in this effort. If we can get that done today, we can have you before our distinguished group tomorrow morning."

The last remark by the Senator had a ring of sarcasm to it from Sadie's perspective and was not consistent with the way he had initially presented himself. It raised a question of seriousness of the commission in her mind as though the Senator was being dismissive. She and Ian hoped that they could become involved with the investigation and expected to be taken seriously. She raised her hand to stop the Senator. Her voice showed her concern as she asked him, "Why is this commission interested specifically in us? Why are we here?"

His response was almost mocking, "Because dear lady your college Dr. MacGown has gone on record saying the planet Earth is going to be hit by another planet. To our knowledge that has never happened before, and although, our commission is charged with investigating all known celestial activity, which has primarily revolved around comets and meteorites, you are our first investigation into another planet."

Sadie's intuition on the Senator's position gained support based on his last remarks and raised even greater concern in her mind, but before she could speak again the Senator looked squarely at Ian and with raised eyebrows said, "No offense Dr. MacGown, but quite frankly we need to determine the seriousness of your claim. We want to know if there is enough validity to it to warrant additional investigation or action on our part."

He paused almost apologetically, "We do understand, however, that your reputation in your field is such that we can't simply ignore you."

"No offense sir, I'm sure you understand," He repeated looking earnestly at Ian.

"None taken, I understand completely, you certainly are not the first to question some of my conclusions. So far it's cost me a marriage, a professorship and an uneven relationship with my children."

Ian's tone was offhanded and irritable, but he immediately pulled back. He did not want to lose this opportunity and realized they were still in the vetting phase of their effort.

Then he paused and looked back squarely at Rosenthal, "This is very important not just to us but…" Ian stuttered to a stop than continued firmly, "or Dr. Haddad and I wouldn't be here. I've already put a lot on the line for the opportunity. I'm willing to surrender whatever else may be left of my life, if necessary, just to be listened to by a group, your commission, who may have the authority and where with all to help complete a task that may literally have earth shaking ramifications. We need your help. We think you need ours."

"It's that important," he paused to get his breath, "Yes! I do believe we are going to be hit by another planet. That's why we, Dr. Haddad and I are here." "We've taken our case to the scientific community and the media without results. You, the government, are our last stop." He stopped abruptly and sat back in his chair.

The senator pursed his lips in thought, "I'm sorry. I may have been hasty and apologize for the doubt created in our minds, however, we've had our share of people announcing the end of the world. None with your credentials, I admit."

Somewhat taken back by Ian's passionate and dramatic response he extended his hand in a conciliatory manner and proceeded matter-of-factly as though there had been no exchange between them.

There was an uncomfortable quiet in the room as the Senator returned to the task he had set for himself of prepping them for the meeting in the morning. Then before he had finished his first sentence he stopped again, looked at Ian, and asked. "What is your personal investment in this Dr. MacGown? I mean what do you expect to get out of this?"

Ian started to speak, paused as though in thought, and said, "Honestly, I'm not sure." He paused again and then continued, "When I was a young man still in school I read something by a Jesuit priest that sometimes sits as a heavy burden on my thinking. It may have been Saint Francis Assisi,

I'm not sure. The gist of it reads, "The greater the perception the greater the responsibility" and the corollary to that is "The greater the perception the greater the sin." I'm concerned that Dr. Haddad and I, through a serendipitous perception, have inherited a very heavy responsibility."

The Senator smirked rather than smiled, probably at his own situation and said, "I understand, either perception, or responsibility or both can be harsh mistresses. It can be difficult to say no to either of them even if it would make life easier; if only for the moment."

He seemed satisfied with a philosophical answer that didn't really address the serious question at hand. He stopped, pursed his lips as he had before and began to speak in what was an extremely sincere but to the point manner.

"Look, I haven't really been honest with you."

Both Ian and Sadie sat back stiffly in their chairs like two people about to be fired.

Schmidt looked over to his friend and winked as if to say, "Don't blow it, just listen quietly," and disappeared into the other room. Ian acknowledged the cue by taking Sadie's hand, giving it a gentle squeeze and looking back in the senator's direction to listen to whatever might be coming.

The senator was ready to continue and spoke without hesitation, "Perhaps you remember back in 1985 when our Congress set up a program called Space Guard. It was in association with a broader worldwide program known as the Space Guard association. This association was aimed at the protection of the Earth's environment against the bombardment of objects of the solar system. It included the countries of Australia, Croatia, Germany, Japan and the United Kingdom. The primary focus of the association was comets and asteroids not necessarily other planets. My commission was built around the Space Guard Program. Our conversation with you will expand our initial charter. It's not much more serious than that."

Having gotten that off his chest he settled back a little and grinning, looked at Ian. "You dropped a bombshell in our midst. For years now we have cataloged hundreds and hundreds of both comets and asteroids, but not one planet that might bump into us." He was becoming a little flippant and Ian tried to pick up on his lead and say something about why he was there, but the senator held his hand up and continued.

"When you get right down to it this whole commission is formed around what you Dr. MacGown may have to tell us. That's the honest unvarnished truth. We have no other planets to investigate other than yours." He did not sound flippant anymore, but exasperated.

Ian's manner was assuring. "I understand your frustration with this endeavor sir, but I believe it can be worthwhile. Dr. Haddad and I will work with you for as long as you allow us to. The story we have to tell is important to the whole world and should not be taken lightly."

The senator looked at his watch and said. "I believe you. This may be as good a place as any, if you agree to take a deep breath and get ready for tomorrow." He nodded agreement as he spoke and Ian realized his opportunity would be in the morning.

"I've had some sandwiches ordered in, if you're okay with that. We'll have some lunch, and then I'll finish my briefing this afternoon for tomorrow's meeting."

After several more hours of discussion that were considerably less interesting than the initial foray the Senator ended the meeting abruptly at 5:30 P.M., smiling graciously and telling them he would see them promptly at 9:30 A.M.

He raised his eyebrows and looked again at Schmidt, "Bob will take care of you this evening. Okay, Bob?"

Ian got up to leave realizing the meeting was over, smiled back at the Senator and said, "By the way about doom's day prophets, I believe you saw my interview on "Sixty Minutes" when I mentioned that Sir Isaac Newton calculated the end of times as 2060AD. He believed Armageddon would come at that time but hid his ideas until his death when he asked his papers be read. Imagine if he knew about Nibiru, the planet we're discussing, and had let us know it was a planet on an erratic path that would account for our demise; he could have saved us some time and effort today. He was right about the apple falling you know."

Ian smiled broadly at the senator, "And here's another one for you, Thomas Paine, a rather famous American was arrested in France during one of his visits there, because he had stated he believed life existed on other planets."

Senator Rosenthal pulled his papers together, grinned back at Ian and said. "Touché, Dr. MacGown, touché."

As he exited the room Schmidt re-appeared waiting to take them back to the hotel.

Chapter 5: The Shinning Ones

Bob Schmidt put his arm around Ian and smirked, "I'm your bodyguard for this evening. I tried to get some secret service men, but they were all busy, so, I'm it. Okay with you and Sadie? I'll pay for dinner and as you pointed out this morning I was always pretty good on defense."

"We would love to have you join us," Sadie chimed in, "Ian always, makes me pay for dinner when we're alone. How could we turn down such a charming offer?"

Schmidt smiled directing his response to Sadie, "What if we just go back to the Hyatt House Article One Grille. I've had many meals there and they're always good. It's close and should avoid any complications with your unusual friends."

Ian, who had been quiet after leaving the Senator's office broke out of his musing with a complaint, "Are you going to make us walk again? Your boss ran us around verbally all day and now you want to run us physically into the ground."

"Come on big guy, suck it up," Smitty rejoined.

Sadie chimed in, "Ian you need a lot more exercise than you get, and beside you were sitting all day."

"Just kidding, let's go," Ian responded walking briskly ahead of them.

Steaks were on the menu and all three including Sadie went for a prime rib special with a sauce nobody had ever heard of. Sadie was the only of the three not to finish, however, pushing enough for another meal in Ian's direction.

After reflecting quietly for at least a long minute or two she looked quizzically at Schmidt and asked, "What's the story on the Senator? He goes from being totally charming to edgy as hell."

"Don't worry, he's a good guy," Schmidt's response was immediate without any hesitation, "If he has a problem it's probably because he went from heading up The Armed Services Committee, which has huge stature, to running this commission. I'm not sure he's sure of his future in the Senate. He has a strong military background, which is how I got involved with him."

Ian, who had been giving only partial attention to the conversation looked up at Schmidt, "how's that Smitty?" he asked, "What does his military background have anything to do with you?"

"Well, old buddy, while you were busy writing books I ended up in Special Forces where Rosenthal was my commanding officer. When he made the jump to politics he sought me out as a special assistant. As far as this commission and his role in it the rumor mill around Washington is that there may be a need for a military man to make it succeed. I know you aren't much for politics Ian, but even you would realize that most of our senators are lawyers."

"Than this thing may be pointed in the direction I think it should," Ian countered. "What Sadie and I are here to talk about will probably not be resolved by lawyers, but more likely by military involvement."

Sadie satisfied that she had gotten a fair response to the question she had asked initially stood up and put her hand on Ian's shoulder and said, " You guys can have at and duke it out, I'm going up to the room to freshen up. I'll come back for an after dinner drink. On that note Ian remember we have a big day tomorrow so don't start after dinner drinks without me?" she smiled.

"Sorry, I'm being a nag and it's not my style. I'll be back shortly," she called over her shoulder as she pushed her chair back to the table and made her exit.

The Hyatt has strings of oversized beads that constitute a screen between the Grille and the lobby of the hotel. Ian watched as Sadie darted up a half flight of stairs leading to the elevators ignoring the small escalator next to the stairs. Ian followed her movement through the beaded screen until she disappeared from his view. He turned back to resume his conversation with Smitty and then suddenly jumped up.

"That's not right. I don't like that. Come on Smitty," he said emphatically breaking into a run towards the steps and elevators.

"What's wrong Ian? What's wrong?" Schmidt shouted as he fell in beside him.

"Two men followed Sadie up those steps," Ian said a little out of breath. "They looked mid-eastern with those same damn black jump suits as last night. They're probably the same two bastards who hit us on the street. Come on," He said now running ahead leading Schmidt out of the restaurant.

Ian and Sadie's room was on the third floor and Ian instinctively ignored the elevators, running up the stairwell and bursting out into the third floor hallway. Sadie was slumped against the wall of the hall looking ruffled and shaken. Ian saw a man at the end of the hall and started to run towards him.

"No Ian," Sadie shouted, "behind you look out."

The blow on the back of his head sent Ian slumped to one knee on the floor. Schmidt, who had followed right behind him moved in front of him ducking under something shinny that spun and hissed in the air above him. Schmidt's size belied his agility and in a continuous move ducked under the flying object, grabbed the man in front of him and slammed him with a thud, hard against the wall. The crack of ribs and a violent expelling of air told the story of the assailant as he slithered to the floor.

A second man unseen by Schmidt wrapped his arms around him from the back trying to turn him over sideways with no success.

Ian still slumped on the floor recovered enough to grab the second man's ankles and drag him down to the floor as Schmidt turned around to meet the new attack. The first man now half lying, half sitting against the wall was waving what appeared to be a 9mm handgun first at Schmidt than at Ian.

"Stop!" he shouted at them and nodded to his accomplice with his free hand towards Sadie, who was still shaking from the ordeal.

As the man moved towards Sadie two more men appeared at the end of the hall and moved towards them. The assailants turned their attention to the new arrivals with an unusual combination of fear and respect, continued waving the gun at Ian and Schmidt than ran down the stairs in fast retreat.

Ian looked down the hall for the other two men who had mysteriously disappeared as rapidly as they had initially appeared. He struggled to his feet and started to walk in that direction.

"They're gone Ian, they're gone. Are you alright? They saved me before you got here. Did you see them?" Sadie blurted out both questions and answers before Ian could speak.

"Are you alright Ian?" Schmidt jumped in still looking around for what might be next.

Sadie grabbed Ian hugging him tightly, "Are you sure you're alright?"

"Yeah, I'm fine, I'm fine." He repeated rubbing the back of his head.

Schmidt stood staring down the hallway entranced with what he had seen, "Who the hell were they? I mean all of them. Those guys," he continued his gaze down the hallway, "looked so weird."

"They saved me, "Sadie said still trying to get her breath, "until you got here, it was so strange," She continued, getting more excited as she talked, "They didn't do anything, but appear out of nowhere, and those men let me go." Her excitement continued focusing strongly on Ian, "Did you see them Ian?" She asked incredulously. "Their faces shone like the "The Shining Ones."

"That doesn't make sense," Ian said shaking his head and then wincing from the effort.

"No Ian, I saw them too," Schmidt said, "Their faces were shinning. What the hell is that?" He asked incredulously.

Ian smirked and shook his head in apparent disbelief, "You would have to go back thousands of years ago to find men with shinning faces, if they ever existed at all." Ian rubbed his head and answered wearily like he didn't really want to entertain the idea even though he was the only one who appeared to have answers. "In history they or someone like them were called the "The Shebtu" or "The Shining Ones", who were descendents of the Elder Gods back in Egypt thousands of years ago." Ian repeated thousands wearily as though he was giving substance to a crazy notion.

Sadie raised her eyebrows and kept shaking her head in agreement as Ian spoke.

"The Shebtu who," Schmidt mocked the sound of Shebtu. "Thousands of years," he said in disbelief, "How many thousands?" He asked, as if it made any difference, still mocking the notion with the sound of his voice.

Then more conciliatory with honest concern that Ian may have been hit harder than he thought, he asked, "Are you alright buddy?"

He looked hard at Sadie, "Is he alright?" He demanded.

"Yeah, I'm alright, they didn't hit me that hard."

Ian saw the concern for his physical well being in Schmidt's eyes as well as for what he was saying. He knew he must sound like the blow to his head had had a greater affect than he was admitting to and reached for something that would explain "The Shining Ones" to Schmidt.

"They're from an old script called the "Turin Papyrus" which reaches back into antiquity. It describes an old list of kings and gods, some of whom were believed to have a shining countenance. How anyone like them could appear here today looking like that is way beyond anything I know or understand."

He took a deep breath, clasped his hands together to keep them away from his head, which was now beginning to throb; looked at Schmidt and continued uncertain that Schmidt might still be interested or understand what he was suggesting, "There is also an interpretation of the literature that describes them as enlightened, wise, all knowing; and in our work, Sadie's and mine, they were associated with "Those who recite formulae.""

Schmidt indeed looked as perplexed at what Ian was saying as to why he was saying it. It made absolutely no sense to him. This wasn't the time for a history lesson.

Ian realized it, pulled up short, but decided to take one more stab at the subject, perhaps just saying aloud what was racing through his head; unabashed at his friend's growing dismay. "Look, there were many of the early patriarchs in the Bible, who were supposed to be possessed of shining countenances. Enoch, Noah and Abraham are all described as having faces that shone like the sun. They were all great important leaders in the past."

With Sadie now trying desperately to wave him off he realized how foolish he must sound. "Look Smitty, my head hurts and I realize none of this makes much sense right now. Maybe it will when I give the whole story to the commission in the morning."

Ian went from one distraction to another and looked down the hall perhaps wondering if they were still there, and realized that for whatever reason the struggle had not caught the attention of anyone else; neither the "Shinning Ones" or anyone from any of the other rooms were in the hallway after all the commotion.

"I think we will serve our cause best, if we don't say anything about this to the Senator. Are you okay with that Smitty?" He asked trying to find some point of departure from his growing dilemma.

Schmidt smiled and shook his head, "I'm not the one who got hit on the head. I'm game to follow your lead, although eventually, we're going to have to track these guys down before they kill you or steal Sadie, Dr. Haddad." He corrected himself for the familiarity.

"I think we can be on a first name basis now Smitty," Sadie said and gave him a hug, "thanks for being there for us."

Ian said, "Come on let's go back downstairs, have a cup of coffee and talk this through. We don't want to ignore it, but we also don't want it to be the focus of tomorrow's meeting."

*

Their food had been cleared but with no sign of a check. "Don't worry about the check," Schmidt said, "I'll make sure they add it to my room."

Ian slumped down in a chair holding his head. Schmidt put his hand on Ian's shoulder and said, "Hang on I'll get you some ice."

Ian didn't object but looked up excitedly, spun around in his chair and shouted at the departing Schmidt, "Where's Sadie? We can't leave her alone upstairs."

"I'm right here sweetheart, don't panic. I came down with you, remember?" Sadie slid into the chair next to him.

Ian forced a crimson red smile. Embarrassment was not his strong suit. "I asked you not to call me that in public, sweetheart."

"It's alright, nobody is here to hear me, and beside they would probably think I hit you in the head rather than cooed sweet nothings in your ear." She seemed completely recovered from her ordeal, but Ian's head was still throbbing and he cradled it carefully in his arms on the table.

She leaned across the table to make eye contact with his bowed head, "Ian, what have we gotten ourselves into? I 'm not sure I'm ready for this."

Ian raised his head and grimaced from the effort. "I'm not sure I am right now either, but I'm afraid our ship has sailed as far as getting out. And you and I know we have an even bigger battle to fight, even if we get past this commission. We made choices, Sadie, even though some of them may have been unwitting ones."

Schmidt reappeared and handed Ian a towel laden with chopped ice. "Here's your ice, Ian."

"Thanks, what's the charge?" Ian's response was uninspired.

"Just tell me what the hell is going on. Who were those guys, and not just your shinning friends, but the guys with the guns? That's serious stuff, Ian."

Ian started to answer and for the first time could see a side arm tucked inside his friend's jacket.

"You mean like the gun you're wearing, Smitty. What's that all about?" It was apparent Ian felt no compunction to give a quick answer to Schmidt's question before getting one to his own.

Schmidt sat back, pulled his jacket closed, and put his hand gently on Sadie's arm to restrain her as she leaned forward to look at the weapon, "I told you I was a special assistant to the Senator. Well, I am a "special", special assistant on temporary duty. I'm supposed to do more than just get coffee for him."

"You guys have been attacked. He's been threatened. He has some other special assistants looking out for him when he's away from the Senate."

"What about the guys in black? Do you know who they are?" Schmidt continued to press for an answer.

"I'm not sure Smitty. I would like to leave any discussion on it till after tomorrow's meeting with the senator, or at least until Sadie and I have made our pitch."

"Okay, okay!" Schmidt shook his head and rubbed his chin. "Okay for now."

The table fell quiet from conversation as Ian sat nursing his head and Sadie sat pensively staring into space.

Schmidt broke the silence. Why are you guys doing this Ian, Sadie?" He looked from one to the other. "I don't get it."

"It's like I told the Senator it's all about responsibility." Ian started to answer and Sadie interrupted.

"It's also about doubt. Ian couldn't live with the doubt that would hang over his head believing he could have and should have taken action important to all of us and didn't. It would fry his soul if it came to pass that people, all of us were in danger; and he could do something to change it and didn't."

"What did he say this afternoon, "The greater the perception the greater the responsibility." He, we know things we have to tell this commission that could change the future forever. Help us, Smitty." She pleaded than grinned flirtatiously at him for the familiar use of his name.

Ian came back to life a bit, raised his hand as if he were ready to address Schmidt's inquiry. "It's like this Smitty. It's a little bit like discussing the difference between one's destiny and their fate. I was born destined to become a famous soccer player, you know that. Then I made a series of bad decisions, which included hooking up with this good looking mid-eastern woman, who began feeding me information from old texts she had deciphered. The next thing I knew, I knew more about one major world shaking event that was going to occur than anyone else in the world, like I told Rosenthal; and fate took over, just too many bad decisions on my part."

"Okay, Ian you always had a sense of humor, but this isn't funny as I'm sure that bump on your head will attest. I'll get you there in the morning and stay with you, but you'll have to do the convincing." His tone was not dismissive, but more of an arm's length attitude or direction. Schmidt was feeling legitimate concern about the men in black jumpsuits and their shinning counterparts.

"Come on, it's time to hit the sack," Schmidt waved them out of the chairs towards the elevators, "hopefully, if tomorrow is eventful, it won't be as bad as today; and if Ian's head hurts, it will be for a different reason."

Schmidt took them each by the arm and led them, hopefully, to a quiet nights rest.

Chapter 6: The Solar Clock

Ian sat in front of a large, long table facing Senator Rosenthal's commission of nine other senators as Rosenthal recited his credentials and his perceived role in being part of the commission's investigation. Sadie sat next to him pulled back from the table sitting with her legs crossed from right to left.

Ian read the name placards in front of each of the senators reciting them in his mind as he scanned across the group.

Illinois - Senator Leon Blessing

Georgia - Senator Josh Holland

Massachusetts - Senator Robert Tarnowski

New York - Senator Bernard Hoesel

Virginia - Senator Richard Brown

Missouri - Senator James Berger

North Carolina - Senator Samuel Ligget

Maryland - Senator Joan Hyatt

Pennsylvania - Senator Arnold Malick

He wasn't sure the grouping made any sense to him. He recognized Senator Brown from Virginia who had some renown as both a scientist and historian, although he had never had any face to face dealings with him.

He also recognized Senator Ligget, who he seemed to remember from a conference he spoke at on Egyptian history. Although he wasn't completely sure, he believed that they probably all had law degrees including Brown and Ligget with the exception of Tarnowski, who Schmidt had told him was a graduate of M.I.T. Senator Blessing, he knew had some association with the Oriental Institute in Chicago, a prestige organization in the annals of archeology, but that was it as far as any expected expertise went in what they were about to discuss.

The only woman on the commission was the senator from Maryland, who kept fidgeting with her notes turning them over and over and constantly waving to one of her aides in the gallery. The aide would jump up, run out and return waving a new pad of paper, which seemed to placate the senator's immediate concern or need.

Ian wondered if he could hold her attention and if she might not become a distraction to the hearing.

"Dr. MacGown will you please address the commission?" Senator Rosenthal's prompting brought him upright from the leaning position he had adopted while scanning names.

"Yes sir. Thank you for that kind introduction. I want to also thank the commission for asking me and my associate Dr. Haddad to take part in your inquiry about Nibiru also known as Planet X."

Ian stopped and looked around the room as though he was looking for a place to hide. He continued, tentatively trying to establish firm footing in his mind for the mission in front of him. He had waited patiently for this opportunity and he didn't want to blow it by sounding unintelligent or like one more dooms day prophet that Senator Rosenthal had alluded to. He moved his gaze from one senator to another being certain that he made eye contact with each one before proceeding.

"I've gone public stating that I believe our planet Earth is going to be hit by another planet. Not a meteorite or large comet, but another planet that in all probability will be bigger than Earth. I know that raises a lot of questions to say the least."

"When do we think it might occur?"

"How do we know this?"

"Can we do anything to prevent it from occurring?"

"and finally, if it does happen, what then?"

"And the most obvious question to be answered first. Do we have any proof that there is any reality to the whole silly idea?"

"No, I'll tell you up front I can't prove it even to my own satisfaction. What we have to offer is an abundance of evidence that must be construed as circumstantial at best, but if not overwhelming in its content should be at least enough to make us all stop and think about the consequences if there is any validity to it."

"For the last eight years Dr. Haddad and I have been part of a joint research effort established within the structure of a Think Tank. The members of this group were not scientists as you might think, but writers who have all in one way or another spent their lives researching ancient writings, sometimes in the form of old parchments, sometimes on the walls of buildings or steles reaching back many centuries, and many more which exist in the form of clay cylinders found in the archeological digs in Mesopotamia in the mid 1800's."

"A story has evolved from a compilation of these disparate writings. It starts with a planet that revolves around our sun in much the same way that Earth and the other planets operate in our solar system except this planet has a long elliptical orbit that takes 3600 hundred years to complete."

"In my story this planet which you may rightly assume is Nibiru is populated much like Earth is today except the timing of the story occurred thousands of years ago."

"At some time in the course of their existence the inhabitants of Nibiru realized that they were losing their atmosphere."

He continued with wrinkled brow inwardly amused at how easily they had let him launch into his absurd story.

"One theory to support the possibility of this occurring would be that their atmosphere was subjected to intense external stress from our sun as they passed in their 3600 year journey, or if you prefer they may have created a hole in their atmosphere from too many carbon emissions. Whatever the case may be, we believe they had reason to venture to our planet Earth. We believe we can assume they were extremely, scientifically advanced if they were able to get here from their planet."

"The reason they wanted to get here was to mine gold to employ a solution they had devised to their problem of lost atmosphere that included sprinkling gold flakes in their skies in an attempt to recapture their atmosphere. That may sound absurd in this conversation, but it has actually been done successfully in recent times as an experiment here on Earth."

"In my story their problem was that they did not have sufficient gold reserves on their planet to complete the task, so out of necessity they came to colonize Earth where they perceived there would be abundant reserves of gold. I hasten to add that this, if it occurred happened at a time long before the advent of modern man."

"For the sake of brevity let's accept the fact that they got here on one of their 3600 year journeys and began to mine gold. Now they were faced with the task of moving the gold to their planet from Earth within the confines of a 3600 year cycle without any established infrastructure as we know it today."

"They would have been miners on a distant planet, we might reasonably assume without reliable ongoing communication with their home planet, but faced with the task of being ready for the next 3600 year passing."

"With your indulgence gentlemen I would like to focus on just that particular aspect of my story for now."

"If an alien population came to Earth with such a defined purpose and a need to maintain contact with a sister planet with an elongated orbit over an extended period of time actually existed and succeeded; what evidence would they have left leading to the present day?"

"That's the core of the discussion we hope to have with you. Because we believe that in examining the evidence we will give clarity to a problem looming in our immediate future that is a threat to all of civilization as we know it."

"And our ultimate goal if we are successful will be to outline action that may lead to whatever solutions may be available to us; if there are any."

"We approach this with the absolute belief that Nibiru does exist and that they sent colonists to Earth at least twenty thousand years ago."

Ian was on stride speaking like a college professor giving his favorite lecture.

"The figure of twenty thousand years is initially derived by examining an archeological site in Egypt known as The Nabta Playa calendar circle. Archeologists who have examined this site and interpreted the evidence there have come to some startling conclusions."

"They believe that the creators of Nabta Playa through a system of steles and monoliths erected at that site were able to track and understand detailed astronomical and cosmological information, which we have only begun to discover and understand in modern times."

"This included distances to various stars and the speeds at which those stars may be moving to or away from us. In creating this site using simple stone structures some ancient culture had created a map of the stars as seen from Earth."

"And that's not all. In addition to the steles and monoliths that were in place at this site they had carved sculptures representing a map of our complete Milky Way Galaxy onto the face of an existing bed rock formation."

"There was much more discovered at Nabta Playa, but I'm afraid any protracted discussion about the details of the site would only confuse the discussion at hand."

"The point I want to make is that it existed thousands of years ago and the builders of these fantastic structures were able to derive cosmological information using only the naked eye; whereas we today in order to develop that same information must rely on the use of very sophisticated modern tools. They didn't have modern telescopes or sophisticated computers. They used only the structures they had built from stone along with a deep and profound understanding of the workings of the stars. However, the evidence they have left is undeniable in expressing to us that their knowledge of the structure of our Milky Way Galaxy was enormous."

He paused, worried, looking for eyes that may have become glazed over, and then continued to build his case.

"One of their primary focuses was the constellation Orion, which we will point out as we continue, was of significant importance to them in achieving their ends and to us in understanding what they were all about."

"We will point out how it is possible today by reviewing the orientation of their steles, which have endured through the ages, to different star alignments, specifically to Orion; to date them to a time at least twenty thousand years ago."

"The question as to why they went to all that trouble when civilization was in its bare infancy begs to be answered."

"Why? Why would anyone here on Earth that long ago need or want that kind of information; and on what kind of scientific base was it established?"

He paused, took a long deep breath for the first time since he had begun his story. He rose from his sitting position standing like an oracle from the past shouting in a kind of whisper.

"The people in my story needed that kind of cosmological information to proceed with and complete their task. They needed to know the comings and goings of their Planet Nibiru."

The members of the commission sat quietly looking back at him with more doubt and concern in their faces than assurance. A moment of doubt gripped him and he wondered if they would let him continue.

After another pause and making eye contact again with each of the senators, he proceeded.

"How would you track the movement of a planet with a 3600 year orbit around the sun twenty thousand years ago without modern day scientific equipment?" He asked almost shouting and then lowering his voice again almost to a whisper at the end of his question.

"They had broad cosmological and astronomical knowledge working for them," he paused again as if to make certain that everybody was listening and then continued gravely to emphasize the importance of what he was going to say next.

"The method they employed to track the passing of long periods of time was a movement in the skies which we refer to today as the Precession of the Equinoxes."

He started to speak with urgency in his voice ignoring hands that were finally beginning to be raised to ask questions he was not yet ready to answer.

"Let me step back and explain how that works and why it was important to these people deep in our past. It is noteworthy that this concept which we refer to as The Precession of the Equinoxes discovered in modern times was thoroughly understood by these ancient people thousands of years ago."

Ian stepped back slightly from the table tilted his head back and ran his left index finger across his upper lip. He was poised like a professor about to give a dissertation.

"Picture the Earth moving around our Sun in an orbit that's on a plane called an ecliptic that we know takes 365 days to complete. This is in addition to the daily twenty-four hour rotation of the Earth. We on Earth don't recognize that we are on such a journey, but rather discern the movement as belonging to the sun, which we see as rising in the east in the morning and disappearing below the western horizon each evening."

"Now if in our minds we can picture another circle outside of this ecliptic and bigger than the orbit of the Earth around the sun, we could divide that circle into twelve equal segments and each segment would represent one of twelve different constellations we would see in our 365 day trip around the sun. We refer to them in our daily conversation as the twelve houses of the Zodiac."

"I'll recite them for those of you who are unfamiliar with them or don't remember them: Aries, Taurus, Gemini, Cancer, Leo, Virgo, Libra, Scorpius, Sagittarius, Capricornus, Aquarius and Pisces. You may know some by slightly different names in the case of Scorpio and Capricorn. In today's world we are concerned with them on a daily basis because we believe our lives are affected by the changing conjunction of the planets in our solar system and their orientation to these constellations."

For the first time there was a response from the commission with Senator Tarnowski clapping and quipping, "Congratulations Dr. MacGown you recited them in perfect order."

Ian stopped and smiled back at the Senator. "At least one of them is listening," He thought to himself.

Ian continued on his mission somewhat gravely, "If in your 365 day travel around the sun you were to look through some prism always at the same time in your journey, say the spring solstice, you would expect to and in your experience would see the same constellation rising behind the sun just before sunrise; because these constellations as we know them are constant and predictable in their location in the sky."

"There is a hook however in that supposition. The experience of seeing the same constellation whenever you looked through your prism on the spring solstice would only last for 2160 years; then you would see a new constellation. From our perspective here on Earth the constellations appear to move, but only after approximately 2160 years, and that only if you look from the same spot, so to speak, at the same time. We choose to look at the time of the spring solstice."

"Now to make sense out of this supposition I must throw another curve at you, please bear with me."

Ian continued moving his hand around in an imaginary circle as he spoke, "The Earth revolves around the sun in a counter-clockwise direction. It has however another interesting and important characteristic."

"It wobbles."

"It wobbles like a spinning top. Picture a top spinning in a counter-clockwise direction but rotating like the Earth around the Sun in a clockwise direction. As the top proceeded in the counter-clockwise direction a spot you may have marked on it with a pen would actually be moving clockwise. That's what happens with our Earth. The remarkable thing about the Earth is that the spot you marked with a pen would take almost 25920 years to come back to the same place even though it continued its path around the sun for all that time. We refer to this as the Precession of the Equinoxes."

Ian paused, waiting for everything to sink in and for whatever questions may have arisen in the minds of the senators. They sat back comfortably in their chairs waiting for more of the story without comment. He wasn't sure if they understood or may have known all about the Precession before he gave his pitch. At any rate the floor was his and he proceeded.

He thought maybe he should give his audience some direction. "What I'm doing with this line of thinking and what I believe the ancients did is build a solar clock; a solar clock that would allow them to count forward or backwards hundreds or even thousands of years with an uncanny precision."

"If you could live forever and keep looking at the constellation rising in the east just before sunset, that constellation would change approximately every 2160 years which is 25920 divided by 12. After looking at all twelve constellations in their 2160 year cycle you would again see the same constellation you had started with and 25920 years would have elapsed.

These are very important numbers and represent the machinery with which to operate a solar clock. These ancient people were aware of this celestial phenomenon and used it to their advantage."

"Now if you do the arithmetic you'll realize that by dividing 25920 years the time it takes to complete one cycle of the Precession by 360 degrees you get an answer of 72. This means that every 72 years you will advance one degree along the axial precession of the Earth."

Ian continued wondering if he was going to run out of time before he got to the real meat of his presentation and began to speak more rapidly.

"In addition to this axial precession the ancients had another tool at their disposal that allowed them to deal in shorter increments of time extending over long periods."

"One of the constellations you would see on your 25920 year journey is named Orion. I mentioned Orion earlier and expect that most of you have probably heard of it in some context. It is mentioned repeatedly throughout Egyptian literature and history, and can be recognized as the figure of a man in the sky with a belt at his waist consisting of three stars."

"These three stars comprising the belt are part of another astrological phenomenon. They can be measured to show very gradual but significant changes in altitude. In other words they rise and then fall again in a very consistent, predictable pattern that can be measured in angular degrees from the Earth."

Specifically one of the belt stars measured at it's highest point at median transit would be at an angle of 58 degrees and 11 minutes above the southern horizon as viewed from the Giga plateau in Egypt. This particular star named Al Nitak takes about 13000 years to descend from the highest to the lowest point."

"After another 13000 years has passed Al Nitak rises back to a position of 58 degrees and 11 minutes at which time it again begins the descent to ground zero."

"This cycle goes on endlessly for time immemorial. It was for the ancients a scale against which they could determine the years that had elapsed by simply measuring the angle of inclination to the Earth of Al Nitak in its 13000 year journey up and down in our skies."

Ian paused again and with raised eyebrows pointed out to the commission members, "I hope the sum of Orion's journey up and down combining two 13000 legs totaling the same approximate 26000 years to complete a Precession of the Equinoxes hasn't been lost to you."

"What a magnificent solar clock they were using," Ian stopped to observe still with awe in his voice.

"There is much more to be told about the mechanics of the solar clocks operation, but that represents the basics."

"For longer periods they could and would mark their journey through time by calculating the 2160 years in each house or constellation of the Precession of the Equinoxes. For shorter periods they could rely on the rising and falling of the three Belt Stars of Orion."

Hands were now beginning to be raised. Senator Holland asked. "What's a median transit?"

Senator Hoesel asked, "By the Equinoxes do you mean the spring and fall Equinoxes?"

Ian replied, "Yes we are talking about the spring and fall equinoxes, however it seems like the ancients were focused on the spring or vernal equinox."

"The median transit can be thought of as an arc across the sky reaching from the North Pole to the South Pole. For our purpose simply think of it as a vertical line reaching up from your toes into the sky. From a ground position you would see Orion's Belt Star moving across the median transit and in measuring the angle as it passed the median from ground zero you could track its movement up and down the median. By measuring the change in the angle you could determine the passing of time over extended periods."

"In summary, once more, if you always stood in the same spot to measure an angle against the rise or fall of Orion's belt star you could determine the passage of time."

"As in the case of the Precession this would also allow you to calculate movement forward or backwards in time."

Senator Rosenthal looked around at the other senators and directed rather than asked, "If there are no more pressing questions, I would like to suggest we allow Dr. MacGown to proceed. Maybe we can get into a little bit more of the meat rather than the mechanics of what he has to tell us. Are you agreeable to that Dr. MacGown?"

"Yes, I am most definitely. To get started I would like to establish some initial dates that I believe will give substance to the story I've proposed. May I proceed?" Ian asked overly politely.

Senator Rosenthal in turn, as though rehearsed with Ian, replied overly politely, "Yes, yes, of course, please do."

"I would like to refer to an observation made by Dr. Thomas G. Brophy in a book titled "The Origin Map" in which he discussed his interpretation of the findings at the Napta Playa archeological site which I mentioned earlier."

"His observation referenced conclusions about what that site revealed to him as an astronomer that he felt correlated with some ancient writings that had been translated from old Sumerian clay tablets. One specific quotation described "the departure of the two Great Gods" from Earth."

"The quotation he alluded to was from a book by Zecharia Sitchin titled, "The 12th Planet." Sitchin translated text from Sumerian clay tablets as follows: "On the seventeenth day, forty minutes after sunrise, the gate shall be opened before the gods Anu and Antu, bringing to an end their overnight stay."

Dr. Brophy's observation was that the time window of forty minutes after sunrise appeared to correlate with a Galactic Center tracking window which he had defined in the Cosmological Sculpture at Napta Playa. That window per Dr. Brophy, "also starts about 40 minutes after rising above the horizon. And on its 17700 BC vernal equinox alignment date the Galactic Center rose very close with the Sun; thus both bodies entered the "declination window", defined by the Cosmological Sculpture, about 40 minutes after sunrise."

Several hands were raised and waving supported by different levels of vocalization. Ian didn't acknowledge any of them but raised his own hand out in front of him. "Hang on, just a minute. Let me tell you what I think this means to us."

Senator Rosenthal interjected himself again, "Gentlemen, please let him finish. Let him make his point."

Sadie sat calmly throughout with legs now crossed from left to right back from the table as though this experience of a group shouting in front of Ian was commonplace to her.

Ian stood with his hand held high and continued in a calm, unexcited demeanor, "It sounds confusing but it represents good science, and I believe tells us two things. First it says there is physical evidence that the people in my story may have really existed, and," he held his breath on the word and, "it gives us a date. It gives us a date of 17700BC when this may have occurred."

"It also suggests that someone was ready to embark on a space voyage from Earth. If you had read Sitchin's book you would understand that the voyage was back to the planet Nibiru."

"There is yet another site, which I think is relevant, that I would like to incorporate in this discussion that also dates to around 17700BC." It was apparent Ian was not yet ready to yield to questions.

He continued unraveled by the small clamor of side remarks that were now like an echo at the end of a canyon.

"There is another archeological site, this one in Bolivia, South America known as Tiahuanaco. It is said in the past to have been one of the largest and most important cities in the Andean world. There has been much written and discussed about this site from an archeological view, but I would like to focus on just those aspects that apply in our discussion."

"First of all scholars generally accept that a combination of large trapezoidal blocks in concert with some huge monoliths more than twelve feet in height at this site appeared to have been lined up to particular star groups. Once more as in the past owners of this site appear to have been studying the passage of time in conjunction with the equinoxes as we discussed before."

"In addition located at this site is a now famous stone structure identified as the Gateway to the Sun believed to be an extremely complex and accurate calendar carved in stone."

Ian paused, "Remember Napta Playa. They had carved sculptures into bedrock formations that had astronomical information and ramifications attached to them. They were also studying different star groups."

Ian was once again searching for a more secure foothold. "I want to be careful not to make this a lecture on astronomy, although it's very important to what's at hand. The specific point I want to make at this juncture is that scientific studies of the placement of these stone structures at Tiahuanaco and their orientation at the time they were built concluded that they were built around 17000BC."

He paused briefly letting the 17700BC date sink in and continued, "The way in which this was determined was by measuring how many degrees the orientation of these monuments were removed from the rising of the sun at the vernal equinox in modern times. Using the figure of 72 years for each one degree shift a figure of 17000BC was attained."

"This figure, of course, lines up with the date we established for Napta Playa, which in turn lines up with the date for the departure of the gods from Sitchin's translation of the Sumerian texts."

Ian wasn't in a hurry and waited for his audience to catch up before his next salvo, "There is something else equally remarkable about Tiahuanaco. There are huge blocks of dressed stones, one weighing an estimated 440 tons and other smaller blocks lying around estimated to weigh between 100 and 150 tons. The question of how they got there from quarries ten miles away in 17700BC is staggering enough, but there's more than that to think about."

"Many, if not all, of these stones show signs of intricate, advanced machining. The kind of machining that would be difficult to replicate today with modern tools."

Ian continued pausing as he progressed to assess his audience's reaction and then raised his hand again for another point.

"I didn't mention one of the most important facts of all in my story. Bolivia represents one of the richest areas in the world for a variety of ores. It would have been a natural place to look for and mine gold, and many of the structures at Tiahuanaco have all the earmarks of a mining operation."

Ian stood up erect and faced his audience anew, "This is only the beginning of what I came here to say, but I believe there was someone from a distant planet here on Earth mining gold sometime around 17700BC."

The lone woman senator from Maryland didn't wait to be recognized but raised her hand and spoke simultaneously. "If they were here as you suggest, where are they now?"

Ian hesitated before answering. He didn't want to lose whatever edge he may have accomplished by getting into a side issue even though it was obviously a very relevant one. He was searching again for that elusive foothold.

"That's a fair question. I say in all sincerity, if I had an answer to your question I would have the answer to many more questions I'm concerned with." He realized he couldn't duck her question without giving ground and took the plunge.

"There have been suggestions that address your question. One possible answer you may find in your Bible where it suggests that the sons of

God found the daughters of man attractive and took them as wives. The suggestion being that they just assimilated into our society."

"Although many people find that idea repugnant from a religious point of view, it may be of interest to the commission that back in 2017 results of a government sponsored genome study uncovered some unusual, unexplainable mitochondrial DNA traces that at that time they were bold enough to suggest could have been of alien origin."

Ian shrugged his shoulders to imply possible lack of agreement on his part. He couldn't at this point in his presentation suggest that the gods he was referring to might be the same gods that were worshiped in modern day religions. He knew he had never successfully won any argument that would end up having religious connotations attached to it, and Senator Hyatt was sitting in front of him with her arms crossed still waiting for an answer.

He looked at her and replied without conviction. "There is another study that suggested that they were successful in repairing their planet's atmosphere and simply returned to Nibiru."

Ian didn't want this to be a stumbling block and tried to maintain the ground he felt he had gained. He threw out what he hoped would be an adequate disclaimer.

"Whether they were assimilated into a race of homo sapiens or simply disappeared I would like to believe for this discussion there is undeniable evidence that someone was here."

He waited for another salvo from Senator Hyatt, but none came, so having successfully sidestepped the issue he jumped back into the fire, standing, scratching his head like he had just remembered something important. He looked again at the commission and said.

"An interesting side note regarding Senator Hyatt's inquiry harkens back to Alexander the Great and Julius Caesar both of whom believed they were descendants of gods. The real story of Alexander's quest was not to conquer the world, but to find his roots, which he believed would prove he was a demigod, or born of a least one divine parent."

Senator Holland's hand was up and waving. He looked angry and spoke vehemently, "Damn it MacGown you keep saying gods every time you refer to these people from Nibiru. Do you think they were gods? How does that stack up against your religious beliefs?"

Ian flushed red, "Whoa, I'm sorry. You're right. I have been doing that and it's not relevant to our discussion today. Please accept my apologies and let me go on with the subject at hand." Ian was back peddling but not fast enough.

Senator Brown was now pointing at him with a raised finger. "You also more or less skipped over how they got here. Are we talking space ships, worm holes? What?" He asked throwing his hands up in the air and continued, "You opened the door on these questions, shouldn't we discuss them?"

Senator Rosenthal called for order. He could see Ian had stumbled and didn't want the commission to dissolve into side issues. He commanded rather than asked, "Maybe a short break would allow us to collect ourselves."

He looked over at Schmidt who was sitting at the side of the room, "Bob, will you attend to our guests and be back in about twenty minutes."

Schmidt hustled over to Ian and Sadie, "Come on I'll get you out of the line of fire, buy you a cup of coffee and let you collect your wits."

Sadie grinned at Schmidt, "You take the right side. I've got the left. We'll carry him out together."

Ian countered, "Hey I'm just getting warmed up. Don't take me out coach."

Schmidt took him by the arm, "Come on, you'll be back in soon enough."

CHAPTER 7: IAN'S DISSERTATION

Schmidt led Ian and Sadie into the Senate cafeteria and motioned them to a table, "Okay, coffee around I assume. The only question is with or without cream and sugar. I'll be glad to get it, since they know me here."

Sadie smiled at his little familiarity and said, "Black please my good man, and thank you."

Ian looked at him and said, "Black please, where is the rest room, my good man?"

Schmidt smiled and replied, "Down the hall to your left sir."

With that Ian was gone and Schmidt promptly returned with three cups of black coffee. He looked at Sadie studiously, "How is he doing in there? Is he going to be okay? I keep listening and watching him and all I can remember is him coming at me back in high school with the soccer ball on his toe heading towards the goal, and there was no way to stop him."

Sadie smiled and laughed, "I can relate to that. He's a very interesting, determined man. I'm afraid a little sad at times. Some of the burdens he decides to take on, of his own will seem to get a little heavy for him, but he never complains, or as you said never stops."

"The only insight I ever get about him is a quote he recites constantly from one of Lord Byron's poems, "If I laugh at anything it is only that I may not weep.""

"The weird thing is that in my mind it is frequently out of context to the situation."

Schmidt grinned at Sadie, "Would it help to know he was doing that way back in high school, but we all just simply ignored him."

Sadie countered, "Sometimes he's hard to ignore, and besides I don't really want to. He's very important to me," winking at Schmidt with her last remark.

Then she sat back more seriously and said more of a question than a statement, "Sometimes I think that smile he alludes to in his quote all the time may be more of a grimace than a smile."

Ian heard the last few words as he approached the table, "How can anyone smile in this environment? Lawyers turned politicians everywhere asking questions before I'm ready to answer them."

"I'm sure you'll prevail. You better drink your coffee, so you don't fall asleep on your feet in there," Sadie taunted with a wry smile.

Schmidt picked up his cup of coffee that was still steaming and gulped it down in one fast motion. The cup returned to the table with a bang as Schmidt jumped up sliding his chair back screeching in protest.

"Come on time to go. We've got to get back in there for Act Two. I for one certainly don't want to miss it."

Ian looked at Schmidt despairingly, as he waved his empty cup at him, "This was not a great idea. Not if I have to stand up there for another couple of hours without a break."

Schmidt patted him on the shoulder, "Hey, I'll be right there. If you get into trouble just signal and I'll bail you out. Even if you simply don't like the way things are proceeding. It may have nothing to do with your coffee intake. And if that doesn't work for you put Sadie in the breech. She has a lot more charm than you do anyway."

Sadie grinned at Schmidt. She was beginning to like him more and more as she recognized more and more his commitment to Ian as a friend.

Ian jumped up, looked at both of them and said, "It's a dirty job but someone has to do it."

Sadie rolled her eyes and still grinning grabbed the opportunity, "Try to be a little more original in your presentation Shakespeare. We don't want people falling asleep in there."

*

When the trio entered the room all ten senators were already seated looking in Ian's direction. Ian made a feint move like he might be ready to run and nudged Sadie for effect.

Sadie ignored him and took her place at the table, casting her eyes up to him in full attention.

Ian put on a serious face, "I would like to apologize to Senators Hyatt and Holland for attributing god like qualities or referring to the people in my story as gods in any way. It may become relevant in some context as we proceed but not just yet."

Senator Hyatt looked perplexed. She was not sure she had received an apology or needed one to begin with. Senator Holland looked reassured and nodded to Ian approvingly.

There was a momentary lull as everyone shuffled for a more comfortable position. Ian assessed his audience once again and began.

"I would like to address Senator Brown's question as to how these ancient people may have traveled to Earth from their planet."

"Remember the 3600 year long elliptical orbit of Nibiru. Maybe if we gave that some clarification we might gain perspective on their situation in making such a journey."

Ian was prepared to proceed with caution. He didn't want to lose them, nor did he want to be diverted to another side issue he wasn't ready to discuss. He took the professor's stance rubbing his chin and appearing uncertain.

"I remember the first time I heard that 3600 year long elliptical figure. I admit I immediately pictured Nibiru coming into sight, and then after a day or two of streaking through the sky, speeding off not to be seen for another 3600 years. That is of course absurd and I would like to paint a different picture for you today."

"The thing that misled me in my initial assessment was the injection of the word "long" into the sentence with elliptical."

"An ellipse by definition may be viewed simply as a squashed circle that has one side longer than the other. It doesn't have to be that much longer to be an ellipse just longer. I'd like to expand that thought to give some perspective to our story."

"To do that effectively I need to digress again back to the year 17700BC as a starting point. If we do some very simple math using our two established numbers of 17700BC and 3600 we can establish another point that I hope you'll recognize."

"Bob, can we have the screen please?" A large screen lit up behind Ian with a simple mathematic statement scrolled across it.

17700 minus 3600 minus 3600 is equal to 10500

Ian pointed to the figures with a red laser beam he had pulled from his pocket, "If Nibiru passed by the Earth in 17700BC and then completed two more revolutions of 3600 years each it would have reappeared on our horizon sometime around 10500BC."

"Some of you may recognize that date. It is accepted by archeologists today as the time that the Sphinx was built. I believe everyone knows about the Sphinx, that it looks like a lion's body with a man's head and is located on the Giza plateau in Egypt."

"I'm not sure if everyone also knows that it faces due east and that if you had been able to view the constellation rising just behind the sun in the year 10500BC at the summer solstice it would be the constellation we know as Leo; so called by us because it resembles the body of a lion. The ramifications of that scenario are really more complicated than that but the implications seem clear. The ancients established another marker that was tied to the 3600 year cycle."

"It would not be unreasonable to assume that at that time they were still here mining gold, or maybe just decided to stay here as colonists. In either instance it appears they were still focused on the summer solstice as an instrument as some sort of solar clock. Their eyes, 7200 years after 17700BC, were still directed to the skies and they appeared to be marking the passing of Nibiru in clear 3600 year segments."

"Since we're tracking their progress in pursuing the 3600 year cycle it might be interesting to note where we end up if we move backwards from the 17700BC date." A click signaled the arrival of Ian's next slide.

17700BC minus 3600 is equal to 21300BC

"Not a direct hit I'll admit but very, very close to the date we talked about earlier as the time of the probable creation of the Nabta Playa site; once more evidence that the ancients were looking to the skies and by my estimate looking for Nibiru."

"Now before I look at our next date I would like to make an observation, only an observation without any real proof."

"It appears that they may have successfully mined gold on Earth and maintained contact with Nibiru for 10800 years." Another click produced the next slide.

21300BC minus 10500BC is equal to 10800 years

"I admit that's a long time and seems improbable but the suggestion stands that if it did occur there are no historical markers to indicate they were having any problems in completing their task."

"Specifically and importantly, there is no trace of any major cataclysm or disruptive activity on Earth in that time period."

"I think this is worthy of note because it becomes significant later on in our discussion."

"In other words it appears that Nibiru was passing by in its orbit peaceably. This is very important as we look beyond the date of 10500BC."

There was an inordinate amount of shuffling by the commission with several hands half raised then dropped. They apparently were going to continue to listen even if it was unwillingly.

Ian was ready to make another step forward and showed it in his body language. He was animated and positive with each statement.

"Now I need your indulgence and rather than laboring what the 10500BC date may mean to us, except that it was seemingly important to them, or they wouldn't have built a monument facing east presumably on the lookout for the comings and goings of Nibiru."

"One more interesting relevant thing lies in the fact that there is evidence of a shift in the earth's magnetic pole around 10500BC which may have been evidence of Nibiru's presence at that time."

Senator Berger couldn't restrain himself and was waving his hand ready to speak and did so before Ian could continue.

Berger was shaking his head, "You can't possibly expect us to sit here and let you skip along dropping dates that you haven't begun to substantiate in any way."

"Are you just making them up? Why should we believe you? Why should we believe any of this?" Berger waved Ian off with his hand as if totally disgusted.

Ian studied him closely wondering if the senator was going to get up and leave, or ask him to leave. He looked over to Rosenthal who sat calmly in the guise of a man not quite sure what to do.

Ian looked back assertively at Berger, "Look, I could bury you with detailed information and we could be here for days dissecting every bit of it for accuracy and verification," His impatience rose to the surface.

He paused and stepped back, "Or you can let me finish in defining an extremely important problem and maybe get on to start defining solutions."

Berger didn't bother to raise his hand again but simply broke into Ian's response, "Dr. MacGown if you don't mind my saying so, right now you just plain sound silly to me. You sound like some high school kid who hasn't done his homework."

At that remark Senator Rosenthal rose up from his chair, glared at each member of the commission and started to speak.

Ian put his hand up to the Senator and held him back. He returned his gaze to Berger, "Look senator you must have something going for you or you wouldn't be part of this commission."

Ian paused, looked from side to side and then back at Berger, "Think about it senator. I must have something going for me or you wouldn't have asked me here. Maybe you should hear me out."

Ian waited for a response that didn't come so continued looking at Senator Berger as he spoke.

"I'm going to continue offering you as much or as little detail as I need to get to the end of this story. I don't mind questions as long as they help the story move along, but I'm not interested in critical reviews at this point on what I have to offer. You can do that at the end when you've heard all of it."

His pause this time was dramatic, "Or you can ask me to leave now."

Having said that he looked not at Berger but at Rosenthal for a response, who simply nodded and said, "Please proceed Dr. MacGown."

Ian looked at the group defiantly before waving his hand dismissively at them. "Alright, I'll just give you the next date and then tell you how I got there and what it means."

"The date is 9577BC."

"That's when I believe the Earth came in close conjunction with Nibiru and left indelible evidence of the event. And by close conjunction

I don't mean physical bumping like two giant balls in the air, but a virtual war between two magnetically, electrically charged bodies in the sky."

Ian now focused his delivery again to Senator Berger, "Some major event happened in that year and in one book that researched it the writers made over fifteen hundred," Ian spat fifteen hundred out as though it was a bad taste in his mouth, "references to other research efforts on that singular event."

"Fifteen hundred references in one book on the subject." He repeated fifteen hundred again in a softer tone now moving his gaze again from senator to senator, "I certainly can't cover all that here but I can tell you what some of the conclusions were."

He was calm again intent now on getting back to what he had to say, "For one thing they concluded there was another reversal in the polarity of the Earth's magnetic pole like that which had occurred in 10500BC again denoting the possible presence of a large celestial body close to the Earth."

Ian realized he had to be more graphic, "If that body was Nibiru, it would have pulled hard at the Earth with a strong gravitational field and the Earth would have fought back, but I can assure you getting the worst of the battle."

"There is evidence around the world that at that time there were hundreds or even thousands of earthquakes in reaction to that strong gravitational pull by Nibiru. In turn, fires were ignited across the earth from the hot flow of lava. The Earth became seared black from continent to continent."

He was uncertain if they were still listening or had finally given up on him and then continued in more of a monologue tone.

"There would have been hurricane type winds probably exceeding a thousand miles per hour fanning the flames, and if you can believe it a pillar of water would have been drawn up from the Earth reaching up miles and miles into the sky as the gravitational pull of Nibiru drained our oceans."

"When Nibiru finally started to move on in its journey away from the Earth, that pillar of water would descend back to Earth creating a flood that would be remembered for centuries after; a flood of biblical proportions," He looked directly at Senator Holland as he ended his sentence.

Nobody stirred. Ian looked to Berger for a response. The response came from Senator Rosenthal who broke the silence that followed Ian's abrupt stop.

"Go on Dr MacGown, we're listening."

Eager to reconnect with his audience, Ian smiled and said in an almost childlike manner. "Hey you all have probably heard about the woolly mammoths that were inexplicably, instantaneously frozen as they were grazing on the Siberian tundra. When this cataclysm occurred it would have had resultant instantaneous major drops in temperatures around the earth that would explain the mammoth's demise into a suddenly frozen state."

"I know that sounds like science fiction, but we all have some level of awareness of stories of the great flood. The flood is not the whole story, but it's something that we all can relate to."

"There's also a lot of other evidence that has been researched and documented. For instance bodies of a huge variety of large and small animal bones piled on top of each other in caves around the world occur in places they shouldn't be."

"Elephants in caves in South America for instance."

"The same kind of thing occurred with fauna encased in frozen lava scattered around the world in places it didn't belong."

Ian paused again to collect himself, "There is an abundance of evidence to support that this did happen, so the big question shouldn't be whether or not it happened but why did it happen in 9577BC?"

Senator Ligget who had been quiet throughout the session finally spoke up, "You're telling us that you believe this Nibiru hit Earth and caused all that destruction. Why do you think it might have been Nibiru? Is that what all of those researchers you alluded to concluded? Isn't it really much more probable that we were hit by a giant meteorite or an asteroid?"

Ian started to answer, but Ligget wasn't through. He stood up dramatically and asked, "Shouldn't there be a crater like when the dinosaurs became extinct sixty-five million years ago? Where's the crater Dr. MacGown?"

Ian smiled glad to hear a new voice in the argument. It was a reasonable question, "Thank you Senator Ligget, I thought you would never ask," Ian looked around at each of the senators before continuing with his next statement which he said slowly emphasizing every word.

"There was no crater in 9577BC."

He waited for a further response from Ligget and continued slowly enunciating each syllable, "With all that destruction there was no sign of a crater. If it was anything but a large celestial body in close proximity without actually crashing into the Earth, there should have been a crater."

Ian leaned forward punching each word at his audience, "There was no crater! It had to be Nibiru."

The commission members sat quietly like a whipped fighter sits on his stool after receiving the ten count. They had nothing to offer to refute Ian's assertion. The only one left standing was Senator Rosenthal who for some reason snickered quietly and said, "Please go on Dr. MacGown."

Ian stood a little perplexed at the situation and spoke up a little more cautiously, "Well that's not all of it. For instance the ancients who are described in the old clay cuneiform tablets stated they believed it was their planet Nibiru that was going to hit the Earth," his tone was definitely more conciliatory, "that's why they instructed Noah to build the ark."

"Most of us have heard of the story of Noah, I believe." Ian was afraid he was treading again on the question as to whether or not the ancients were being called gods by him, and moved ahead quickly. Senator Holland looked like he was about to raise the question again then shrugged it off.

Ian had become tentative, not sure if he had made a major point or dug a hole for himself, and proceeded almost apologetically, "The other bit of evidence I believe is derived from the 9577BC date itself when there is so much evidence that some major celestial body did come into close proximity to the Earth."

Senator Ligget unabashed spoke up again, "Why so exact? Why 9577BC? Why not simply say 9500BC or 9600BC?"

Ian's answer was short and to the point, "Researchers who reviewed hundreds of radio carbon dates of surviving artifacts from around the world that focused on that event, found an astonishing correlation to the 9577BC date." He then smiled once again and looked back to Senator Ligget.

"To your point, however, if you are a student of history and are aware of the story of Atlantis sinking into the ocean, you might also be aware that the Greek philosopher Plato gave a date of 9600BC that he believed was the time of the sinking of Atlantis. There is an obvious, seeming correlation between that 9600BC date and the 9577BC event. Although the 9600BC date as you suggest is a possibility, it is more folk lore than history without a basis of research. I believe, however it does tend to support the occurrence of some major cataclysm in history."

Berger was back hand raised in the air waving in a way that was sarcastic without words, "Dr. MacGown you are a great story teller," he drew each word out for emphasis, "but I think I've forgotten or gotten lost in the woods like Hansel and Gretel as to why you are here."

Ian drew back and grinned, "Ah, Senator Berger," he was beginning to like the relationship he was building with the Senator from Missouri, "of course you want answers now, right now."

Ian's brow wrinkled with thought, "Yes, I remember you asked me here to tell you if the Earth will be hit by another planet."

Ian stopped and smiled again at Berger, "Yes Senator I believe, although I'm not absolutely certain of the date, it will be hit by Nibiru sometime as late as 2100AD or as soon as 2038AD."

Berger shot back at Ian, "You're not funny MacGown."

Ian kept smiling, "I wasn't trying to be funny. This isn't a funny situation." His repeated emphasis on the word funny drew the smile from his face.

Berger looked in disbelief, "You're saying 2038BC, a specific date with no proof. You have got to be kidding. How can you keep this farce up?"

Ian was becoming irritated with his adversary, "That wouldn't be that funny unless I was kidding, would it. I'm not kidding."

Senator Rosenthal attempting once more to maintain decorum asked quietly, "How serious is that 2038 date? That is literally tomorrow."

Ian became more sober and studied in his answer and looked at Rosenthal who was nodding his head up and down for agreement, "Let me finish up as quickly as I can and tell you how we got there. There are other possibilities for dates that may make more sense but those other dates still pose a major concern."

He had cast the die and now was going to have to put some money on the table. Berger had goaded him and he was upset at himself for taking the bait.

He looked at Sadie for reassurance and winked at her. Maybe they were ready to listen.

He began, "To make any sense out of this I need to explain the best I can how I believe the orbit of Nibiru may relate to the Earth's orbit."

He clicked several times and stopped on a slide showing the Earth and Nibiru.

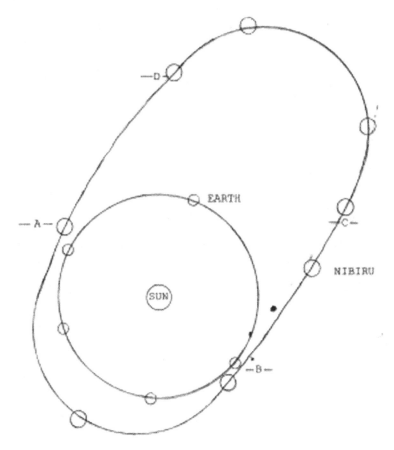

Bear with me in looking at this problem with this very rough drawn sketch and picture the Earth, if you can, circling the Sun, as I've shown in its 365 day orbit in what is essentially a flat elliptic.

"Now in your mind picture Nibiru swinging at one end of its elongated ellipse around the Sun, ergo Earth, as shown on the slide. It's possible from this slide to imagine, that at some time, probably very, very rarely, but sometime in the course of thousands of years, the respective orbits of Earth and Nibiru are going to be on a collision course as suggested by points A and B. At points C and D, however, at the long ends of Nibiru's orbit it's unlikely that we would even be aware of its existence."

Ian perused his audience looking for a reaction and decided to proceed without comment from them, "Now here's an important subtlety. Since Nibiru travels in an elongated orbit it naturally has one portion of its orbit relative to Earth that takes longer to complete than the other as I've suggested on this slide. From my slide it's easy to see that travel from point A to point B in a counter-clockwise direction should take less time then travel from point B continuing around in a counter-clockwise direction back to point A."

Berger couldn't restrain himself. He called out, "Sheer genius, Professor, sheer genius."

Ian didn't flinch. He had to use Berger's goading to his advantage, not fight it, "Ah yes, of course Senator Berger you knew that, but did you also realize that the time that occurred between the pole shift in 10500BC and the cataclysm in 9577BC, when there was a second pole shift, represented the number of years for one quadrant of that 3600 year orbit with the four quadrants reading as AB, BC, CD and DA."

"Now I need to establish relative distances in each of those quadrants, which I chose to do in years traveled."

"Sheer genius, wouldn't you say Senator," he grinned at Berger and moved forward not waiting for another response.

"So let's do some easy arithmetic," He waved his red laser beam, "We believe we may have been in close conjunction, enough to cause a pole shift, with Nibiru in 10500BC at point A, and again in virtual contact in 9577BC at point B."

"We are offering as a supposition that in the year 10500BC Nibiru may have been at point A causing some disruption as a result of its close proximity and continued on to point B on at which time the cataclysm occurred on 9577BC."

"Did it actually occur that way? We'll probably never know for sure. Could it have happened that way? We think there's a high probability."

"Now, with that as a probability, if I may do some additional simple arithmetic; 10500BC minus 9577BC equals 923 the number of years to travel from point A to point B."

"If I assume it takes the same number of years to travel from point C to point D, because ellipses are symmetrical, I arrive at a total of 1846 years by combining the travel at the ends of the ellipse."

Berger was shaking his head and hand simultaneously, "First we get a ridiculous history lesson and now a ridiculous arithmetic lesson. Do you have anything relevant to tell this Commission Dr. MacGown?"

Ian took a deep breath and grinned back at Berger, "Yes I do. If you subtract 1846 from 3600 and divide by two for a resultant 877 years you will have described the number of years to travel from B to C and to travel from D to A, and by that reasoning, describe four quadrants of the ellipse of Nibiru."

Ian shouted over the din that followed his audacious response to Berger, "I submit to the possibility that there may have been regular approaches close to Earth by Nibiru on a cycle that repeated in 923 years intervals followed by 877 years, followed in turn by 923 years and again 877 years; and so on."

His insistence was enough to bring relative calm to the group, "I purposely qualified, may have been, because there are other potential time intervals which we'll be discussing later." Ian paused, waited for quiet and continued cautiously.

"Events that followed in the many years after the 9577BC cataclysm, although circumstantial, show a possible pattern of continued close contact at these kinds of intervals that resulted in ongoing, cataclysmic events for our Earth and concurrently past civilizations."

"This cycle of 923 and 877 years is the one that initially caught our attention; and now that I've got you focused on those numbers I'm going to ask you to focus on some other similar numbers or cycles that we need to address."

None of the senators flinched, but sat resigned, some with hands clasped together, others with arms locked across their chests waiting for Ian to stumble.

Ian was driving that soccer ball towards the goal and there was no way to stop him, "Our second premise was based on the belief that before, and I must emphasize before, the 9577BC event Nibiru operated on a legitimate 3600 year cycle."

"Our historical and scientific research combined has led us to believe that Nibiru's speed as a planet traveling around the Sun was undoubtedly altered by the encounter with Earth in 9577BC. We believe it slowed down and the 3600 year cycle was altered.

"If this is a correct and reasonable assumption then we must look carefully at how Nibiru may have continued its journey after 9577BC. Specifically, we must ask did it remain on its original cycle of 923 and 877 years or are there other possibilities?"

Berger couldn't stand it and once more interrupted before Ian could say any more, "I must say my dear Dr. MacGown the more you clarify things the more confused I get."

He looked around at the other Commission members. "Does anybody have a clue about what this garrulous individual is trying to tell this Commission?"

Senator Rosenthal broke the momentary silence that followed, "I do and I don't think we should take it lightly. Unless any of the other Commission members have something more pressing to attend to I suggest we continue to hear Dr. MacGown out."

"However, if anyone would like to dismiss themselves from the Commission at this point, it will be without prejudice on my part." He stared directly at Berger. Berger shuffled in his chair. Nobody else moved.

Senator Rosenthal looked back to Ian, "Dr. MacGown I do think we could use a little more explanation as to what you believe happened after what you refer to as the event in 9577BC."

He looked around at the Commission members who seemed unsettled, looked back at Ian and said, "I believe before we do that maybe we should break for lunch."

Ian looked back at the senator with moderate distress in his eyes, "This is not a good place to break, but if you will allow me to show some alternate scenarios when we come back before going on with what happened, I'll be fine," His voice had a ring of disappointment in it.

Rosenthal nodded to Schmidt. "Bob, will you take care of our guests?" Schmidt answered with a high five and moved towards Ian and Sadie.

As Schmidt approached them Sadie quipped loud enough for Berger to hear, "Why don't we just leave him here, there's not much left of him."

Berger stopped ready to make a comment, thought better of it and walked away.

Sadie looked at Schmidt, "What is his problem? Why is he even on the Commission?"

Schmidt bowed his head so as not to be heard by anyone but Ian and Sadie, "Be careful, he has some clout and will use it when provoked. Come on let's get lunch."

*

Ian flopped down into a chair at the same table in the cafeteria where they had coffee earlier and looked at Schmidt. "Smitty, what is that guy's problem? If he has so many issues with our subject why is he on the Commission?"

Schmidt smiled at his old friend. "Don't sweat it Ian. It probably has nothing to do with you. He actually has great interest in what's going on."

"In fact, he wanted to head the Commission, but they gave it to Rosenthal, because as I told you they wanted a man with some military experience. I think Berger of the two is actually, probably more qualified. I understand he graduated at the top of his class at MIT and went on to do graduate work in astrophysics. I'm not sure where he got it, but he may have his doctorate in that field. I know for sure he did a stint with NASA in some capacity before getting into politics. That's a lot of background for someone, who frankly looks pretty young, and he's not just another lawyer playing politics."

Schmidt looked around again before offering a warning, "Be careful, Berger has a lot of friends in the Senate. He can hurt you. Right now he's just grinding an axe with Rosenthal."

Ian snarled back, "Frankly I'm not sure I give a damn about what or why he's doing anything."

Sadie who had become quiet put her hand on Ian's arm, "What we're trying to get done is a lot more important than some petty territorial dispute between senators, be cool Ian."

She paused and then grinned at the two men, "Sorry, I guess I wasn't very cool with my remark in there."

Schmidt gathered them up and directed them towards the food line, "Come on, let's get some lunch."

After a quick scramble on the cafeteria line and gobbling their food down, they all sat back as if to take a deep breath. Schmidt pushed his empty plate to the center of the table, looked around one more time to see who might be within ear shot and looked back at Ian.

"Ian I have to be honest and warn you buddy, these guys have already decided they are going to try and blow up your planet Nibiru. All they want from you is a date, an exact date to work to in implementing what they consider a good solution. That's why Berger is on your case every time he thinks you might give an exact date. Is that where you are? Are you ready to give them a date?" Schmidt asked showing concern in his eyes.

Ian didn't answer but sat with his lips slightly parted and then spoke as though blessed with a great revelation.

"Those sons of bitches, they've been playing me. Maybe it's time I play them a little bit." Ian stopped mid thought as though he had another great revelation.

"That's why Patel is behaving so erratically," he shouted, "That's why they came after Sadie, because she's the key to us succeeding. Patel's afraid they will try to blow up Nibiru."

Both Sadie and Schmidt sat up straight at the name of Patel. Sadie said, "Hush, Ian you're being too loud."

Schmidt looked at Ian with a raised eyebrow, "Who the hell is Patel?"

Sadie answered quickly for Ian, "He was the member of our Think Tank that was so strongly oriented to the Preservation side of things."

Ian winked at Sadie as if to say, "I've got this," and directed his attention back to Schmidt. "Patel must have found out about the Commission's intent to try and blow up Nibiru. He would be solidly against that because he believes all life is sacred where ever it exists, and he does as I do believe there may still be life on Nibiru."

Ian continued dryly as though what he was saying wasn't that important and should be known by everyone, "He's from one of those sects from India that believe you shouldn't kill even the least of all living things especially people who may be responsible for our very existence."

Schmidt looked again to Ian, "Is he, this Patel, or this whole situation going to be a problem?"

Ian grinned, "No, it's no problem. Not for the moment. In fact I can use it to steer things a little more our way now that I'm aware of the whole situation. The Commission will listen for as long as I chose to talk, or until I give them the date they want. Thanks Smitty, I didn't realize I was flying blind in there."

"As a matter of fact it's time to get back in there. Come on, let's go. I feel refreshed." He got up and pushed away from the table and headed back without any attention as to whether or not either Schmidt or Sadie was following him.

*

Ian faced the Commission members scrutinizing their faces and wondering what they had discussed at lunch. Senator Rosenthal gave him a hint.

"Dr. MacGown, please pick up where you left off. We were discussing dates when you thought Nibiru might approach our Earth once again."

"A thin disguise," Ian thought to himself.

"There are additional dates we may want to discuss. I think I can more easily bring them into focus by establishing the optional paths we think Nibiru may have taken after 9577BC. The evidence we have strongly indicates two obvious possibilities. It either continued on a regular 3600 year cycle which I have already described or continued to slow down to a slower yearly cycle. It seems very unlikely that it would have speeded up."

"Since this is all speculation on my part as to whether or not Nibiru may have slowed down; or if it did how much it may have slowed," Ian took his time, he was feeling good about where he was in the conversation with the new found knowledge he had gained from Smitty. Feeling they would listen for as long as it took for him to make his point he took a deep breath and continued.

"Not knowing anything about the speed of planets," he glanced over to Berger, "We simply made some reasonable assumptions based on our previous work. We assumed it was unlikely that Nibiru speeded up, although we were able to find some obscure evidence of planets slowing down after a celestial encounter with another body."

He clicked ahead to another slide, "I admit information on this slide may be more guess work than science, but it does show the calculated effect of possible slowing by Nibiru and dates that may result from the slowing."

Rotation cycle in years	3585	3590	3595	3600
Possible contact date	2038	2055	2071	2097

Ian winked at Berger as the slide went up and thought to himself that was dumb, Smitty warned he could be a problem.

The Commission carefully studied the slide looking for more than was there, with the obvious awareness that it didn't begin to answer the question that was on everyone's mind. A strong sense of anti-climax pervaded the room.

Senator Ligget spoke up first, "Dr. MacGown can you explain how you got to those particular end dates? We can see the numbers you used but don't understand how you established them."

Ian replied, "I'm sure you realize these are only probable dates based on assumptions we made. What we're suggesting is that the actual date based on those assumptions could be anywhere between 2038 and 2097."

Ligget blinked realizing that Ian had just repeated essentially what he had asked.

Ian began to offer more explanation then hesitated and asked the commission members for a reprieve, "If I may I would first like to introduce some additional historical dates with explanations before attempting to clarify these dates."

The Commission members simply shrugged their shoulders as if to say, "What now?"

Ian ignored their reaction and went on with his diatribe, "There are two sets of dates to consider in this exercise. The first are dates in our recorded history of troublesome times marking significant events such as flooding and or major volcanic activity."

"There is also a second set of dates representing activity by ongoing civilizations after the great flood or if you prefer the 9577BC event. The activity or people I want to bring to your attention all had the same characteristic. They had their eyes to the skies apparently continuing to study the movement of Orion and the Precession of the Equinoxes."

"I submit to you that the survivors of 9577BC had retained enough knowledge to understand that Nibiru could return with its devastating consequences; and they would study the skies for thousands of years setting alarms on their solar clocks to warn them of the repeated passing of NIbiru.

"After that fatal time in history when their world almost ended, they built even more sophisticated solar clocks. It almost had to be that they were no longer concerned with mining and transporting gold, but perhaps with the future survival of civilization and the planet Earth."

"They were trying to protect what they had, and in order to survive had to keep track of something they knew was waiting for them, coming at them again, albeit perhaps far in the future and they felt a responsibility to warn future generations of an impending doom."

"There is evidence of all this, only circumstantial, but I believe convincing evidence."

He smiled to himself at how quietly the Commission sat and listened, "Let me show my next slide." He said quietly.

"This is an array of dates that followed the 9577BC event using the yearly rotational numbers of 923 and 877, which are derived from using a 3600 year cycle and assuming that 923 years after 9577BC became normal to that cycle."

"This was our initial assumption."

Ian stood silently as each member of the commission studied his slide. He broke the silence that had settled on the group, "I'll give you a chance to digest it and then would like to review some specifics."

"I'm not necessarily excited about this slide. On one hand it's very busy. On the other hand it leaves so much out. We can look at it as a start, however, to begin to look in some sequence as to what happened after that cataclysmic event in 9577BC."

"Before looking at what followed 9577BC I need to remind you again as shown on this slide that over 20000 years ago someone built Napta Playa so they could track the movement of the Belt Stars in the Orion constellation and in turn the Precession through the Equinoxes. They had established the first solar clock to track large spans of time."

"They used this knowledge to coordinate a visit by two beings from another planet in 17700BC, and in 10500BC built the Sphinx, again to focus on Orion's Belt as the instrument of their solar clock."

"Okay, let's look at what the information suggests. I would like to take you through it, reading from the time of the cataclysm in 9577BC,

to point out what I believe to be significant dates and events that seem
to coordinate with probable passings of Nibiru. The time spans between
the various dates indicated are 923 and 877 years respectively. The years
we discussed, we believe, represent four quadrants of Nibiru's cycle."

Signs of Nibiru		Solar Clocks
	2100AD	
China in floods and turmoil	1223AD	Tenochtitlan, Chaco Canyon
Easter Island settled after a cataclysm	300AD	Angkor Wat
	577BC	Chichen Itza
Knossos destroyed	1500BC	
Sudden collapse of major civilizations, volcanoes	2377BC	Great Pyramid
	3300BC	Stonehenge
	4177BC	SUMERIAN CIVILIZATION arrives around 4000BC
	5100BC	
Major floods in Australia	5977BC	Napta Playa Calendar circle in use
	6900BC	Catal Huyuk
	7797BC	
	8700BC	Gobekli Tepe
CATACLYSM Atlantis sinks	9577BC	
Utah salt water flats formed	10500BC **	SPHINX
	17700BC **	Gods take off from Earth
	20377 BC	Napta Playa

"The event in 9577BC was certainly not planned, although we believe the ancients knew it was going to happen; in any event it changed everything as events following 9577BC indicate."

Ian used his laser pointer to focus on dates on the slide and began.

"Before I get into these dates, I think, as a side note it's interesting to note that the Salt Water Flats in Utah are believed by scientists to have been formed around nine to ten thousand years ago, when they would have been a body of water made up of salt water, that miraculously evaporated all at once; obviously at the time around the 9577BC event."

He redirected the laser beam back to the story he had to tell and went on, "For two rotations of Nibiru in 8700BC and 7797BC there must have been ongoing devastation with survivors simply trying to stay alive, ala Noah and his ark."

"One of the very interesting archeological site that has been excavated in recent years is a site in southern Turkey known as Gobekli Tepe which has dressed monoliths around twenty feet high with unusual carvings on them and focused on the rising and falling of Orion's Belt. They appear to have been erected some time close to 9577BC date, either just before or right after that event. You could reason that either the ancients were trying to determine the probable time that Nibiru would arrive or that perhaps as survivors they were already looking to the skies worried about the future."

There was no response to Ian's introduction of Gobekli Tepe as being important so he went back to the familiar story of Noah and his ark.

"Another interesting side note that may attest to the scientific advancement of those ancient people is a popular notion in today's scientific community that Noah didn't necessarily have actual species of all animals and things, but DNA samples that could be used as survival kits. Even at that he would have had an arduous task in front of him to reinvent civilization."

Berger exasperated once more said, "Please get on with it Dr. MacGown."

Ian quickly focused the laser beam back and forth between the dates of 6900BC and 5997BC without any additional comment about Noah and his ark or Gobekli Tepe, "It's interesting to note that Catel Huyuk a civilization that flourished in southern Turkey around 6900BC was believed to have been established by survivors of the great flood; people who were able to pass old skills and knowledge forward to ultimately recreate remnants of a civilization that they had lost. Their homes were made of mud-bricks with flat roofs, which made them similar to many other ancient cities."

The Commission members sat silently and Ian was ready to move ahead, "As I move forward to these next dates I must go back to the analysis by Dr. Brophy of the Napta Playa archeological site. He observed that three of the major stele at the site represented Orion's Belt at a date later than earlier dates we had discussed. Specifically he felt they represented Orion's Belt on the meridian around solstice from 6400BC to 4900BC."

Ian pursed his lips tightly before continuing. "I know it's another giant leap, but what if there were survivors with that same technical knowledge they had in the past continuing to use Napta Playa to scan the skies? Circumstantial evidence or another monumental coincidence, take your pick?" He paused for a reaction from the Commission.

Berger slumped back in his chair and shook his head. He was ready to let someone else be the attack dog for a while.

Ian went on, showing excitement and directing his pointer this time to the years 5977BC and 4177BC.

"This is a big one," he whispered like he had a secret to tell, "Sumer in Mesopotamia is accepted today as that place where civilization as we know it had begun."

His tone again became that of a lecturer and he broke into a new diatribe, "Civilization literally erupted in Sumer with tall brick buildings, the use of furnaces and the kiln in baking and producing pottery. The Sumerians had mathematics, astronomy, laws, arts and musical instruments. They built cities and suburbs in creating a cultured society, and the most significant achievement of all to make that possible; they invented writing and were able to maintain records for everything, whether it was for business or personal use on clay cylinders. This all happened 6000 years ago around 4000BC."

"When archeologists started to excavate Sumerian cities back in the mid nineteenth century, and as they continue to do today, they found thousands of clay cylinders with a strange script on them that held many secrets of the past."

Ian knew he had a lot of loose ends that were beginning to fray and it was time to attempt to pull things together. He pointed in Sadie's direction, "It's from Dr. Haddad's work in deciphering some of those old clay cylinders found in Sumer that we're here today on this important mission."

Ian pulled up and looked at the group. "I'm sure you get where I'm going with this. When the various cities that had been built by the Sumerians were excavated by archeologists they discovered over seventeen different levels of occupation starting at around 2500BC and finding the lowest level at 4000BC. And it wasn't just a mud hut. It was the base of a temple."

"Now look again at this chart when there was a passing of Nibiru at 5100BC and again at 4177BC. Remember I said these dates represent only one possibility as to how Nibiru tracked after the big event."

"It certainly looks, however, like the Sumerians and the Nibiruians may have been the same people. I could offer a lot more circumstantial evidence that gives credence to this idea, but I would prefer to leave you with the thought that they returned sometime around 4000BC and established a civilization similar to that which they had on Nibiru, and in all probability similar to that which they had established here on Earth prior to 9577BC."

This time Senator Blessing who had said nothing since they started raised his hand insistently and gave Ian a hard stare. "I've read a little bit of

Sumerian history and believe that we are all descendents of the Sumerians, but are you telling us we are all Nirbiruians?"

Blessing stuttered, trying to get Nibiruians out, whether it was from a speech problem or a kind of stupor for having to deal with such an outrageous idea was uncertain.

His thrust at Ian created a roar of laughter with Berger and Ligget laughing until tears flowed from their eyes.

Ian stood silently for a second or two, then looked first at Ligget and Berger, then back at Blessing, smiled and said, "Senator Blessing that's a very reasonable question and I don't have a good answer for you. What I can tell you is the question has been hotly debated since the early part of this century; sometimes from a religious point of view, sometimes from a scientific point of view. In either instance it doesn't make any difference to what we must address here today."

"We can all continue that debate if we survive another cataclysm. If not, it may not matter."

Ian looked around at the commission members who had become silent and pensive in response to his very serious response to Blessing's question.

He addressed them again very soberly. "I would like to look now, if you are all agreeable, at some other very significant dates that I feel correlates strongly with dates when Nibiru may have passed closely to the Earth."

"In the time periods correlating with Nibiru's 3300BC and 2377BC passing's some very great, familiar structures were built by our ancestors that as in the past were focused on the skies and specifically on the movement of Orion's Belt. Many great Henges the most famous of which is Stonehenge were built in Great Britain. All of these today have been recognized as solar calendars, albeit they may have used different methods; they all focused on the constellation of Orion"

"In Egypt, on the Giza Plateau, one of the greatest most sophisticated solar clocks and calendars ever built still exists. The construction of this solar clock included no less than seven monuments, including the Great Pyramid, which were aligned in such a manner as to track precisely the movement of Orion's Belt, and in my estimation the movement of Nibiru as it passed repeatedly, although in long intervals, close to Earth."

Ian's voice had a tone of desperate on in it as he addressed the group anew. "What other purpose could they have possibly had; and who other than someone with more technology and astronomical knowledge than, I believe, we have today could have created and built those extremely complex structures?"

The commission was silent. Ian continued, "That's not all." He stated emphatically, "We still don't have a good explanation for structures in the Americas like Chichen Itcha, Tenochtitlan and Chaco Canyon, all of which are focused on the summer solstice and the movement of the Sun and the stars; and by my thinking Orion's Belt."

"Few people realize that the Hopi Indians in America had three religious buildings in the same configuration on the ground as the three Orion Belt stars. This is the same as the three pyramids on the Giza strip in Egypt which reflected the same configuration as the Belt Stars, again, on the ground."

This would have to be a monumental coincidence that two apparently different cultures, on two different continents, would be so engrossed with the orientation and movement of Orion's Belt stars unless they had the same concerns and purposes."

"And oops I almost forgot Ankor Wat in Cambodia focused on a constellation different than Orion, but seemingly with the same intent."

"These disparate structures built around the world all ask the same questions."

"Who really built them and why?" I think we know the answer."

The commission remained silent. Ian didn't know if they had finally given up on him and were letting him vent his spleen or had decided to hear him out.

Berger in a way came to his rescue. He asked sarcastically, "Is that it? Can we tell from that when your mystery planet will get here?"

Ian replied carefully. He was being played and he knew it. He wanted to be careful about how this ended, not to give any more ground then he had to at this time.

He looked back at Berger, "I can understand you might be skeptical, but take a look at the other side of the chart."

"For instance we found evidence that there was major flooding in Australia at 5977BC."

"Around 2377BC tree rings showed slow growth and there was widespread volcanic activity around the world. Coincident with that, history tells us that between 2000BC and 2500BC a large number of major civilizations around the world collapsed simultaneously. This would have included the Akkadian, Afghanistan Hilmand civilization, the Indus Valley in India, the Hongsan Culture in China, Israel, Anatolia and Greece. The list is endless it seems. You can check some of these in your history books and others in the family Bible."

Ian ignored Holland's bristling at the mention of the Bible as a part of his rhetoric and went on.

"A thousand years later around 1223BC, which is close to the 923 years we suggested as one leg of Nibiru's rotation, there was another major widespread collapse of civilizations including the Mycenaean's of Greece, the Hittites of Anatolia and the Shang Dynasty of China; and the whole Northern Hemisphere including central Russia suffered severe climatic distress. These conflagrations caused huge dislocations of many people around the world changing the course of history."

Ian was on another roll not to be stopped. "Just a little more and I'll quit," he quipped.

"There also were significant collapses of major civilizations in South America around that same time of 1223BC including the Olmecs;

and a relocation of the Aztecs to higher ground to avoid an oncoming tsunami."

"It's interesting to note in support of all of this that the Mayans in Mexico claimed that they were survivors of survivors."

"Unfortunately the Conquistadors deprived us of any detailed history when they conquered Montezuma and the Mexican people and destroyed much of the literature that would have given us insight to that particular history."

Without pause Ian pointed to the next item on his chart.

"Sometime around 312BC Easter Island was settled by people, who many generations later would tell Captain Cook when he rediscovered them, that they thought they were the only survivors of a great cataclysm. The initial settlers and generations after them would build hundreds of great statutes that they would station on their coast lines, with eyes to the sky looking for we know not what, but we can guess."

Ian was taken back when Rosenthal suddenly interrupted him and said, "Dr. Mac Gown, we need to talk about a date. When will Nibiru approach the Earth again?"

Ian seemed unsure of himself for the first time since he started this arduous task of explaining how Earth was in imminent danger. He shifted his weight backwards and said hesitantly. "I can't give you one now, not this minute, but with your help for Dr. Haddad and me we know how to get one. That's why Dr. Haddad and I are here. We need your help."

The cat was out of the bag and Ian's conversation came in rapid spurts. "In our efforts within the boundaries of the Think Tank I alluded to earlier we came upon some old scripts that talked about Nibiru and its orbit."

"Let me regroup a little bit here with some additional information. The alignment of all the planets in our solar system keeps changing as they spin in their respective orbits; different alignments can cause different situations. We can today, as were the ancients, able to calculate these alignments in tables called Ephemerides Tables."

For the first time since Ian had begun his story Senator Berger shook his head in a very positive way. Ian continued but could not take his eyes off of Berger, who was now hanging on his every word.

"He said, the information we found was very specific about how the ancients calculated the orbit of Nibiru and its precise movement using their Ephemerides Tables, which we believe contains information on Nibiru as well as the other planets in our solar system. Unfortunately, the information we found did not include the actual tables or their calculations, but gave us clues as to where they might be found."

"Those clues, if we are to take advantage of them would require Dr. Haddad and me to travel to Egypt."

Ian was speaking to the group, but directing his comments now to Senator Rosenthal. "As I'm sure you are all aware since the major outbreak of violence in that area of the world in 2015 Egypt has closed their boarders to just about everyone. Dr. Haddad and I thought, hoped, that maybe the U.S. government could get us into Egypt."

"That's why we have been so aggressive in presenting our case about Nibiru. We wanted to be sure you would listen and take us seriously. The information we're after is in Egypt and as we all know is important to the whole world."

Senator Brown, who had not spoken during the whole session leaned forward and firmly, demandingly asked, "How do we know you can get the information you allude to or that you'll recognize and understand what you're looking at if it bites you in the ass. Is that going to be a problem for you?"

Ian hesitated just for a second. Sadie who had been sitting with her right leg now crossed atop her left knee a little bit back from Ian uncrossed her legs moved closer to Ian grasped the microphone from his hand and pulled it towards her. "No sir, it will not be a problem," she said emphatically, "not in finding the information or in understanding it when we see it."

"Ah, I thought so," the senator showed his delight, "Those eyes too deeply involved in all that's been said. Dr. Haddad, I presume," he quipped although she had been introduced at the beginning of the session. "I've heard about you. I thought you would be…"

"A man," Sadie finished his sentence for him.

"Older," Brown grinned back.

Ian reached over and retrieved the microphone. "Dr. Haddad has studied languages of this generation and for many, many generations past. She has studied in every mid-eastern country that exists in their most prestigious institutes, and can read and decipher all of the ancient languages including Egyptian, Sumerian, Assyrian and Hebrew."

Ian knew this moment would come regarding Sadie and was ready, "Dr. Haddad can stand in front of any stele or Egyptian wall and read the script verbatim without notes. She can leave that wall or stele; get on a plane, travel three thousand miles and tell you when she arrives exactly what she read."

Ian wasn't done. He wanted to be sure they understood, "She spent ten years working at Luxor Temple in Egypt with the University Of Chicago as part of the Oriental Institutes Epigraphic Survey team that copies and publishes texts from inscribed walls. Dr. Haddad can read old Sumerian clay tablets like you would read the Sunday newspaper."

Senator Rosenthal threw up his hands above his head smiling at Sadie, "We give. We surrender to the good Doctor of Languages." He wanted to say lady, but thought better of it.

"What do you need from us? I believe we can get you into Egypt or any place else you need to go? As you have pointed out repeatedly Dr. MacGown this is important."

The room became suddenly very quiet. Senator Rosenthal waved down hands that had been raised by several senators. He looked at Ian and Sadie and nodded to Schmidt, "Bob, please see that Dr. Haddad and Dr. MacGown get some dinner and have them back here at 8:30 in the AM; as for the members of the commission please remain here. We need to discuss our options in proceeding."

Schmidt walked to the exit and motioned to Ian and Sadie to follow him. "Okay guys here we go again back to the hotel which is probably our best bet for a good meal and some rest."

Ian and Sadie fell in behind him without additional comment, heads both slightly bowed in deep thought about the day's proceedings.

Ian stopped abruptly and looked back at the conference room as if to get one last glimpse about what was being said there. He was still absorbing the sudden change in his situation.

Schmidt saw his hesitation. "Come on Ian we've got to go."

Ian stepped forward and grasped Schmidt's arm. "Just like that we're out of there. That doesn't make sense."

Schmidt turned grasping Ian by both shoulders and looking him squarely in the eyes grinned at him and said, "Hey you're ahead on the score card, don't blow it. You did great in there. I've seen them tear some others up in the first five minutes. Pack your bag you're going to Egypt. I'm probably going with you."

Ian grinned back, "But you're not Egyptian."

Schmidt smirked, "Yeah, right."

Sadie moved in and gave Ian a hug. "You did a great job in there sweetie, I never doubted you for a minute. By the way that was pretty hot stuff you said about me in there."

Ian hugged her back whispering in her ear, "That's your charm Sweetheart, the things you say to me, that's your charm."

Sadie pushed him back away from her, "Oh no, not Bogart again. Come on, let's get some dinner."

They followed Schmidt to the street and Sadie stopped short looking across to the corner, "Oh God, not them again, they're worse than dealing with Bogart all the time." Ian looked surprised not at seeing the black jump suited ones again, but at how well Sadie responded this time to their recurring appearance.

Schmidt looked at her reassuringly. "Don't worry we've been watching them all day. I've got two men on them waiting for any move they make. Come on I promise dinner will be quiet."

*

Ian broke the silence that followed another round of prime ribs at the Hyatt House Hotel restaurant. "This is getting monotonous, although I'll say the cook certainly knows what he's doing."

He grinned at Sadie as he slid her half eaten meal onto his plate. He looked at Schmidt quizzically, "Smitty, are you sure you have those guys under control?"

Schmidt who had been lost in thought ignored Ian's query and looked at him earnestly as a five year old boy would. "Ian, how much of all that stuff you're feeding these guys do you believe?"

Ian grabbed the moment, sat back in his chair with his arms crossed in front of him and asked, "Who wants to know?"

Schmidt shook his head as he answered, "Who the hell do you think? Those guys outside asked me to come in and ask you. I'm serious Ian. What do you believe is real about all this?"

Ian realized his friend was serious and took a moment before answering, "I really believe all that I had to say today and I'll tell you what, there's more that I'm afraid to bring up because it's not really relevant and I don't think you would believe any of it. In fact you would probably think I'm ready for the loony bin."

Schmidt knew his friend well enough to know that there were even odds that he was being led on, but decided to take the bait for the sake of conversation. "Okay, hit me. Let it all hang out."

Ian sat back once more and grinned. "Okay you've heard about flying saucers, UFO's right. Do you know how they make all those crazy turns and suddenly disappear. They use the lines of force of the Earth much the same way an electric motor operates with the electro magnets in the stator of a motor. The motor generates torque the way the UFO's generate speed and acceleration, or more correctly the UFO's generate speed and acceleration the way a motor generates torque only using the Earth's lines of force."

Schmidt just laughed at his friend remembering conversations like this back in their high school days. He snickered and asked, "Is that all you've got?"

Ian was enjoying himself after a trying day that had substantially more consequence to it than his banter with Smitty.

"Okay, try this. You know Einstein's Theory of Relativity. One part of that says if you leave the Earth and speed away approaching the speed of light time begins to slow down. I'm sure you've seen the old movies where the guy comes back from a trip in space the same age as his parents. Okay here's the deal Nibiru for all intent and purpose is a space ship compared to Earth and travels at speeds exceeding 100,000 miles per hour."

"Now, have you ever wondered how those angels in the Bible were always coming to our guys and telling them what was going to happen next? What if the angels were from Nibiru ala a space ship traveling at fantastic speeds though space and returning periodically to what might have been their past; or future if you like."

Sadie who had been listening quietly and patiently gave Ian a look, "Ian, stop it,"

Schmidt waved her off, "No, let him go. I'm enjoying it. It's not the first time he's held me his clutches of wild ideas. Come on Ian, what else have you got?"

It was still early in the evening and Ian was light hearted "Okay Smitty try this. Have you ever wondered why we as a species sunburn? How many other hominoids can you think of who also burn in the sun?"

Schmidt furrowed his brow and shrugged his shoulders silently acknowledging he knew of no other.

Ian sat the trap, "Why are all the Scandinavians who live farther away from the equator so light in complexion and those people who live nearer the equator darker in skin? Don't you think that the people from Nibiru in their long journey away from the sun would tend to be lighter in complexion to allow them to absorb the more limited amount of sunlight available on Nibiru.?"

Ian paused for effect. "If they came to Earth they might even have a shining countenance like those guys in the hallway last night."

Sadie pushed dramatically back from the table, "That's it. I can't take any more after today. He never tires Bob. He'll have you here until midnight listening to his theories; it's time for bed."

Ian held up his hand to hold Sadie off, "Just one more for my inquisitive friend then I'll go, "Smitty, did you realize that the old Sumerian texts say the elders lived as much as a thousand years, like Methuselah for example. What if their lifespan was tied to their rotation around the Sun, you know a 3600 year rotation is ten times our 365 so they live ten times longer. What do you think?"

Sadie gave another of her hard looks to Ian, "He doesn't care Ian. We're all going to bed."

Schmidt took her cue. "All right, let me bring my guys in from outside. They'll spend the night in the hallway just in case."

Ian patted Schmidt on the shoulder as they stood up, "I wish Berger was as a good a listener as you are. His imagination quotient must be close to zero."

Schmidt returned the pat to Ian's shoulder. "You did a great job today dealing with a tough group on their own private mission, or if you'll pardon the pun, commission. Come on, back to your room. Check the windows, make sure they're locked. I'll see you in the morning."

CHAPTER 8: OLD TEXTS

Ian skipped breakfast wolfing down only a cup of coffee and a small donut. "Too much beef and dessert last night," he thought to himself. "Where's Sadie," he asked out loud though the only one he could see was the secret service guy hovering in the Hyatt Hotel restaurant doorway.

"I'm right here darlin'" came the reply from behind him in a sweet southern accent.

"Why do you keep sneaking up on me like that? And besides, there are no southern belles from the middle-east. You're as bad as Berger."

"Do you mean the sneaking part or the accent? I don't recall any complaints last night. In fact I thought we were in complete agreement last night," she bent down to him at the table and gave him a kiss behind the ear.

Schmidt entered loudly, "All right, break it up we have a problem and a lot of work to do."

Ian frowned as he looked up from the table, "What problem, other than the one we fought all day yesterday?"

Schmidt smirked and said, "Come take a look outside, you'll see what I mean."

Ian jumped up from the table, took Sadie by the hand holding her firmly in his grip and followed Schmidt to the hotel entrance. They could hear loud chanting as they got closer to the street. "Save Nibiru, Save Nibiru."

Schmidt turned and stopped them before they reached the street, "There are around fifty protesters out there trying to save the planet they think we want to blow up. For some reason Ian they think you're the bad guy occasionally calling your name along with some adjectives, and I haven't heard "sweet cakes" used yet."

Sadie stood behind Ian with her right hand on his left shoulder as though she were peeking around his larger frame. "How did they get out there?" she asked, "How did they know we're here?"

Schmidt turned away from the crowd of protesters to face Ian and Sadie head on and said shaking his head, "Get this! Senator Hyatt left the meeting yesterday afternoon and called an impromptu news conference to bring the media up to date on the progress of the Commission."

Ian flinched, "Smitty, you said this was a closed session. What the hell is the matter with her?"

Schmidt just kept shaking his head. "I don't know. Just one more person who needs a little more attention then they're getting, I guess. People like her have a way of screwing things up it seems without even trying."

He stopped in the middle of what sounded like it was going to become a diatribe, turned and looked back at the noisy protesters and said, "Whatever, I've got to get you back with the commission in less than twenty minutes from now. I talked to Rosenthal earlier on the phone and he's sending two more men over beside the two we have here and we're going to move out of here. Crowd or no crowd," he said emphatically. "My job is to get you there," he said this time with too much emphasis.

Schmidt's portrayal of someone on an important mission wasn't clearly understood at first by either Ian or Sadie until Sadie broke out in laughter breaking the tension that had taken over the three of them.

"Oh my god, not another Bogart or was that Sean Connery. Is that you 007?" She asked coyly.

Schmidt smiled sheepishly. Imitation was not his forte'. "Sorry guys, sometimes this stuff gets to sounding childish to me and I'm afraid I react accordingly. I see reinforcements coming our way. Are you ready to go?"

Ian looked at Sadie who shook her head she was okay. He led the way to the door. "We're ready, let's go," he called over his shoulder to Sadie mimicking Schmidt's earlier attempt at bravado.

The secret service men who had been standing in the doorway in front of them joined up with the two reinforcements and formed a box of four big men around Ian and Sadie with Schmidt walking outside just off the sidewalk next to them. They looked formidable enough, so much so that the protesters simply continued their chanting facing the news media that was now present with cameras rolling, preparing for the evenings news. The chants faded into a murmur as Schmidt led them into the Hart Senate building dropping the four bodyguards off at the entrance.

*

Ironically, they were earlier than the prescribed 8:30AM time, but the Commission members were already seated. No changes Ian thought to himself except Senator Hyatt had moved her mike and nameplate to the immediate right of Senator Rosenthal and sat very placidly at his side. "No consequence for her actions," Ian thought, "just a better seat." Then he grinned inwardly and thought, "Maybe he just wants to keep her where he can keep an eye on her." He muttered softly to himself but out loud, "Keep your friends close and your enemies closer."

"What? Sadie asked as she sat down next to him.

"Nothing," Ian replied, "Just getting my thoughts together."

Senator Rosenthal called them to order. "I am aware as I'm sure you all are that whatever cover we may have thought we had for this commission has been blown. I must warn you that any future outside communication regarding matters discussed in the confines of this commission will be met with immediate censure. If you do not understand the need for this or are uncomfortable with this requirement please leave before we start this next session. Am I clear? Does anyone require clarification on how we will proceed?"

Ian watched Senator Hyatt as Rosenthal spoke and thought how innocent she looked. She had acted probably without guile, but also without good sense or responsibility. "Not very becoming of a U.S. Senator," he thought, "in whom we put our trust."

Senator Rosenthal pulled him up short. "Dr. MacGown this Commission is ready to work with you and Dr. Haddad. I'll be perfectly candid in telling you we accept and are ready to deal with the possible future presence of NIbiru, but what we need is a date. What can we do to help you to get us that date?"

The Senator who had been speaking with the fingers of both hands intertwined out in front of him threw his hands open as he ended his sentence.

Ian couldn't help it, the old joke popped into his head, "What no foreplay?" but he responded affirmatively and positively.

"We're ready Senator, however, I need to fill you in on some of the details of our research that's very pertinent to this effort."

Ian paused as he had before with this group giving them time to air any thoughts or grievances they may have that would affect his next input. He asked himself, "Were they with him, willing to listen or were they still just lying in the weeds wanting that fateful date?"

"Go on please Dr. MacGown, we're prepared to give this whatever it takes to reach a solution. That noisy crowd outside probably won't go home until at least five o'clock." The Senator found some reason to grin at Ian as he completed the last statement.

Ian for no reason retorted, "Not my crowd, they can stay as long as they want."

Sadie shuffled in her chair and glared at Ian. Ian looked across the room and could see Schmidt grinning broadly at his brash reply to Rosenthal.

He could read Schmidt's mind, "If they weren't here to harass his buddy Ian, why were they here at all?"

Ian looked back at Schmidt one more time, shrugged, then turned and looked more seriously at the commission and began anew his protracted plea for understanding about his personal mission.

"Remember our brief discussion about the date of 10500BC at which time it is believed by most modern scholars today the Sphinx was built. The belief is that the Sphinx was built by ancients identified as the "Shining Ones", so called because they were believed to have a shining countenance. Although, the aspect of this shining countenance is supported somewhat in the Bible and other literature I would prefer to ignore it for the moment and bring it into context later."

"These "Shining Ones", as they were called, were aware of both the Precession and Orion's Belt. In concert with that knowledge in 10500BC they established a starting point in time, which at a later date would be known by the Egyptians as "Zep Tepe", the "First Time". For the "Shining Ones" this was the beginning of the 25920 year cycle known as the Precession and co-incidentally was the start of Orion's slide up and down the meridian. It was a marker from which they could measure the passing of thousands of years back into the past or forward into the future. It was the "First Time" on their solar clock."

"In our parlance today it would be when both the big hand and the small hand on the clock were pointing at twelve o'clock."

"We believe, and history found in old texts records, that they from their extensive knowledge of the cosmos knew that there would be a catastrophe in 9577BC, and at that time left information somewhere in Egypt that could be retrieved later."

"We're not sure what happened after the 9577BC event until sometime around 4000BC which as we discussed earlier is when the ancients or Nibiruians, as you please, returned and established a new civilization. They came armed with the same astronomical knowledge that the "Shining

Ones" had possessed. It fell on the ancient Egyptian culture, however, to establish and refer back to "Zep Tepe", the "First Time." A time, however, as we reviewed, that significantly, had been established by the "Shining Ones" back in 10500BC prior to the great cataclysm."

Ian waved off the hands that were raised apparently with many questions, "Bear with me just a little longer please. Let me try to piece this together."

"In the epoch that followed from 4000BC around 2500BC the time the Great Pyramid and the complex of buildings oriented to Orion's Belt were built; a group of priests centered in the Egyptian city of Heliopolis were heavily involved in observing and recording the motions and movements of the Sun, the Moon, and the planets in our solar system, and many other star systems."

"They were astronomers of the highest order who tied all their studies back to "Zep Tepe", the "First Time". They were the elite of the elite in the Egyptian culture imbued with great knowledge which they used to serve their Pharaohs and Kings. The core of their knowledge had been passed down to them through the ages. In fact Egyptian legends tell us that the extraordinary technologies of which they were aware and employed were handed down to them going back to the time of the "Shining Ones"."

"They believed many of their Egyptian temples that were built were reconstructions of temples that had been built in the time of "Zep Tepe" and destroyed in the 9577BC event."

Ian thought to himself, "I'm almost there, if they'll just listen a little longer."

He paused again, continually trying to take the pulse of his audience. Sensing they were still with him, he spoke even more assertively with yet another element to his now protracted story.

"It was these priests in this time period of 2500BC who were compiling funerary texts, which on the surface, were designed to describe or guide the path of deceased pharaohs after death to the Duat; a place in the sky in the approximate space where Orion is located. These religious writings and funerary texts were discovered in modern times inscribed on the surviving tomb walls of pyramids throughout Egypt. The most famous of which are the Pyramid Texts, but others such as the Coffin Texts and the Book of the Dead, which tell the same or similar story, were also studied extensively by the priesthood of that time and subsequently found and deciphered by modern scholars."

Senator Berger interrupted, "Dr. MacGown, please…"

Ian refused to surrender the podium and waved Berger off one more time, "Just one more step Senator, let me finish."

"We believe those funerary texts are significant today because they were in fact a guide that described and could be used to understand the Precession and the movement of Orion's Belt. It was the priests, who were the holders of knowledge, way of conveying to their pharaohs where they were in the precession of time on a solar clock."

Ian stood with both hands raised in front of him shaking them up and down repeatedly for emphasis, "Understanding of those funerary texts would allow them to go back to "Zep Tepe, the "First Time", and from there calculate how far forward they had advanced in time; and with that knowledge, how close they were to the next passing of Nibiru."

Ian pulled up ready for a deep breath, but before he could continue Berger stepped in, "We admire your research and conclusions Dr. MacGown, but where is this taking us?"

Ian didn't flinch and answered immediately, "To the Temple of Edfu on the west bank of the Nile. Dr. Haddad and I need your help to get us there; to Edfu. At Edfu we believe we will find additional texts that will ultimately tell us when Nibiru will rise again in our skies."

Several hands began to wave. Senator Holland was first to speak, "Why Edfu, what's in Edfu, where is Edfu?" His questions strung together like a piece of lattice tatting.

Ian stopped and put his hands up in surrender, "Hey please, let me tell you, let me answer those questions. I know I may not be making a lot of sense; there's simply too much to tell, but the bottom line is Dr. Haddad and I must go to the city of Edfu in Egypt to study old texts that will allow us to complete information we've been working on. Information left there in text form by that elite Priesthood we discussed. Information we believe will allow us to find those lost Ephemerides Tables that we discussed earlier that track the motions of planets in our solar system around the Sun. We believe the ancients included Nibiru as a planet in our solar system; and believe if we can find the Ephemerides Tables we will give you what you need to calculate an exact date when Nibiru will pass close to the Earth again."

There was a silent, but uniform sense of "finally" that settled over the Commission. Senator Ligget broke the hush that "finally" brought, repeating Senator Holland's question, "Why Edfu?"

Ian looked relieved and a new sense of calmness could be read in his demeanor as he addressed Ligget's question. "Edfu is an ancient Egyptian city. There are extensive texts written on the walls of an existing temple and attendant buildings located there. The texts at Edfu are different than those I mentioned earlier and are known as the Building Texts."

His pause before continuing was calculated and dramatic, "These particular texts record the history of "Zep Tepe", the "First Time"; history that has been passed down from the "Shinning Ones" through the ancient priesthood. If we can get Dr. Haddad in front of those walls, we believe, she can decipher and tell us where and how to find those lost Ephemerides Tables, which in concert with what we learned from the Pyramid Texts, will give us, you, the answers we all need."

This time Senator Rosenthal spoke up, somewhat harshly, "Why couldn't you just tell us this up front, why all the protracted dialogue?" He sounded more than a little exasperated.

Ian took his, now signature, pause and looked as though he too was questioning, "Why so protracted?"

"Because you wouldn't have believed me, I'm still worried that you may not, and I'm prepared to spend two more days convincing you, if necessary."

Senator Rosenthal sat back in his chair grinning at Ian and grudge ling admiring his grit, "That won't be necessary Dr. MacGown, you've done a good job. I would take you to Edfu, myself, if I thought it was the best way to get the job done. We all understand how important it is to establish that date. Is there anything else we need to add at this juncture?" he asked.

Ian raised his hand to speak, "There is one more thing. Dr. Haddad has also deciphered remnants of an old Sumerian poem that if we can complete and couple with the Ephemerides Tables may offer not only a date, but some type of solution as well to our problem. Let me put the poem up on the screen for you." He pressed his ever present clicker one more time and the remnants of the poem appeared.

Ian spoke as they read, "As you can see some parts are much more legible than others and although in total it doesn't make a lot of sense, there are aspects of it that are intriguing."

… skies were …………
Man……………………………………….……
……Nibiru……coming……
To embrace…………Earth

An……………that would………
………………….that would kill

……Gods…………………………………
The path……………………………
Decided…………Moon…………
A sacrifice…………………

Trip over………………………
…………their cry…………………
Trip over the moon
Great…………be gone………

> But......Gods.......................best
> Left Earth.....................
> ....suffering
> Poor Earth..................................
> For...

Ian was smiling, "What no applause for this great poetry? We believe that the poem, because it gives a suggestion that the Sumerians in writing the poem, eons after the fact of the cataclysm, were relating that the ancients may have had a solution to the coming 9577BC event. A solution, perhaps, that simply didn't work; but the history of the effort was passed on. Maybe, and I know it's optimistic, but perhaps in some of our probing in Egypt we can find out why it didn't work."

Senator Berger smiled and in his sardonic best said, "The Gods help us if history repeats itself."

Senator Rosenthal now in total command, and seemingly less than enthusiastic about Ian's poem, sloughed off the remark by Berger and directed attention back to Ian, "Dr. MacGown do whatever you can that will in any way help us. We will get you and Dr.Haddad into Egypt past any current restrictions that may have been put in place since our unfortunate conflict in that area recently. We understand your concern with those restrictions and will do our best to see that you come to no harm.

He looked around at the commission members and soberly stated, "I'm sure we all understand there are risks for all of us that must be taken if we are to avoid another great cataclysm; and in that we must all give our utmost support."

He stopped abruptly, looked at Schmidt who was standing in the wings and announced, "My assistant Bob Schmidt will make all necessary arrangements and will accompany Dr. MacGown and Dr. Haddad in this important endeavor. I see no need for any additional conversation on the subject at this time. What we need is action."

Ian bowed slightly to the Commission and spoke softly but assertively, "Thank you for listening and for your support."

Senator Berger leaned forward and in a whisper said, "God's speed, God's speed."

Ian and Sadie followed Schmidt to the door tilting their heads forward to pick up the sound of the protestors in the street.

As they approached the street Sadie suddenly spun turned around and started back, head down moving with determination. Ian grabbed her by the arm spinning her back facing him, "Sadie, what are you doing?" he asked his brow wrinkled with concern.

"We have to go back. We have to tell them about…"

Schmidt who had stopped, turned and grinning at both of them said, "Don't worry, they already know. They just don't know his name is Patel."

CHAPTER 9: EARLY DEPARTURE

Ian slipped the plastic card into the slot allowing him and Sadie entry into their room and immediately noticed the red light flashing on the telephone. "They had just left Schmidt and no one other then Commission members knew they were here," he thought to himself.

He punched "O" and waited for a response. "One minute sir, I have a call waiting, please hang on," the female voice was lilting, but somewhat annoying.

"Dad, are you there?" His son's voice at the other end of the line made him smile broadly.

"Scotty, how are you, how did you find me?"

Scotty snickered, "Get serious Dad, you were all over the news yesterday. People outside your hotel protesting, yelling out your name, it wasn't that hard finding you. The biggest problem after I found you was convincing the operator to put me through. She had to check with your old friend Bob Schmidt. What's he doing there?"

"Scotty it's really great to hear from you. The answer to your questions would require the longest diatribe you've ever heard from me and I'm all out of those for the moment. Besides you've always known what a kook your father was and didn't require explanations."

"Hey, no Dad, I think I'm coming more and more in your direction, although Mom and Julie both still think you're nuts. I guess one out of three isn't that bad. Actually with me on your side it's two against two."

Ian was listening quietly glad to hear a positive response from his son, whose voice fell off and then came back with enough volume to make Ian pull the phone slightly away from his ear.

"In fact, get this, I've been accepted into an advanced space program by NASA, I start next week. I wanted you to be the first to know. That's why I called." His excitement at this point was like a top tenor reaching a crescendo.

"Scotty, that's amazing, I wasn't sure how serious you were about this. I wasn't sure they would recognize real talent and I can't tell you how glad I am it's working out for you. Where will you be stationed? Can you give me any details?"

"No details, not now Dad, but as soon as I can I'll be back at you. It was important to me to let you know that both of us, you and me, think something funny is going on up there that needs to be investigated."

"Dad, I can't talk that long, it took me a long time to get through to you, I've got to go now. I'm sorry, I've been a little behind schedule all day trying to catch up to you, but I'll call you soon. I love you Dad." The ominous click at the other end left Ian standing with the phone at arm's length as if the phone was broken.

He looked at Sadie, who had sat down on the side of the bed, waving the phone, smiling and said, "Scotty, he's been accepted by NASA into a new advanced space program."

Sadie stood up and gave him a hug, "That's wonderful Ian it's what he wanted isn't it."

Ian looked concerned, "It can be dangerous."

Sadie retorted, "Yeah, too bad he didn't fall into that calm, sedentary life style like his father. Come on we're supposed to meet Bob downstairs for one more roast beef dinner before breaking out of here." She tugged at his arm pulling towards the door. He pulled her back pressing her tightly to him and nuzzling her cheek.

She responded with a tight hug pulling him to her bosom and whispered in his ear, "Later, maybe, we'll see how dinner goes."

"I'll be here later, Sweetheart. Don't be late."

Sadie laughed at him, "Oh my god, not Bogart again. That man is insatiable. Come on Bogy, we must eat. How else can I keep up my strength?" She tugged again pulling him to the door.

*

Schmidt sat drinking a cup of coffee. "Where have you guys been? I was getting ready to order without you."

"Scotty called me, saw us on the news and figured out where we were."

Schmidt grinned, "I know, I put him through to you."

Ian looked soberly at Schmidt. "He's going into NASA's space program.

"Oops, you okay with that Ian? Schmidt asked.

"I'll have to think about it. I'm not sure. At any rate it's his choice." Ian shrugged and picked up his menu.

Sadie piped up cheerily, "Hey good news they have Mexican tonight. No roast beef, change is good."

"Well enjoy it, because you'll be eating somewhere else tomorrow and it's unlikely you'll feel good about it," Schmidt's response was clipped and to the point.

*

A soft knocking at the door roused Sadie from her sleep. She shook Ian, "Ian wake up, wake up someone's at our door."

She pulled herself up high enough to see the digital clock across from the bed over the TV, "Ian, be careful it's three o'clock in the morning."

Ian sat up slowly slipping his legs down to the floor leaving him sitting on the side of the bed facing the door. He didn't move, but cocked his head slightly in a listening manner. "I think it's Smitty, what's the hell is he doing at three in the morning. The guy's crazy."

Ian went over and looked through the peep hole in the door ignoring Sadie's admonition to "be careful." "It's Smitty," he said more of a question then a realization.

Smitty whispered, "Ian, open up."

Ian opened the door and Schmidt pushed his way in. Sadie pulled her covers up tightly under her chin.

Schmidt still talking in hushed tones leaned back against the door said, "Come on get dressed and pack, we're leaving right now. I'll be in the hallway waiting." He slipped back into the hallway not allowing any negative response from either Ian or Sadie.

Ian smiled at Sadie who was still half lying in bed with the covers tightly to her chin and said, "Guess this is it, come on, we better get dressed."

Without a word Sadie was on her feet taking her pajamas off and throwing them into a nearby suitcase all in one motion.

At three twelve AM they were standing in the hallway with Schmidt, who grabbed the door as they exited and slowly closed it behind them without a sound. He put his index finger to his lips and shook his head to be sure they understood, "no talking."

Schmidt directed them down the stairwell carefully looking out before exiting into the lobby of the Hyatt House hotel. He didn't want any of the kind of surprises that came with opening elevator doors and coming face to face with someone you didn't want to see. They hurried across the lobby into the driveway in front of the hotel perfectly timing the arrival of a black limousine with headlights off. As Schmidt hustled them into their escape vehicle and they drove away, Ian thought, "I can't even hear the damn engine running."

Ian looked at Schmidt who sat across from him on a jump seat, "Where are we going at three o'clock in the morning "O", covert one? I hope it's to Egypt and we're leaving in the middle of the night just to accommodate the time change."

Schmidt who hadn't said a word yet smiled and answered, "We have a plane to catch."

Sadie broke her silence, "Does it have a bed?"

Schmidt answered shaking his head knowingly, "Beds may be in short supply for a while."

Sadie ignored him resting herself against Ian and closing her eyes.

They rode for about a half an hour and pulled into an open hanger at what Ian recognized was Bolling Air Force Base along the Potomac in the city's southwest quadrant. There were no lights on in the hanger and Schmidt motioned them quickly out into another waiting limousine. No lights went on in the limo as the doors of both limos swung open, then were slammed with a loud thud that Ian was sure could be heard for a least a mile. Whatever effect they were shooting for was certainly attained by his measure.

Several engines roared simultaneously and their limo lurched forward with high beams blaring. Three other limos exited with them at the same time from the hanger almost running into each other and each turning and driving in a different direction.

Schmidt sat with his arms crossed and winked at Ian and Sadie, "We'll be flying out of Andrews Air Force Base.

The trip to Andrews should have taken ten minutes, but they drove up and down a variety of streets for at least forty minutes by Ian's estimate before turning sharply into Andrews Air Force Base.

Schmidt literally pulled them out of the limo and guided them to a waiting Army cargo plane sitting on one of the tarmacs with engines running. They flopped down on what looked like beach chairs with seat belts and watched Schmidt pull the door of the plane shut and take his place across from them. The plane was already beginning to taxi as Schmidt hollered at them to fasten their seat belts.

They could feel a sharp bank and then leveling off as the plane gained altitude. Sadie looked at Schmidt and asked, "Does your wife know you do this kind of thing?"

Ian didn't wait for Schmidt to answer and asked, "Where we going?"

Schmidt leaned back in his seat adjusting his seat belt for comfort and answered crisply, "First stop is Tel Aviv."

Ian countered, "And…"

Schmidt smiled, "We'll get you to Edfu. It might take a while though."

Sadie looked at him with raised eyebrows, "Does your wife even know you're gone?"

"She's glad to get me out of the house," he laughed closing his eyes as he spoke, "you better get some sleep if you can; we can talk later."

The plane landed at Ben Gurion International Airport with just enough bump to make everyone sit up and groan in unison from the effects of their uncomfortable seating.

As they were ushered out of the plane by Schmidt Sadie looked around recognizing where she was and said, "Great, this airport has some of the best shops in the world. I can pick up all the things that probably didn't make it to the plane."

"Actually, that's good because we have to mingle with the crowds before we catch a …" Schmidt was cut off.

"Sherit Taxi, right," she said wisely, "we're going to Jerusalem next to get a bus aren't we Smitty," she couldn't resist the familiarity.

Schmidt looked around to make sure no one was listening and said, "Sadie…"

She didn't let him finish again, "I've made the trip a hundred times. The bus from Jerusalem takes us to Cairo and then…," she stopped and smiled at him again, "then it's up to you Smitty."

Ian joined the banter, "I'm right here if either of you need me."

Schmidt just shrugged his shoulders and laughed, "So much for the low profile."

Sadie laughed and said, "Smitty, if you weren't so old fashion we could take the high speed train that's been running now for at least five years."

"Low profile Sadie, low profile," Schmidt said insistently. He recognized this was her territory and he was going to have to call his shots well.

"A Sherit Taxi leaves in about forty minutes. That should give us just enough time to pick up some things and move on. Come on the shops are this way." Schmidt motioned them towards the terminal building.

Sadie stepped ahead of him, "I know," she said.

*

Inside the terminal building all was going well, when a short grizzly looking man in mid-eastern garb suddenly ran by Sadie and grabbed the sack of items she had accumulated for the next leg of their journey. The grizzly one made it two steps past Sadie and was unceremoniously tripped up by Ian, who had seen him studying Sadie, and had anticipated his thievery. Schmidt who turned around in time to see the event unfolding took one step and put his heavy size twelve shoe on the man's chest.

Thoroughly outmatched the man tossed the sack back in Sadie's direction, who picked it up and instinctively checked inside. The small crowd that had stopped to look was now staring at Schmidt, who still had his foot on the man's chest.

Schmidt looked at Sadie grinning sheepishly, "Low profile, low profile," he said as he removed his foot.

"Yeah, right," She replied and headed towards an exit, "the Sherit's this way."

Sherit Taxis run day and night between Tel Aviv and Jerusalem and are designed for about ten people. There was only one other young woman sitting in the taxi as they entered, tightly holding a young tot to her side.

She kept staring with a faint smile at Sadie, who sat quietly between the two men throughout the trip to Jerusalem.

As they exited the taxi Sadie put her hand on Schmidt's arm ready with another question. She couldn't understand why they hadn't gone directly to Cairo from Tel Aviv. Schmidt was beginning to understand this pretty lady and before she could ask said, "My contact's here. She has everything we need to get us to Edfu."

Both were taken aback when the young woman from the taxi walked over to Schmidt and without a word handed him a leather bag that had gone unnoticed before, hanging from her side; then turned with her tot in hand, walked slowly away, then turned and smiling at Sadie said, "Shalom Dr. Haddad."

"So much for a low profile," Sadie said softly then offered an admission of probable guilt. "I studied at Hebrew University, even taught some classes there. She was probably a student in one of my classes. Hebrew University is one of the finest in the world you know."

Ian looked at Schmidt and grinned, "We'll have her wear a Burka when we get to Egypt."

Schmidt looked back at Ian and addressed Sadie in the third person, "Has she also studied in Egypt?"

Sadie ignored Schmidt and tugged at Ian, "The counter we want is this way," she said, "Its bus 444. We go to Eilat and stay overnight then on to Cairo from where we…"

"I've got it my lady, from there we take a nice sleeper train," Schmidt interjected, "It says so right here in my soft leather bag."

*

The train station wasn't crowded. In fact if a large group of Japanese hadn't been traveling that day it would have seemed empty. Schmidt was uncomfortable with the situation and had hoped they might have gotten lost in a crowd. Instead they stood out like two tall Caucasian men traveling with a mid-eastern woman.

Sadie sensing the apprehension of the men smiled and recited, "The train has air conditioning, a lounge car, and nice sleeper berths. We should be rested when we get to Edfu. It should take us about twelve hours, right Smitty."

Schmidt shook his head and turned to Ian, "Too bad she doesn't carry a gun, you could just leave me here."

"Be careful, she might…" Ian grinned at Schmidt.

"What carry a gun or leave me here?" Schmidt asked looking suspiciously at Sadie.

"Hmm, let me think about it over a drink. I should probably find myself some nice guy in a black jumpsuit and hook up with him. Guys like that have been giving me a lot of attention lately." She stepped off the platform onto the train and headed down the train corridor towards the compartments. She walked a few steps, turned to Schmidt who was following Ian and asked, "Which one?"

"Do you want the fold out version or the two bunk variety, your choice madam?" Schmidt was the perfect gentleman.

"She'll take the fold out version. They're right next to each other, right Smitty." Ian quickly answered for Sadie. "That way you, Smitty can have your choice of an upper or a lower in the other compartment."

Sadie shook her head okay to the deal made for her. "Whatever you guys want, just get me to the lounge car."

Schmidt gave a "thumbs up," and pointed to the door immediately in front of Ian. "That's your room, it's a deal, see you in the lounge in five minutes."

Schmidt stood inside the door of his cabin until he heard the door of Ian's and Sadie door open, and then stepped into the corridor. "Hey, how's that for good timing. Come on Sadie, let's get you that drink."

As they entered the lounge car they could hear Japanese voices calling out to each other in boisterous conversation. There was only one other man dressed in a sari wearing a turban that shouted out incongruously, "India."

Sadie who was leading the way through the narrow corridor stopped and put her hand on Ian's arm. "Dr. Patel," she blurted out in obvious astonishment.

Schmidt tried to push his way past Ian, who held him back saying, "It's okay, Smitty, it's okay."

Dr. Patel rose from his seat and motioned them to come, sit next to him. Sadie stepped forward and gave him a warm embrace. Ian extended his hand and clasped Patel's hand graciously. Schmidt stood moderately dumbfounded then accepted the hand extended to him by Patel.

Patel, smiling, looked at Sadie and asked, "How is our little Oracle of Delphi?" He looked at Schmidt knowingly and said, "You visit her in her temple of languages, ask her any question and she'll give you answers."

Schmidt warmed up to the analogy and replied. "I'm beginning to understand how knowledgeable she is."

He paid for the remark with a kick to the side of his ankle from Sadie.

Ian started to speak, but Patel interrupted him. "I'm not responsible for some of your recent misfortunes. You know I'm not a violent man," He paused showing a sign of embarrassment, "however, I may have inadvertently turned the dogs loose on you." He grinned sheepishly at his analogy.

"Whose dogs are they Doctor, if not yours?" Ian spoke as though he had been holding that question on the tip of his tongue.

Patel motioned to all of them. "Please sit. We can talk."

Ian and Sadie sat down across from him while Schmidt slid into the seat next to Patel, who showed no uneasiness at his presence.

Patel stared intently at Ian and addressed the question he could read in Ian's eyes. "I don't know who they are. I became aware that your government intends to attack Nibiru at its next crossing. I realize they believe they would be trying to destroy the planet before it destroys the Earth; but there may still be life on Nibiru."

"I did express my concerns to various other governments, I admit, but I did not receive anything more than a simple dismissal from them as though I was a mad man. There was no indication from their responses," He paused and interjected, "although, I did also speak to other members of the Think Tank; but got no significant response from anyone that would indicate any aggressive action by anyone."

Ian asked somewhat tentatively. "What are your plans now Dr. Patel."

Patel sat back and laughed. "I'm probably going back to India and look for a place to retire."

Ian looked skeptical and went straight to the heart of the matter. "I don't believe you Dr. Patel. Why are you here? How did you manage to get on this train with us? What do you want?"

Patel didn't flinch, but smirked at the barrage of questions. "I might ask you Dr. MacGown, why are you here?" He didn't wait for an answer. "You are rising to meet a challenge thrown in your lap, so am I; and it appears we must be in opposition to each other. You have chosen to protect at any cost, my choice is to work to see that civilization as we know is preserved."

Ian's concern etched across his brow. "We don't have to be at odds with each other. We think we may be able to define a solution that will protect and preserve life on both planets."

Two men in black jumpsuits appeared at the doorway to the lounge car. Patel stood up, stepped out into the corridor and spun around facing Ian squarely on, "I don't believe you. Be careful Ian, you are on a dangerous mission." He took Sadie's hand and kissed it. "May Allah be with you?"

He bowed slightly to Schmidt and walked away towards the two waiting men.

Schmidt looked at Ian. "Keep your friends close and your enemies closer. Which one is he, Ian. Did he approach you as a friend or an enemy?"

Ian pursed his lips as he answered. "An old friend, a new enemy, he can be very resourceful and very dangerous." Then as an afterthought he added. "At least he's out in the open. We know he's there."

Sadie asked plaintively, "Can I have my drink now?"

In unison they all seemed to realize that the chatter of the Japanese was gone, replaced by the clatter of the wheels of the train driving them forward, probably to another encounter with Patel.

Sadie said dryly again, "Do I get my drink now?"

Ian put his arm around Sadie and shook her gently. "Sure, if it'll put you in a better mood, some of your friends get pretty heavy."

Sadie replied, "Old friend, new enemy."

Schmidt said soberly. "Make sure we all stick close to each other, finish our drink at the same time and get back to our compartment at the same time."

Ian quipped. "We wouldn't think of leaving here without you and will do our best to protect you."

"I'm serious Ian, we know they're on the train with us and it's at least another ten hours before we get to Edfu. We need to be careful. Keep your door locked and stay inside. Come on, it's not too early to get some rest." Schmidt was up ready to head back to their rooms.

Sadie repeated, "What about my drink?"

Schmidt slumped back into his seat, tried to get the attention of the Egyptian waiter and said, "Keep your friends close. I'll wait with you."

*

Back in his compartment with his friends safely tucked in for the night Schmidt sat uncomfortably on the lower bunk, sifting through the package of credentials and tickets that had been handed to him in Jerusalem. He started at a shuffling of feet outside his door and saw the knob on the door slowly turning. He threw the package to the top bunk and pulled himself quickly up to the top bunk. The door burst open and three men sprang into the tiny room. Before their feet were set Schmidt came down off the top with both feet knocking two of the men to the floor and grabbing the third around the neck as he landed. None of the four men could move without catching an elbow, foot or fist. The man in the headlock broke loose, ran back through the door, and was cold cocked with one punch from Ian, who now stood blocking the doorway. Schmidt towered over the other two who offered no resistance.

"What do we do with them?" Ian asked.

Schmidt picked one up by the shirt collar and banged him against the corridor wall, "Tell your Dr. Patel the gloves are off. Someone's going to get hurt." He tossed the man down the corridor and reached for the second one who scurried away. The third looked furtively at Sadie, who was standing in the open door of her compartment and reached into his jumpsuit pulling out a gun. Ian put his hand squarely across the man's face and slammed his head hard against the wall of the corridor. The man slumped to the floor with the gun still in his hand. Ian picked the gun from his hand and handed it to Schmidt. "Here this is your department."

Schmidt reached for the gun then hesitated. "No you keep it. You may need it later."

People stood in the aisle not sure what to do. Sadie said in a loud Egyptian voice "Too much drinking, it's all over"

Ian looked at her. "Yeah, like that's going to fly with guns all over the place."

Schmidt looked at Ian and said, "These guys might carry guns, but they're rank amateurs. I signed you up for the room I'm in and then purposely let you shift. They're good enough to get the information about

- 125 -

where you were supposed to be, but not good enough to pick up the shift."

He looked at Sadie. "It's obvious you're the one they're after, so stick close."

Ian put his hand out to Schmidt. "Well I think that's enough excitement for tonight. Let's try to get some sleep. Thanks Smitty, you're a good friend."

Sadie walked over and gave Schmidt a hug, turned around without another word and went back into her compartment.

Schmidt watched as Ian closed the door behind him, took a quick look around, went inside, and lay down on the bottom bunk fully dressed; ready for some rest and the early morning.

Chapter 10: Edfu Temple

"Okay, where do we go from here chief?" Schmidt posed the question to Sadie from the train platform at Edfu.

"How would you like to take a horse and buggy ride? That's how you get to the temple from here," Sadie grinned.

Schmidt reached into his sack and said, "I have the tickets right here."

"I'm not sure they take tickets," She said raising her eyebrows.

"Tickets take many forms, you know that. Come, on, pick a horse, any horse," He encouraged.

The ride to the temple was indeed by horse and buggy, but not through tree lined cobblestone streets as you may imagine, but rather through Egyptian streets with old two and three story buildings on both sides. Sadie rode between the two men, who spent the whole trip looking deep into passing alleyways on either side wondering if Patel's hoodlums would try anything again.

When they arrived at the Temple their horse and buggy was tied up in a row of similar rigs in what looked like the starting gate of the Hambletonian.

The Temple of Edfu is the second largest in Egypt after Karnak and is one of the best preserved. The walk from where you leave the horse and buggy to the Temple is spectacular. As you approach the main entrance which looks like it is at least fifty feet high, it dominates the horizon in front of you.

Schmidt looked to Ian and asked, "What's the big deal about this place? Fill me in so I know what's going on." It hadn't occurred to Schmidt to inquire until he had the grandeur of old Egypt in front of him.

Ian looked back at Schmidt then to Sadie, "Fill him in Sadie, like Patel said you're our Oracle of Delphi."

Sadie stopped walking and put her hand on Schmidt's arm to hold him in place and like a tourist guide launched into, what sounded to Schmidt, like a canned pitch.

"The walls of this temple are filled with writings known as the Building Texts, which record the history of "Zep Tepe," the "First Time." Remember, Ian talked about that in front of the Commission."

"Zep Tepe" was the age of the gods, a time long before the rise of Egypt's grand culture. The Egyptian's, themselves, stated in their folklore that many of the great advancements of their day were actually handed down to them from a much earlier culture that existed before the great cataclysm. In fact, Smitty, this Edfu Temple is supposed to be a reconstruction of one that existed at 'Zep Tepe," the "First Time."

She continued, "All the writings on the walls of this temple are known as the Building Texts and they record the history of that "First Time", when the gods ruled."

Schmidt interrupted her, "Whoa, what gods?"

Sadie couldn't hold a grin back, "The "Shining Ones", Smitty, remember the guys in the hallway at the hotel."

Schmidt held his hand up to stop her, "I do remember, but you called them the Shebtu."

"Okay, you're right, but they're really the same. The Shebtu come later after the great cataclysm. The important thing is that the "Shining Ones" existed before the cataclysm and got wiped out by it," she paused, "Let me try to summarize for you."

Schmidt smirked at her, "Please do, you have my full attention."

Sadie picked up the pace, "The Building Texts on the walls inside describe a temple associated with the time of "First Creation," or "First Time." This Edfu Temple was built on top of an older temples foundation, which we believe was the temple where the "Shining Ones" created the tables we're looking for. The accounts on the walls of this temple we're about to see allude to an end to the time of "First Creation" following a violent conflict. We believe that conflict was Ian's big event in 9577BC. The "Shining Ones" according to legend perished following the conflict, but were followed by a second generation of divine inhabitants, the Shebtu, who were known as the builder gods."

Sadie looked to Ian for assurance, "Did I get that right?" She continued without an answer, "Anyway the Shebtu according to old scripts were in possession of powerful relics from the "Zep Tepe," "First Time." It's believed that they stored those relics in a subterranean chamber, which has never been found, but may be what we're looking for."

She paused and looked to see if Schmidt's eyes had glazed over and said mildly apologetically, "I just pull the information together, Ian organizes it."

He grinned at her, I'm with you, go on."

"The Shebtu were known as the "Followers of Horus." This Edfu Temple is the Temple of Horus, who is believed to be an old Egyptian King."

She grasped Schmidt's arm firmly, "Okay, Smitty, here's the tricky, most important part. We believe that Horus, who is very well known in Egyptian literature, was in actuality Nibiru, and that the "Followers of Horus" in old Egypt were actually tracking Nibiru's movement."

"Because Nibiru, Horus, the Shebtu and those tables we're looking for are all connected, we believe that in tracking the Path of Horus, which is described in Egyptian history, we can find the tables." She ended with a flourish pulled him along and said, "Let's go."

Ian put his arm around Sadie's shoulder and said, "We have a spot for you that will give you an opportunity to present your case in front of a United States Senate Commission. Are you available?"

Sadie shrugged him off saying, "Right now I'm a little busy and really don't have time for cranks."

Schmidt looked at Ian and pulled Sadie back in his direction, "Dr. Haddad is previously employed," than walked towards the Temple, shaking his head at the inane conversation, prepared for whatever mischief Patel might have set in motion. He was greeted by two massive pylons with granite falcons, the image of Horus, on each side as he entered the temple into the Court of Offerings.

The Court of Offerings is surrounded by columns on three sides decorated with reliefs, which continue around the court along the bottom of the wall. At the back of the Court of Offerings Schmidt could see another pair of black granite statutes of Horus leading into another hall, which was a large rectangular open air building with two rows of six pillars supporting a roof that was still intact; and looked like it had astronomical paintings on the ceiling symbolizing the sky.

Sadie nudged him and pointed to a building beyond the second hall, "That's the Festival Hall, which is the oldest part of this temple, and where I need to go."

Schmidt looked around at all the different reliefs on the various buildings and, in an afraid to ask voice, asked, "Do we have to go through all of this or just that building?"

Sadie answered quickly, "No, just one small area, but I'm going to need a flashlight and you're going to have to get me past a locked gate Smitty."

She turned facing him, with Ian playing look out to make sure no one could over hear her, "Here's the deal Smitty, beyond the Festival Hall," she pointed, "is the Hall of Offerings. There's a stairway with a locked gate, which is why I've never been able to read the reliefs on the stairway. You'll have to get the gate open for me. Once inside I'll need a flashlight because it's not lighted."

"Thanks for the advance notice," he snickered, then pulled a small flashlight from his bag and handed it to her, flicking it on and off quickly to demonstrate its brightness. He also produced an unusual looking cutter that looked like it relied on twisting a small piece of metal around a leather strap, which in turn forced two other metal cutting edges tighter and tighter. She was immediately satisfied that he could get the job done and started to turn away heading for the Hall of Offerings.

Schmidt pulled her back, "Hey, what are we looking for there?"

She smiled, "You ask a lot of questions for someone unacquainted with archeology," She was really beginning to like this guy and his dedication to her and to Ian. He had a right to ask questions, "Okay, the elders we talked about used to have a New Year Festival, when the image of Horus, the Falcon looking bird, was carried up an ascending stairway, which will be on our left, to be revitalized by the Sun, then, carried back down the descending stairway. It was part of a ritual. For what we want there are reliefs on the walls of both stairways which depict that event. We will need the flashlight to read them."

Schmidt looked confused as Sadie added to her diatribe, "Remember I told you, Ian and I believe Horus is really Nibiru and the carrying of his statute up and then down the stairwell is symbolic of Nibiru's passage around the Sun. We think there may be clues written in those reliefs that will tell us where to look for the tables we need."

"Gotja, sorry to hold you up, let's go," He tugged at Sadie's arm who was still standing looking at him to make sure he understood.

They approached the gate, slowly checking around them as they walked, making sure no one was paying any attention to them. Sadie and Ian shielded Schmidt as best they could as he performed his magic with the miniature cutting tool. Sadie slipped by the open gate and Schmidt followed her up the stairway while Ian maintained vigilance at the entrance. About an hour went by when Ian heard Sadie making her way back down the stairs calling softly, "I've got it."

Ian turned briefly looking towards the stairs when two men blindsided him driving him away from the door in a tangle of three bodies. Schmidt heard the commotion and started out to help Ian. He was met by a man that all Schmidt could think of at this precarious moment was, "He must be seven feet tall." There was no escape the giant grabbed him holding him in a bear hug pumping him up into the air, than back down against the ground. Each time Schmidt's feet hit he thought his feet and ankles would break. At the third impact he set his left foot for balance and drove his right knee into the giant's groin. The giant dropped him sending him falling backwards, but still standing. The huge behemoth was now on his knees in front of him holding the family jewels. Schmidt looked at him and thought, "Now we're the same size," and drove a right hand, twisting hook, into the giant's chin causing him to teeter backwards and then flop on his face.

Schmidt looked to his left, saw Ian standing erect over his two assailants, and started to run after Sadie who was being carried away by two men, each holding her under her arm pits, as her legs flailed wildly in the air, reaching for the ground that wasn't there.

As the men ran with Sadie in tow a man in a white robe with a shinning countenance loomed in front of them causing them to change direction like halfbacks running to open field, when a second man in a white robe with a shinning countenance appeared in their path. They shifted course again and a third white robe stood ominously in front of them. Sadie landed on her feet, half crying half laughing as they dropped her and ran.

She turned to Ian and Schmidt now laughing with tears in her eyes, "Did you see that? Who are those guys? How do they do that?"

Ian shook his head in disbelief. None of the other people inside the temple had stopped what they were doing or seemed to be aware that anything unusual had happened. Sadie was standing in the middle of the temple court laughing hysterically.

Ian and Schmidt walked slowly over to Sadie. Ian put his arms around her, "Are you alright?"

Sadie couldn't stop laughing, "Just fine, of course, I'm just fine. Hasn't that ever happened to you?"

Ian held her a little tighter, and now people who seemed to be standing still a minute ago were beginning to notice them, "Are you okay? Did we get what we needed?"

"Yes," she said exasperation ringing in her voice, "we need to go back to Cairo, to the pyramids"

Sadie looked intently at Ian, "What I just read in there refers to the Great Primeval Mound, which we know is the natural outcropping of rock that lies under the…"

Ian didn't let her finish, but whispered, "Great Pyramid."

"There's more Ian, I have it in my head. It tells us where to look inside the Pyramid when we get there. This could be it," Sadie was glowing with excitement.

Schmidt said, "We can take a boat back up the Nile, a plane out of Luxor airport, or that damn train that you seem to enjoy so much. All roads lead to Cairo."

Schmidt shook one ankle than the other, "I'll do anything but walk."

Sadie smiled at his easy manner after so much trouble and replied, "If I can't take the train I'm not going."

Ian took the lead towards the exit pulling them both along, "Let's go."

Chapter 11: Hall of Records

"No sign of Patel," Ian looked around the lounge car in the sleeper train as he slipped easily into a comfortable seat. Schmidt sat across from him looking forward and back, "You're right. No one here again except that noisy group of Japanese tourists."

Sadie who had not yet found a seat slid into the seat next to Ian with a complaint, "You guys are not very polite. I'm lucky there are four seats or I'd probably be standing. The least you could do is order a drink for me, maybe two after the day I've had."

"You're lucky I didn't let that big fellow get a hold of you," Schmidt quipped, "He kept saying your name over and over, Sadie, Sadie."

"Stop it," She kicked at his ankles as she admonished him, "and in spite of your ill humor I want to thank you again for being there for us."

Ian jumped in quickly looking to share the praise, "Hey, I had to handle two of them."

Schmidt countered, "Yeah, but together they were less than half as big as my guy."

Sadie's head was now on Ian's shoulder with her eyes closed more than halfway to being asleep.

Ian grinned at Schmidt and looked at Sadie, "Forget the drink I guess."

"You can bet on that, she's out."

Schmidt looked seriously at Ian, "Ian I don't get it, how did you guys ever get into this?"

"Are you kidding, you invited me in back at the Montgomery Inn."

"Naw, that's not true, we both know we were using each other. Rosenthal used me to draw you in. What got you to the point that you answered my call?"

Ian paused and glanced out of the window of the speeding train like the answer may have already passed him by, "The Think Tank I mentioned was working as a team trying to answer questions that basically revolved around "how."

"How did someone thousands of years ago build something as magnificent as the Great Pyramid?"

"How were they moving large stones that weighed hundreds of tons around and elevating them in place to build these fantastic structures."

"How did they seem to know more about the universe, then we do today?"

"The evidence they left behind was mind boggling including the whole notion of UFOs and space travel, but we were still repeatedly stumped as to "how," so we gave up and began to ask "why?"

"Why had they done all these things we couldn't understand? And then we began to ask "who," who were they? Once we stopped asking how, and focused on why and who, Nibiru came into sharp focus. It had to be an alien presence and for most of us someone a lot smarter and with more longevity then we had accumulated."

"Here's the hook for us in this effort Smitty, an important part of the evidence that had been accumulated over many years seemed to be centered in Egypt. The Egyptologists, who had developed all the evidence as well as the Egyptian Government insisted that the concept of aliens, ergo Nibiru couldn't be accepted. They insisted then and continue to insist that the great Egyptian culture simply evolved; and in so doing squelched important evidence they had that may have supplied direction to an inquiring world. So here we are today sneaking into their backyard looking for more answers."

"Sadie and I both believe there is a solution that the ancients understood and they would have left evidence to be found at the time of need. The problem is that they left it somewhere in Egypt with people who are reluctant to have it found. Then you throw Patel into the mix and we have a bundle of problems that you Sadie and I are left to untangle."

Sadie at the sound of her name sat up and asked, "Did we order drinks yet?"

Schmidt looked at the two sleepy, weary people across from him and said, "I've got a better idea. We still have at least ten hours until we get to Cairo. When we were back at Edfu after our little adventure, I called a contact in Cairo, who can get us into the Pyramid tonight. Why don't we get some rest for the remainder of the train ride and be ready for tonight."

He looked around again and grinned, "I haven't seen any sign of Patel's cronies. They're probably still running from those shinning apparitions, so we should be safe. If they do show up I'll just shine my flashlight on my face and scare the hell out of them."

Sadie shook her finger at him, "You had better be careful they might not care for you laughing at them. I didn't see them fighting off that big guy for you."

Both Schmidt and Ian sat back grasping the same realization at the same time, "No only Sadie," Ian sputtered, "Only Sadie do they rescue."

Schmidt without comment to that point said, "Come on, we need some rest. It's probably going to be a late evening."

*

Their arrival at the train station in Cairo was greeted by what appeared to be a tall Egyptian man wearing a turban and a beard with a New York

Yankees tee shirt and Bermuda shorts. Sadie looked and was disappointed to see that with such an audacious getup he was wearing sandals instead of tennis shoes. The man quickly pulled Schmidt aside and some exchange was evident. With the exchange complete they were whisked into a van with peeling white paint and a picture of the Great Pyramid on its side.

Sadie thought to herself, "Now everyone will know where we're going. They don't even have to follow us, just meet us there."

It was dark, past midnight, but horns of frustrated drivers and taxis still blared loudly. The drive was shorter than either Ian or Sadie remembered from previous trips, but it was Schmidt who said with surprise, "Here already?"

The Egyptian man, who still had not said a word jumped out of the van with the motor still running and signaled them to follow him. He led them up over at least ten large stones some of which were almost as high as Sadie is tall. Ian and Schmidt more or less hauled her up following the path the Egyptian had set for them. Sadie complained, "I know there's an easier way. Why didn't we just use the tourist entrance, the Robber's Tunnel."

Schmidt answered, "He's in a hurry," Which made absolutely no sense to Sadie.

At the entrance a door immediately opened to them. Their driver handed them a flashlight and began scrambling back down to his van. He turned to Sadie and said respectfully in Egyptian, "Shalom, Allah be with you." He turned to Schmidt and with a huge grin and an English accent said, "See you later mate."

Sadie watched the departing driver then turned to Schmidt and Ian and said, "Even his Egyptian had an English accent, I knew right away." She paused then looked to Schmidt inquisitively and asked, "Will he be back?"

Schmidt took a deep breath and said, "I hope so." He turned the flashlight, which was large like a spelunker would use, down the Descending Passage of the Pyramid and stopped short when he saw the four foot high ceiling and the narrow width of the passage, which seemed to be not much wider than his shoulders.

Ian grinned, "Come on big guy, the last time I did this I couldn't straighten up for a week."

Sadie added to his grief, "So you'll know what you're in for Smitty it drops down at a twenty six degree angle for close to three hundred and fifty feet and it's only four feet high before we get to the Subterranean Chamber, which is our destination. You'll have to stoop way down."

"Thanks for the tip," Schmidt said from a squat position resembling an Asian ascetic, "how high did you say it was in here?" Schmidt could hardly talk, despair slithering out with each word. He looked like an upside down letter el about to fall down. He alternately tried squatting and scooting forward like a Russian dancer and then reverting to the el position.

Sadie rejoined without sympathy, "I told you about four feet high."

Ian joined in seemingly more comfortable even though he was almost as tall as Schmidt, "At least that big guy won't be able get at you down here."

After about fifteen minutes of arduously, essentially crawling on hands and knees the two six foot plus, creaking old men pulled up straight into the Subterranean Chamber of the Great Pyramid.

"How high is it in here?" Schmidt asked, relief and concern intermingled in his voice. He began moving the flashlight around from wall to wall and then off the ceiling as if to answer his own question.

"More like ten or eleven feet," Sadie replied sounding relieved." Even at five and a half feet tall the walk down the Descending Passage is not a cake walk.

"Okay, what are we looking for Sadie? Where do we start?" Ian followed Schmidt's light around the chamber looking for a clue he wasn't sure he would recognize.

Schmidt continued flashing the light from wall to wall, "This place is huge compared to that chute we just came down. How big is it Sadie?"

The reply was certain and quickly stated, "Its 46 feet by 27 feet for a total of 1242 square feet."

"Are you sure," came back the sarcastic retort, "you don't have your calculator with you."

"Don't need one, besides what we're interested in is that big hole in the floor; be careful you don't fall in."

The flashlight which had been entirely focused on walls and ceiling quickly found the big hole in the floor.

"What is that?" Schmidt asked with astonishment and then flashed his light to a ladder showing three steps protruding from the hole.

"It's called the Bottomless Pit, but as you can see it has a bottom or the ladder wouldn't be there. It's actually over twelve feet deep," Ian leaned forward attempting to look down into the pit as he spoke.

"When it was first discovered back in the 1800's Smitty they weren't sure how deep it was, so they called it the Bottomless Pit."

Sadie's voice was ominous as she entered the conversation, "We have to go down there, all of us."

Schmidt's response had a tad of hesitation to it, "Is that what you found out back at Edfu?"

Ian grabbed the protruding steps of the ladder, gave them a shake for stability and proceeded down into the Bottomless Pit calling back to them as he descended, "I'm going to need some light down here Smitty. What are we looking for Sadie?"

Schmidt shone the light into the pit and motioned to Sadie to be next and smiled, "Ladies first."

As he started down he called to Ian, "How deep is it?"

Ian answered sounding like he was indeed at the bottom of something deep, "At least two of my body lengths."

Sadie shouted back at Schmidt, "Wait till I'm down, It may not hold two of us."

With three of them standing in close quarters at the bottom of the pit Ian asked Sadie again with a little more urgency, "What are we looking for, this is crazy."

Sadie mocked him, "I have to close my eyes and click my heels three times," she stopped and said, "it's almost that bad." She gave Ian an elbow to move him back from the wall of the pit she was facing, "I have to point the fingers of my left hand into the cleft of my chin and then at that same plane line up my right hand parallel to it, raise my right hand and place it against the wall."

She completed her maneuver and silence fell over the group. Nothing happened.

Schmidt broke the brief silence, "Maybe we should call Mary Poppins."

Sadie turned ninety degrees pushing both men out of her way with an extra elbow directed at Schmidt and repeated the maneuver against a second wall with no results and no comments.

She turned to a third wall mumbling, "It doesn't make sense one of those walls should have done it."

Schmidt couldn't resist, looked at Ian and grinned, "Maybe she's losing her touch."

Sadie was irritable now, growling at him as she tried the third wall, "There's supposed to be a revolving door here somewhere."

A slow creaking revolving door seemed to be in sync with her growling and turned inwardly away from them. A soft blue tinted light filled the huge cavity in front of them without spilling into their unspectacular container. Schmidt self-consciously switched off the light in his hand. They all held back in awe of what was in front of them expecting the door to swivel close.

Ian stepped into the light, "Come on this is it. This should take us to the Hall of Records."

Sadie stepped up next to Ian, but Schmidt wasn't ready to move that fast. He shot a worried look at Ian, "Hey, where does the light come from, there must be someone besides us down here."

Ian paused and looked around as if he expected to find a better answer then the one he was about to give, "Smitty, without any idea what I'm talking about, and absolutely no way to prove it, I'm sure that light has been shinning for thousands of years waiting for someone like us to barge in here unannounced."

He pointed down the hallway in front of them, "I'm sure that if we walk about as far as it would take to put us under the right paw of the Sphinx we'll find the Hall of Records, which will tell us all we need to know and then some." He grabbed Sadie by the arm and said, "Let's go," following the light in front of him down a beautifully lit corridor.

*

They stopped abruptly as they entered a room more brightly lit then the hall that had led them there.

In front of them was what appeared to be an amazing halo-gram of a man in shinning white garments and a face that shone like the Sun. "Good day," he said, "We've been waiting for you, all that we know, all that you need to know is here at your disposal." Then he disappeared.

There were steles of all sizes lined up in a room about the size of a ball room. They were laced with hieroglyphics from top to bottom. Sadie approached one and began to read it aloud to Ian and Smitty, "It's a kind of a menu like you would find on our computers. This one is all about husbandry and agriculture." She placed her hand on the menu entry for crops and a large hologram showing dozens of different crops with pictures and dialogue in hieroglyphics under each picture appeared.

Schmidt with raised brow asked Sadie, "Okay what does it say?"

Sadie looked intently at him and replied, "It says Smitty should eat more vegetables."

Sadie moved along past each stele touching it briefly and moving on to the next, "Here's one on how man was created. Do you want see it?"

Ian started to answer, stopped, thought for a minute and said, "No, not now," he paused again, "maybe never. Look for the Ephemerides Tables, that's what we need. If we don't find those, nothing else may matter."

Sadie persisted, "Ian you've got to see this It's a recorded discussion between Enlil and Enki at the Council of Twelve about the coming flood and the future of mankind," she flashed the hologram up in front of them and began to read.

ENKI: "The Creator of All Things implanted a procreation gene in all of us to populate the universe."

ENLIL: "Yes, we are aware of that, but our own planet is over populated to the point of requiring a census to decide on the number of acceptable births each year."

ENKI: "We've compensated for that by giving them only one tenth of our life span."

ENLIL: "They're too noisy. Let the coming of Nibiru be their end. They have too many of our bad traits. They're inclined to war and covet all things material. They lack compassion for their brethren and procreate too rapidly."

ENKI: "They're still learning. We should save the best of them."

Sadie looked at Ian, "It goes on for some time. Do you want to hear more? There's so much here to learn, to know."

Ian didn't answer her, but looked perplexed. The information at hand was truly fascinating but not what they needed. He motioned her to the next stele.

Sadie obediently pushed against the next stele and began reciting anew, "Did you realize there is no absolute limit to the universe and it really did begin with "one that became all things." And even though it has no limit it exists with other universes." She looked at Ian who had been following her along as she perused each stele, "Does that make sense to you?"

Ian shook his head, "I'm not that kind of scientist Sadie. You know that. Keep looking."

Undaunted she asked him a new question, "Did you realize that time really is a continuum. It says the past and the future are as one, and that you can move from one to the other. Wouldn't that be time travel? Maybe that's how they got here Ian."

Schmidt who had been moving slightly behind Ian asked, "How who got here?"

Sadie answered a bit sarcastically directing some of her pent up emotion in front of all this knowledge at Schmidt, "Whoever built all this. Whoever developed the tables we're looking for, whoever exists on Nibiru, that's who," She finished emphatically.

Ian interjected patiently, "Keep looking Sadie."

She smiled back at him from the next stele. "Would you like to know how to make a computer chip?" She didn't wait for an answer but moved forward, "Wow, this is eerie it suggests that there really were things like the Minotaur from Greek mythology, like in the labyrinth in Knossos."

"How can you tell all that, you can't see anything but that pillar in front of you?" Schmidt demanded.

"I'm just reading the menu on each one," she answered coyly, "would you like to see more?" As she asked, a hologram with hieroglyphic writing and pictures of strange creatures flashed in front of them, one half man half bull.

"What does it say," Schmidt asked somewhat in awe?

Sadie studied the hologram for a minute and answered with a frown, "It says we shouldn't be fooling around with cloning, that procreation of all things is a natural process not to be messed with. It says the universe will be populated throughout time," she paused, "get this, by the Creator of All Things."

Ian snapped at them, "We're going to be depopulated if we don't find those tables. Come on Sadie, keep looking."

"Sorry, sorry, it's unbelievably interesting," she said as she started to move a little more rapidly along the steles.

She paused again at a new stele and began reading out loud, "This is absolutely fascinating it explains in detail how they made the Great Pyramid. It tells how they used music to levitate those seventy ton granite blocks into place and even lists the musical notes that were used." She continued to study about the Pyramid when Ian gently took her by the arm and moved her to the next stele.

"Sadie please, there won't be any more pyramids if we don't find those tables.

Without another word she moved to the next stele at hand and said, "Ian you are some sort of genius I think, but I'm not sure. This one talks about something that sounds like a black hole, the most powerful force in the universe and it shows what looks like the planets." She pushed something again and another hologram appeared showing the planets spaced properly in a three dimensional picture of the solar system.

"There's a lot here it might take me a while to read it. Look," she said enthusiastically, "it shows Nibiru with the other planets just like Egyptian depictions of our solar system."

She scanned some more and stopped abruptly, "Look here's a picture of the surface of what they refer to as the fourth planet from the Sun, which we know is Mars, and it clearly shows something like the Sphinx with a lot of other buildings around it. This is absolutely fantastic. There must be answers for everything in here."

"Sadie, come on," Ian's impatience was at a peak.

Sadie responded by filing more rapidly and then stopping with an, "Aha, here it is Ian. Oops, it just registered with me. This is the Hall of Records. There is no actual inventory of items or things so it's unlikely we'll find the Tables here," she straightened up taking a very studious stance, "but it should tell us where to look, if not where we can actually find them."

She began rapidly scrolling through a huge amount of Egyptian characters at a pace Schmidt thought to himself he would not be able to read in English at that speed. Finally, she slowed down and began muttering rather than speaking, than broke into a full dialogue, "Here it is, I think I've got it. We need to go back to Jerusalem." She stopped reading and turned and smiled at the two men.

Ian sputtered, "Why Jerusalem?"

"Because it mentions a place of sacrifice and assent, solid and sacred, Ian that could only be the Dome of the Rock on the Temple Mount," Sadie was now shaking her head in unison with Ian, who was reaching conclusions with each word she spoke.

Schmidt joined the conversation, "I know the Dome of the Rock, but why there? It sounds like you're jumping to conclusions." He continued skeptically, "I want to get out of here, but with the right information. How sure are you?"

Schmidt's new skepticism caused a ripple of concern for both Ian and Sadie. They both stopped short in their effort to find the tables and focused on Schmidt. Ian asked, "What's up Smitty?"

Schmidt looked like he had been keeping a secret, "Look, I've been keeping in touch with Rosenthal as we've moved through this little adventure of ours. He's getting worried. Apparently there have been mobs of demonstrators outside of the Senate Building every day since we left and it's beginning to get ugly. He feels he needs those Tables to offer up some kind of concrete plan."

Ian ignored Schmidt's pitch and went back to his original question to try and justify focusing on the most recent stele in front of them, "The "Rock" is supposedly where Abraham prepared to sacrifice Isaac, ala a place of sacrifice and it is also the "Rock" from which Muhammad's winged horse leapt into the sky, accompanied by the Archangel Gabriel, on the "Night Journey" into heaven from the Qur'an; ala the assent."

Schmidt and Sadie were staring at Ian as he spoke. It was obvious his mind was racing in several different directions and they were both wondering where he would stop. Sadie spoke first, "Are you saying you agree with me?"

"Yes, yes absolutely, we need to go to Jerusalem, but not to the Dome of the Rock, just next door, to the Al Aqsa mosque, and," He added emphatically, "We're not done here yet."

"Why the mosque," Sadie asked uncertainly as if that didn't make a lot of sense to her.

"What else? If you know where to look, why aren't we done here?" Schmidt asked exasperated.

Ian looked first at Sadie, "I'll explain later about the mosque," then he turned to Schmidt.

"Listen Smitty, if Rosenthal needs those Tables that badly now, he also needs to understand the meaning of the poem I read to the Commission."

Ian looked back at Sadie, "Keep reading Sadie, there must be something about how Nibiru tripped over the Moon, or maybe why it didn't trip and hit the Earth."

Ian returned his gaze to Schmidt and said, "If there's any other solution than simply trying to blow up a planet that may be twice as big as we are out of the sky, we should look for it while we're here. The ancient's knew a lot more than we do today; maybe it's here in these records."

Sadie had already begun to look at other steles for some clue that would reference back to the poem. She wandered throughout the steles trying to hook onto that one lead to answer the question Ian had posed that now hung like stale air in this sacred place of knowledge.

Ian and Schmidt wandered with Sadie touching different steles as she did releasing holograms of pictures and hieroglyphics' that they didn't understand, into the air, occasionally calling one to her attention they thought might be the answer they were looking for.

After hours of searching, and bumping into each other over and over Ian called out in a harsh whisper like he didn't want anyone but Sadie to hear, "Sadie, come here, look at this. The only thing I can read and understand is the date. It reads as the equivalent of 9577BC, the time of the cataclysm."

Sadie gave him a gentle push out of the way, "Let me see it."

"It describes the time leading up to the cataclysm almost like the Bible says. They were telling people to build boats and then goes on to describe efforts to deter Nibiru. There was concern because they knew there were still people on Nibiru."

Her voice began to tremble like a small child telling of a bad experience. "They were going to try to set the path of the Moon in such a way as to cause Nibiru to bounce off of it away from the Earth." She let out a little gasp of realization as she read further, "They knew they would be unsuccessful, since they had a limited nuclear capability. What they needed existed only on Nibiru and was out of their reach."

"They knew they were doomed. I don't understand this, it doesn't paint a clear picture. The poem is here but it looks like it may have been written by someone who came after the Earth had regenerated as a kind of satire mocking the fact that Nibiru didn't completely destroy them. I can read it to you if you wish."

Ian was soft and respectful in his query, "No, that's okay we can talk about it later. Does it say what they would have done if they had had the nuclear capability?"

Sadie shook her head before replying, "I'm afraid it's very simple, but I don't see how this could be an answer. It says, for the course of one full moon nudge the moon to a path calculated by the Tables of Destiny away from its normal path to meet great Nibiru to deflect to another path. It just doesn't say how to deflect it. It says they didn't intend to try and attack Nibiru with nuclear devices but needed nuclear material as fuel."

Sadie grabbed Ian by the arm, "Listen to this, it describes the Tables as a cauldron to catch the movement of Nibiru, to catch the blood when Nibiru appears. What is that Ian?"

Ian frowned, "I don't know, I don't get it."

Schmidt was more assured in his response, "We do have the nuclear capability, we could do it, but we need to find those tables."

Ian asked quietly, "Is there anymore Sadie? Is that it?"

Sadie shook her head, "Sorry, that's it. It does say something about who wrote the poem, he was……"

Ian cut Sadie off and broke into a smile, "I've got it, your comment about the cauldron means we have to find those tables," he looked again to Schmidt, "Can you get us out of here Smitty and take us to Jerusalem?"

Schmidt smiled back, "I thought we would never leave," He shouted over his shoulder and headed back through the passage towards the "Pit."

As they exited the Hall of Records the hologram that had greeted them met them at the entrance, "Thank you for coming, we hope all your needs have been met." He recited in Egyptian.

"What did he say?" Schmidt asked.

"He hopes you're happy Smitty," Sadie quipped.

The assent back up to the surface was easier than the descent. Leaning forward up hill is easier than downhill and all the necessary doors and portals to the outside opened without resistance almost willingly as if to rid itself of an intrusion.

They exited through the "Robber's Tunnel," which is at ground level and were met by the Egyptian man who had driven them there, who, in gestures, directed them to be quiet and crouch down out of sight. He began to move away from them and waved for them to follow him. After ten or fifteen steps he stood up straight and waved furiously at them to follow him. Ian who was out in front could see the white van about one hundred feet away and signaled to Sadie and Schmidt to follow. Sadie bolted forward toward the van while Schmidt lingered looking all about him when a shot rang out. Schmidt drew his gun ready to fire back at whomever. The Egyptian man threw his hands up in the air motioning to Schmidt to put his gun down and move to the van.

Schmidt could see two men who looked like soldiers about one hundred feet away, but they were facing away from him. He ran and jumped in the van with the others as it sped away sending showers of sand and gravel flying behind them. Sadie looked out the back window and could see the soldiers facing away from them firing into the air.

Schmidt and the Egyptian were arguing. Schmidt shouted, "What was all that all about?"

The Egyptian, equally loud, answered in English, "You were late. There was a shift change, I had to make arrangements. Forget it, where are you going now?"

Schmidt sat back more at ease and answered, "To Jerusalem, you're driving," then asked, "Can you do it?"

His answer came in Egyptian, "Only if you let me get gas."

Sadie got into it before Schmidt could erupt, "He's yanking your chain Smitty he needs gas."

Schmidt just shook his head, "Anwar, you're such a pain in the ass."

Anwar hit he accelerator and grinned as the van lurched ahead, "Then you still love old Anwar."

Sadie thought, "Finally, a name," then leaned forward patting Anwar on the shoulder, "we'll all love you if you get us to Jerusalem."

"No problem madam, we're here to serve," Anwar answered as the van swerved off sand and gravel onto a modern highway not quite like the yellow brick road, but leading to Jerusalem.

Chapter 12: To Jerusalem

Sadie, sitting slumped against Ian in the back seat of the van was suddenly thrown forward against the back of the front seat when the van lurched to a stop with a shriek of squealing brakes.

Voices rang out loudly. Anwar was cursing and protesting in Hebrew through an open van window about how he had simply dozed off for just a minute. A guard not making any attempt to hide his irritation about some infraction by Anwar threw the door of the van open and dragged Anwar to the ground.

They were at an Israeli check point at the border between Egypt and Israel and the screaming match that followed looked bad for Anwar. As the argument raged on one of the guards threw his hands up in frustration and walked away leaving the second guard and Anwar entangled in a furious argument with the guard grabbing Anwar by the shirt and shaking him violently.

Sadie peered out of the van window and watched as a subtle exchange from hand to hand took place through all of the scuffling between Anwar and the guard; then watched as the guard grabbed Anwar again and threw him first back against the van and then forcibly pushed him back into the driver's seat. The guard then slammed the door, which had remained open, as the van sat and continued to idle loudly. Then in a dramatic motion directed Anwar through the check point making a threatening motion with his rifle and screaming in Hebrew he never wanted to see him again.

The van lurched forward and Ian who had never moved slumped back against the wall of the van and began to lightly snore. Schmidt who had feigned disinterest by appearing to be sleeping continued to sit in the passenger seat with his hat pulled down over his eyes and muttered, "The old misdirection game. Shame on you Anwar, you're too obvious; but I guess we're on our way to Jerusalem."

Anwar replied politely steering with one hand and brushing himself off the best he could with the other, "Just another day at the office mate, just another day at the office."

A quiet, easy, silence descended on the group as the van bumped along to the gentle rhythm of Ian's snoring, until he abruptly sat up straight and launched into conversation as if what he had to say was a continuation of a dream.

"You know I keep thinking about what we saw in the Hall of Records and those tables being referred to as the Tables of Destiny," Ian continued like a stream of consciousness, "and the direction we received to go to the Temple Mount." He paused and shook his index finger out in front of him to make a point, "That's where the Knight's Templar's were directed. They ended up spending nine years digging through hard rock beneath the Mount before they found what they were looking for. That's why I want to go there, to see where they were digging."

Sadie looked at him with some interest and some small part of amusement at his sudden declaration.

I thought we had already decided to go there," she stated rather blandly then continued, "what do you expect to find there Ian?"

Schmidt turned around from the passenger's seat to face Ian, "Yeah, what specifically are we looking for I thought it was for the Tables."

Ian grinned at them, "Here's the deal the Templar's were supposed to have found things of great value under the Temple Mount. Things like scrolls about Jesus' life and great treasures like gold and silver. Some legends say they might have found the Ark of the Covenant and some scholars and theologians believe they found the Holy Grail, but," he was not ready to be interrupted, "focusing on just the Holy Grail, if they did find it, what did they actually find? The actual substance of the Holy Grail has never actually been defined"

"I've been thinking about the line that Sadie read back at the Hall of Records that we didn't understand. It said the Tables were a cauldron to catch the blood which flows when Nibiru appears."

"Joseph of Arimthea was supposed to have used the Holy Grail to catch Christ's blood. What if the idea of a Holy Grail is a kind of euphemism for a sacred protective object that may take different forms ala a silver chalice or a set of Ephemerides Tables. The Grail is believed to be a sacred object that had great powers," he paused dramatically, "what could have greater powers then these Tables we're trying to chase down? What if the Holy Grail and the Tables of Destiny are one and the same?"

Sadie sat back in a reflective mood and Schmidt interjected, "And your point is that the Templar's found the Tables and took them away some place."

"I believe they found something. Current thinking is that they found the Holy Grail, ergo, I believe the tables, and took them back to Scotland, probably to Rosslyn Chapel."

Schmidt grinned, thinking to himself, "We're beginning to sound like Abbot and Costello." He sounded exasperated, "Okay then you think the Holy Grail and the tables might be the same, and may be in Scotland. Then why are we going to Jerusalem?"

Anwar, who had been quiet since the check point incident piped in, "Why are we going to Jerusalem mate?"

Ian shot back, "Because when I get to Scotland, I want to know exactly where to look. I believe if I can see the actual spot on the Temple Mount where the Templar's were digging then I'll know where to dig in Scotland."

"I'll explain. The Dome of the Rock currently dominates the Temple Mount along with a small mosque called Al Aqsa. The first temple built on that site was much smaller built by King David's son, King Solomon, who chose the temple as a place to house the Ark of the Covenant and other important religious treasures."

"That temple was destroyed and looted of its treasures including the Ark of the Covenant by King Nebuchadnezzar around 586BC. It was rebuilt in 515BC not much bigger than the first version."

"The third time, King Herod the Great of Judea took the lead in rebuilding and expanding the original temple into what is today the Temple Mount. That lasted until a Jewish revolt against the Romans all but destroyed everything but the Western Wall, which we all know became a holy site of worship."

"My interest lies in the fact that at one time there were great treasures there including the Ark of the Covenant, which lends credence to some legends which hold that the Holy Grail was also part of the treasure; and that the Templar's found the Grail and took it to Scotland. Since the Templar's did their digging when the temple was in the configuration of Herod's Temple, I would like to see that exact spot where they dug."

Anwar shouted excitedly, "I can show you. The tunnels mined by the Templar's were re-excavated back in the 1800's by some British Royal Engineers. They found that the tunnel goes down vertically for eighty feet through solid rock and then spreads out under the Mount. No wonder it took them nine years to do it, hey," and he added, "You were right on when you mentioned the Al Aqsa Mosque, that's where the tunnel would be today."

"Deal," Ian replied without hesitation, "and I'll be glad to pay you for the effort."

Schmidt broke in, "No way are we paying this guy for that kind of help, he's been lying to us all along. His name isn't even Anwar. Please meet Major Arron Glickstein with the Israeli Army."

Ian started to laugh and Sadie looked shocked. In a reflex action she hit Anwar on the back of his neck and asked, "Why, all the ruckus back at the check point then, why didn't they just let us through?"

"Because they know only Anwar," the Major replied with a chuckle, "This is a time of peace in 2019 between Israel and Egypt even though Egypt is currently upset with the U.S. We recognized the importance of your mission Dr. Haddad, so I was sent along to grease the skids for you without upsetting Israel's relationship with Egypt."

Ian shook his head, "I guess I'll have to spend more time reading the score card to see who's on what team."

"I'm on your team," the Major volunteered, "and I'll get you to wherever you want to go in Jerusalem and then fly you to Scotland if you would like." He smiled at his next revelation, "I'm also a pilot for the air force when I'm not driving around the sands of Egypt," he quipped restraining the urge to laugh at his own short bio.

Sadie started to laugh, "Why do all the men in my life think they're clones of James Bond?"

Schmidt said, "Hang on, let me summarize. Ian wants to look or climb down some dark hole in the Temple Mount, so Major Glickstein, alias Anwar, can fly us to somewhere in Scotland to find the Holy Grail, which is really the Tables of Destiny we've been looking for all along. Did I leave anything out?"

After a very brief silence the Major asked, "Where in Scotland?"

Ian's answer was crisp and to the point, "Rosslyn Chapel driver, if you please."

Sadie asked the obvious question, "Why Rosslyn Chapel?"

"Okay I keep thinking about the Templar's, some things I remember about the Freemasons, and Rosslyn Chapel, all of which appear to be all tied together. Let me tell you some things about Rosslyn Chapel first that are not well known."

Ian picked up quickly at the opening, "Rosslyn Chapel like many ancient structures is perfectly aligned to the cardinal directions much like those I discussed with the Commission and similar to ancient solar temples, or as I called them solar clocks. It has a distinct astrological orientation that isn't consistent with either its location or designed purpose."

He looked at the three of them for some sort of response. Anwar had his head cocked in Ian's direction so he could hear. "You guys are familiar with the Freemasons and their supposed connection with the Templar's. It's believed that the Mason's are an extension of the Templar's and conversely they're both tied to Rosslyn Chapel, which has the Templar's signature all over it; which as I pointed out may in turn have some astrological significance and ergo a connection to our tables."

Schmidt said, "So what's the point about the Freemasons, my uncle was a Mason."

Ian paused and twinned his fingers together like a master storyteller about to spin his greatest yarn, "Here's a for instance, as I understand it some of the initiation rites of the Masons correspond strongly to some of the solstices and may tie to the Precession of the Equinox," he paused again, "hang with me on this next idea because it may be more innuendo then fact. There are three important pillars at Rosslyn. The most seemingly important one is called the Pillar of the Apprentice, which plays heavily in the initiation rituals of the Masons and seems to have significant cosmological orientation to it."

Specifically at the base of the Pillar of the Apprentice eight snakes are sculptured, which have been identified and associated with an old myth that we find in many cultures around the world known as the World Tree."

Sadie jumped into the conversation, "That's from Nordic mythology where the World Tree is called Yggdrassil and has the eight snakes curled around the roots of the tree."

Schmidt laughed and said, "How do you spell that, and what's the point?"

Ian took the lead back, "Exactly Sadie, because in ancient times the World Tree represented the cosmological center for mankind. It was supposed to bind together heaven, earth, and hell into the Christen Tree of Life. The crown of the tree was supposed to comprise the twelve constellations of the Zodiac and the spiraling branches were supposed to symbolize the planets. The point is that the Templar's built a reference to all this, plus a lot more cosmological knowledge, into a structure that we believe may hold a very important piece of information on how our solar system works. Then put this together with the fact that the Masons have an initiation ritual that references the Pillar of the Apprentice and that same ritual suggests they understood the Precession probably from knowledge handed down to them by the Templar's."

"It's circumstantial and just a lot of loose ends, but the Templar's must have had some knowledge of the cosmos unusual for their time, knowledge that they may not have understood but realized it's greatest use would be in the future." Ian stopped to see if he still had an audience, who in fact seemed fascinated by what he was suggesting.

Encouraged, he continued, "One more thing that keeps ringing round in my head, the building of Solomon's Temple, which became Herod's Temple, goes back to an old Egyptian priest and architect named Hiram Abif, who designed the first Solomon's Temple. Many if not all of the Freemason initiation rituals seem to tie back to Hiram Abif, who was an Egyptian priest imbued with ancient Egyptian knowledge."

Ian raised his hand up to hold back any comments, "In addition to all of that some of that ancient Egyptian knowledge may have found its way to Solomon's Temple via the Qumranian's of Jesus' time, who tied back to ancient Egypt and were instructed to put their most treasured scrolls under the Holy of Holies, ala Solomon's Temple."

"Here's what I'm driving at," he continued, "I read that back in 1307 a Templar was arrested and in the course of his interrogation regarding the initiation rituals of the Order, when he was shown the Christian Cross, it piqued my interest that he said, "Put not your faith in this, for it is not old enough."

"Do you get it? That may mean that knowledge that the Templar's found may go back to ancient Egyptian times before the rise of Christianity and maybe back to the "Shinning Ones," who we know had extensive cosmological knowledge."

Schmidt grinned at Ian, "Is that why we're going to Jerusalem or to Scotland?"

Ian answered shaking his head, "I know it's complicated and gets a little ragged around the edges, but I'll explain later after I've seen the dig site of the Templar's, besides that looks like a bustling civilization ahead."

Anwar shouted out exuberantly, "You're right mate, Jerusalem, straight ahead."

CHAPTER 13: ROSSLYN CHAPEL

Schmidt and Sadie waited patiently by Anwar's van while Ian explored the depths of the Temple Mount. Schmidt leaned against the van talking to someone on his cell phone in hushed tones occasionally showing small bits of pique and distress.

Sadie paced the length of the van making military turns repeatedly and saluting Schmidt showing sarcastic compliance with his admonition to, "not go too far." When she had tired of her charade and Schmidt finally stopped talking on the phone she asked, legitimate concern in her voice, "What's up? Why all the hush, hush talk Smitty?"

Schmidt nodded in the direction of two men half a block away from them, who seemed to be inching their way in Sadie's direction. He moved his hand to where Sadie had seen his gun and answered, "Maybe they can tell you." He stood up straight from his leaning position to face squarely towards the two men.

Sadie held his arm smiling slyly at him, "Great we're going to shoot someone in the holiest city in the world; that should be well received by the local gentry, and will most certainly help our cause."

Schmidt grinned at her, "Just posturing Sadie, a little muscle flexing to let them know I see them."

The two men, suddenly looked startled, and moved off in a ninety degree direction. As they moved away Ian and Anwar came walking like they were in a foot race with each other. Ian pulled open the van door, jumped in and said, "Okay, come on, let's go."

Anwar was already around the other side getting into the driver's seat. Sadie moved in behind Ian and motioned to Schmidt, "Come on, they're ready to leave, you better get in or they'll leave without you."

Schmidt slammed the door on Sadie's side and moved in next to Anwar in the passenger's side, "Where are we going? To Scotland I presume," he answered his own question as Anwar pulled briskly away from the curb.

Anwar answered, "To Scotland via Ben-Gurion Airport, I made the arrangements while Dr. MacGown was sightseeing. We have a jet for you and a great pilot."

He grinned broadly at Schmidt, who shook his head in disbelief grinning back at him, "There's nobody in the world, crazy enough to let you fly one of their jets in that outfit."

Schmidt spun around in his seat to face Ian, who appeared to be in deep thought about something, "Did you find what you needed Ian," he continued before Ian could answer, "We are developing major problems."

Ian's reply was curt, "Yeah, I think so. What problems?"

"I talked to our ambassador at the American embassy and he said the whole world is going crazy about this Nibiru thing. People who never heard of Nibiru are marching in the streets, protesting the slaughter of innocent children on Nibiru." Schmidt was ready to continue, but Ian quipped, "They may not even have children, but simply all live forever."

Sadie slapped him on the shoulder, "You're not funny Ian, what else Smitty?"

"The usual you would expect. Groups of parents concerned for their children here on Earth, if nothing is done to protect them, marching against those worried about Nibiru."

Schmidt continued, "There is one group insisting they are descendents of Nibiru colonists, while another insists that the Nibiruians are interlopers and should be put on a space ship back to Nibiru. It apparently is not clear who the Nibiruians are, although several groups have volunteered to identify them. In summary they're all meeting in the streets with clubs and guns."

"Patel's pacifists are being blamed for at least one shooting and death out in front of the Capitol Building and," he was not through, "it is happening all over the world. How could so many people have gotten involved in such a short time, Ian? You were just recently in front of the Commission trying to convince them that Nibiru even existed?"

Ian shook his head in reply, "I have no real answers. Apparently there are groups in the world organized just waiting for a cause, any cause. They'll jump on either side of an argument, if only to be heard."

Sadie, who had listened quietly, interrupted to add some passion to the discussion, "We need to find those Tables to give people something to believe in; to believe everyone's children can be safe."

"What did you find at the Mount Ian, anything that contributes to a solution?" Schmidt asked.

Ian was quiet for a second like he was still focused on the riots, "I found a vault where it was supposed to be under the Mount, and I believe it will help us to fashion a key to a similar vault in Scotland."

Anwar alias, Major Glickstein interrupted, "Sorry Dr. MacGown, but we're coming up to the airport and it looks like there might be a little activity there," he took a different, more serious tone with them and said, "Okay, we all need to pay attention. There should be a plane waiting for us with the engine running. I'm going to pull the van right up to the door of the plane. Everyone move quickly, don't stop for anything, make sure you have everything with you. There's a runway cleared for us. Get in and fasten your seat belts."

The van ran out onto a runway without resistance, and headed towards a small executive jet parked on a runway away from the terminal. As the van screeched to a stop in front of the jet a group of at least thirty people broke past guards at the terminal and started running towards the plane carrying banners and screaming in Hebrew and English, "Save Nibiru, save Nibiru."

At the same time two cars careened around another plane parked at a distant gate heading for Major Glickstein's plane, which was already loaded and taxing down the runway.

Two men stationed next to the jet stepped forward and fired guns into the air which sent the throng of thirty or more in fast retreat. With the crowd in fast retreat the two men jumped into Glicktein's van, which had been left standing with the motor running, and chased the two interloper cars down the runway as they attempted to run in front of Glickstein to prevent his takeoff.

Schmidt, who had taken the co-pilot's seat next to Glickstein, whistled as he watched the van accelerate and overtake the two cars, firing at the tires of the two assailant cars making a direct hit on the first one sending it careening off the runway into a bunker designed to stop run-away planes.

Schmidt was still in awe, "Anwar did you see that? What do you have in that old Junker, it made those guys look like they were standing still, and who the hell are those body guards of yours, they're really tough."

Anwar didn't respond, since the second assailant car was weaving wildly trying to position himself in front of his left wheel to prevent him from gaining speed with the runway getting shorter and shorter. The driver of the car turned his head, looking back trying to run under Anwar's wheel. When he turned his attention back to his path on the runway three men in shinning white garments appeared standing directly in his path. As he instinctively spun his wheels to avoid them his front wheels hooked onto the edge of the concrete runway and sent the backend of his car flying over the front leaving the car lying in the dust with a huge thud.

Anwar looked over at Schmidt grinning as the plane climbed out gracefully across the Mediterranean towards Scotland, "Just another day at the office mate, just another day at the office."

Schmidt looked over his left shoulder at Anwar, "Did you see that, did you see those guys in white."

"What guys?" he answered, "I didn't see any one but those guys lying in a heap. What are you talking about mate?"

Schmidt shook his head wearily, "Nothing, it was a great takeoff, absolutely great."

Schmidt called back to Ian and Sadie, "You guys all right back there, everything alright?"

Sadie answered, "Just another day at the office mate, no worse than being carried off with no one to save me, but a bunch of sunny faced, white robed heroes."

Anwar said, "What did she say?"

Schmidt turned back in his seat, "She said she's fine."

*

Anwar glided the plane softly onto the runway of Edinburgh Airport and taxied to a remote tarmac away from the terminal. Schmidt turned back from his seat facing Ian and Sadie, "I've been in touch with Rosenthal, who says this thing has grown to huge proportions. Apparently Senator Hyatt has been offering interviews about the Commission's work to whoever will listen. Once the reporters got wind of it the next step was the internet and it literally cascaded around the world. Apparently you were not the only ones concerned about Nibiru, Ian."

"The primary focus of the protests seems to be centered in Washington with secondary emphasis in Cairo and Bombay.

"Why Cairo," Sadie asked?

"It doesn't make sense, but the Egyptians think that because we went there for information, per Senator Hyatt, the Egyptian Government is involved with the destruction of Nibiru. Apparently the group, who feel they are direct descendents of the Nibiruians are headquartered in Cairo and take issue with that prospect."

He continued somewhat wearily, "As for the Bombay contingent that seems to be the work of your good friend Patel. They're rioting in the streets and killing people as they protest the possible innocent deaths of people around the world and on Nibiru. Do you get that Ian? I sure don't."

Anwar leaned into the cabin of the plane with his ever smiling face, thrust an Uzi into Schmidt's hands and waved a second one over his head, "Then you may not want this when we meet up with Patel, although it may be a good idea. I've been having him tracked since you mentioned meeting up with him on the train to Edfu. My information says he is in Scotland traveling with ten or more people, although everything looks better than I thought at the airport."

Schmidt nodded assent to receiving the message and tucked the Uzi under his arm, "Thanks Anwar, what about Rosslyn Chapel, are we all set?"

Anwar shook his head vigorously, "We'll have a lot of support. There are people of authority lined up with whatever tools you may need. All we have to do is get there. We can leave whenever you're ready. There's a Scottish army vehicle waiting on the runway for us with some sort of Chaplin from Rosslyn ready to help."

Ian held back, "Hold up just a second, there are a couple of things we all need to understand about Rosslyn Chapel before we get there. It is a sacred, spiritual place, but it's not really a church. One of the most obvious features that you'll see is that there's no alter from which to conduct a service. It was meant to be a chapel for a church that was never completed. The interesting thing is that the basic footprint was intended to be a replica of a portion of Herod's Temple, which is why I wanted to go to Jerusalem. I wanted to see where the Templar's did their digging and how it might correspond to Rosslyn Chapel. My concern now is that we may have to deal with a clergyman, who may take issue with our digging in his sacred, if not holy, site."

Schmidt started out of the plane talking over his shoulder as he exited, "Come on, we'll just have to deal with that when we get there."

Sadie tugged at Ian towards the exit, "He's right you know you can't fight a battle until you know who your enemy is." She turned and was on the ground facing Schmidt, "That's not like Ian, he's usually gung ho."

Schmidt started to reply, "It's been......" When Ian came bouncing out of the plane, "Come on, let's go, are we going to stand here all day? What's the hold up?"

Sadie grinned at Schmidt, "There that's more like it."

Anwar who had exited as soon as Ian finished his short diatribe pulled an army vehicle that looked like more like a Hum Bee than anything else, to the side of the plane, "Get in," he hollered over the roar of his new found toy, "we need to move."

Ian was in first and slid next to a sixtyish, grey haired slender man, whose only indication that he might be clergy was his white collar. "I'm Reverend Loring at your service. I believe you want to dig some sort of hole in Rosslyn Chapel."

Ian snickered and smiled simultaneously, "Yes sir, but it won't be a very big hole, just big enough to retrieve something very important, and only with your permission. I'm Dr. Ian MacGown, it's a pleasure to meet you. My associates are Dr. Sadie Haddad, Bob Schmidt, and Major Arron Glickstein of the Israeli Army."

The Reverend replied with a smile, "It's a pleasure to meet you all, and I must say Major I think your Israeli uniforms are quite striking."

The Reverend stopped smiling and assumed a different demeanor, "The proprietors of Rosslyn Chapel have been in touch with your Senator Rosenthal and are fully apprised of the very difficult situation confronting us all. They understand you may have to in some way do some surface damage to the Chapel, although I, for one, hope it will be minimal. I have been instructed to provide you with whatever tools you may need and have them waiting at the chapel."

He paused as if there was something more that had to be said then continued, "There is a long standing tradition and belief that a vault beneath the Chapel may contain something as valuable as the Holy Grail, although I'm sure Dr. MacGown, you know as I do that complete definition has never really been given to the content of the Grail." He paused again, "Recognizing the importance of your mission, we can't deny you the permission to retain and use whatever you may find, but beg your indulgence to at least share with us whatever you may find."

The Reverend gave a slight sigh as if he had more to divulge, "I'm sure you are aware that some geological ultrasound tests have been made in past years and indicated that there is indeed a large vault underneath the Chapel," he raised his hand to indicate he wasn't finished, "and some other ultrasound tests also indicated there is a tunnel running from Rosslyn Castle to the Chapel. Perhaps you should look in the Castle to see if you could enter from there." He smiled graciously at Ian as if to say, "There I've said it all."

Ian nodded politely, "Thank you sir, I wasn't aware of the connection to Rosslyn Castle and as far as sharing what we find we certainly understand and will, considering all other urgencies, share all that we find with you."

"Good, thank you, my junior assistant Mr. Diggs will be waiting to help you with whatever you need. He knows all the ins and outs of the Chapel better than anyone who has ever served there." He finished with a flourish, "Are we there yet, Major, were the instructions I gave you sufficient?"

Anwar replied, "They were fine sir, and it appears the Chapel is right around the corner so to speak, and everything seems to be all clear. No apparent sign of Dr. Patel."

There was a hitch in Anwar's voice and he tried to catch the Reverend's eye in his rear view mirror, "Sir I must admit I am not entirely aware of a Castle. Can you enlighten us?"

The Reverend who had assumed a somewhat grave manner after his short diatribe smiled again glad to be of additional service, "Of course, Rosslyn Castle," he emphasized, "is just a few hundred meters south of the Chapel. It's very, very old and for the most part is in shambles, although is still available for tourists. It was built back in 1304…"

Anwar spoke in a hushed voice, "Sorry to interrupt sir, but we have arrived. Thank you for the information on the castle." He turned to Schmidt and said, "It looks quiet."

Schmidt who taken the passenger's seat agreed, but with a somewhat grave tone to his voice, "Yes, it almost appears too quiet." Then he added looking at Anwar, "Can we expect any support from the locals, if we need it?"

Anwar turned his head looking both to his left and his right, "Maybe, but it will be very low profile. We probably will never see them unless we need them." He abruptly stopped his conversation with Schmidt and shouted in a hushed tone to the back seat, "Okay, we're here, let's go," and brought the vehicle to an abrupt stop about fifty yards outside of a short stone fence surrounding the Chapel.

Reverend Loring got out of the Hum Bee and started towards the Chapel muttering, "There's no need to make an old man walk so far, Mr. Diggs is here to let us in."

As he finished his sentence, Mr. Diggs, the junior assistant, who appeared older then Reverend Loring, appeared at the front entrance waving at them to hurry, "Come on, come on, I just chased some other men away in a funny looking vehicle like yours, but I recognized the Reverend right away. Why did you park so far away?" He patted each one of his visitors on the arm, "No time for hugs and kisses, we have some work to do." He then stepped back looking from one to the other of the newcomers waiting for instructions holding his gaze suspiciously on Anwar.

Ian extended his hand to Diggs, "I'm Dr. MacGown, an old Scotchman like you. I need to look around a bit and then I'm probably going to need your help. My associates are," he pointed to each as he introduced them, "Dr. Haddad, the pretty lady, Bob Schmidt from the U.S. senate and Major Glickstein of the Israeli Army."

Diggs stepped up and took Anwar by the shoulders and said, "I hope things pick up soon in your country son and they can get you some better uniforms." Then he slapped his knees with his hands and fell into a short convulsive laugh.

Anwar looked at Schmidt grinning, "It comes with the territory mate it never ends."

Ian had already begun pacing the length and width of the chapel writing quick little notes on a sheet of paper he had folded several times to make his task easier. He shouted to Sadie, who had wandered off to a corner admiring the beautiful stained glass windows that would have been befitting of any of the great European Cathedrals built by the Knights Templar's.

"Sadie, come here. Look at these numbers, the footprint of the Chapel seems to match exactly what those of Herod's Temple would have been. I paced them off when I was at the Temple of the Mount."

His excitement brought all the others quickly around him to look at some numbers that for the moment made sense only to him. Without any more discussion he brushed by the small assembled group and began counting the pillars that on two sides extended the length of the chapel. He then walked to the entrance of the chapel and carefully counted off three pillars which left him standing between them in the middle of the two opposing walls. He muttered, "Just as I thought, this is the spot I think would correspond to where the Templar's would have dug."

Sadie was grinning tilting her head upward, "Ian look," she pointed to the ceiling directly over where he was standing. There was a large circular knob in the form of an arrowhead in the middle of the arched roof pointing down to the top of Ian's head, who without moving craned his head backwards to look up and observe this new find. He then awkwardly looked down between his feet and with palms turned upward facing the ceiling carefully stepped off the spot and said, "This must be it, but that's too easy. Where's the hook?"

Sadie said, "It looks like some sort of keystone, and the hook may be, how we get it out of there?"

Diggs stepped forward, "Yes I've looked at it many times wondering how important it might be. Look there is no mortar or anything to bind it to the stones next to it and I believe it to be made of granite."

Ian smiled at the old trooper, "Thank you Mr. Diggs, I believe you're right. Now how do we get it out of there?"

Everyone was now leaning across the stone looking at the keystone afraid to step on it even though they had all just walked on it less than a few minutes prior.

Their group silence in answer to Ian's question was broken again by Mr. Diggs, "I've got a small sledge and some good size chisels along with two crowbars bigger than this fella in my truck. I'll get them for you." He started quickly, but lumbering towards the back of the chapel assigning the fella designation to Schmidt who he patted as he went by him.

Schmidt looked at Anwar, "If that's granite, and it sure looks like it, this could be tough even with his tools; or should I say especially with only those tools."

Anwar grinned back at Schmidt, "You may be right, if I recall granite is dense and heavy, and those tools he's offering don't sound promising."

"One hundred and sixty eight pounds per cubic foot," Sadie quipped, "That's the weight of granite."

She continued, "Since that block looks to be two feet square and probably no less than four to six inches thick it must weigh at least between one hundred and ten and one hundred and seventy pounds. That's not much for two big guys like you even if it's a little thicker than I guessed."

Anwar shook his head, "No argument, just tell us how to get it started. It looks like you couldn't even get a thin piece of paper between it and the block next to it."

Schmidt couldn't hold back a huge grin aimed at Sadie's ever present command of the situation at hand, "He's right Doctor, what do you recommend?"

Sadie smiled slyly, "Well since you boys seem a little skittish about the whole thing I thought I might give it a whirl. That is if you're all right with it."

Ian who had stood staring at the probable entry to the vault where he wanted to be looked at her, "Sadie what are you doing?"

She looked back at the three men without a smile, "I'm serious. I read something back at the Hall of Records on how the Egyptians were able to levitate seventy ton granite blocks using only sound. What I read was just a series of notes repeated over and over," she stopped and now was grinning, "I remember the notes and Ian will tell you, I have perfect pitch."

Their discussion was interrupted by the clanging of two large chisels on the floor in front of Mr. Diggs who stood standing with what looked like a ten pound sledge hammer in his hand. He picked up one on the chisels and said quietly, "I'll start."

Ian said, "Hold on just a minute," he looked squarely at Sadie, "you're serious, aren't you."

"Never more serious, let's go, times a wasting." She directed Schmidt and Anwar, "I have to stand on top of it. If I get it up into the air then each of you simultaneously, push it to the side." She turned to face Ian, "If you love me you'll catch me no matter which way I fall when the stone hits the ground."

With no more said she stepped to the middle of the stone and started chanting chords over and over while everyone watched in a kind of stunned silence.

There was no immediate response and disappointment settled quickly over the faces of the onlookers. Then almost imperceptibly a millimeter of edge began to show on the sides of the stone. Sadie kept up her cadence over and over for fifteen to twenty minutes when it became apparent that the stone was floating freely almost six inches above the ground. Ian signaled to Schmidt and Anwar who leaned down ready to push the stone away from the opening in the floor. He faced up in front of the chanting Sadie and nodded to the two men, who in unison gave the huge stone a push to the side. It fell hanging halfway over the opening as Ian stood with arms open ready for the catch and grinned as Sadie stepped gracefully to the side without assistance, avoiding the clattering stone as it landed with a final thud. As though planned and without further instruction Schmidt and Anwar each grabbed a corner of the stone and spun it off to the side fully exposing the vault below.

Ian said somewhat incredulously, "There are steps."

Steps the width of the opening led down into the vault and because of the depth of the vault extended to some point beyond the scope of the vision of the group, who were all now bending forward, looking into this hole they had created.

Schmidt held Ian back as he stepped forward, "It's your party, but I think I should go first." He motioned to Anwar, "Come on, let's check it out."

Sadie laughed, "And if you find someone down there to protect us from, how do you think they got in there?"

Ian ignored the minor spat and started down the steps affirming, "It's my party." They could see his back as he approached the end of the long stairs when he let out a long loud whistle, "Wow this place is huge," his voice echoed back at him, "Huge!"

Reverend Loring held Mr. Diggs back, "We'll keep watch for now, let them look."

Sadie, Schmidt and Anwar filed past him in that order eager to see what lay beneath. They each went in opposite directions at the bottom of the steps, searching the perimeter of the huge vault. Schmidt shouted out from one of the corners, "Hey, there's a door here." You could hear him grunt and it was apparent he was trying to move a massive old structure.

Anwar called over to him, "Wait, don't, we may not like what we find behind it."

Ian who was standing next to four large trunks neatly arranged in a line against a wall that had inscriptions carved in gold inlay over three of the trunks called them over, "He's right, come and look at this first."

Sadie who had positioned herself next to Ian moved from one to the other reading each one out loud.

Si tatlia jungere possis sit tibi scire posse --- If thou canst comprehend these things thou knowest enough

Theca ubi res prestiosa deponitur ---A place where a precious thing is concealed

Res ipsa prestiosa --- The precious thing itself

Schmidt looked at Ian, "They don't have locks on them, what are we waiting for? It's your party."

Ian stepped up to the first trunk and with no more effort than one would use in his grandmother's attic flipped the lid open to reveal scrolls neatly tied with gold ribbon filling only the bottom of the trunk. None were piled on top of each other. Sadie picked up one, gently untied the gold ribbon and carefully opened it.

Anwar looked over her shoulder and said, "I can read that, some of it, maybe parts of it. I can see it's in some kind of old Hebrew."

Sadie kept reading, "Yes, it's all about the life of Jesus, who he was." She picked up another and repeated the process, "This will be very interesting for Reverend Loring."

Ian opened the other three trunks. The second one held more scrolls and the third held a variety of gold goblets, robes lined with gold thread, and implements of the time of Jesus that would be used in dining. Anwar picked up the largest, most ornate of the goblets and held it up to the group, "The Holy Grail?" He posed the question to them to answer.

Ian, who stood staring at what appeared to be a large scroll sitting alone at the bottom of the fourth trunk answered, "Maybe yes, maybe no. Sadie, can you look at this. Tell me what it is, what it says."

Sadie picked up the lone scroll murmuring as she carefully unrolled it, "It's much larger than the others."

She puckered her lips, and gave Ian a faint smile, "Tables of Destiny, these are the Tables of Destiny." She repeated the phase written on the wall above the first trunk, "Si tatlia jungere possis sit tibi scire posse --- If thou canst comprehend these things, thou knowest enough."

Schmidt began dialing his cell phone, "I've got to let Rosenthal know. Damn it, no signal down here, we need to get out of here. Come on, we got what we've been looking for."

Reverend Loring's lilting voice called out from above, "Are you all right? Did you find what you were looking for? Is everything all right?"

Schmidt started to answer when two successive shots rang out in the chapel above them. He had taken two steps up when he heard the soft thud of a body hitting the hard floor of the chapel.

"Oh dear lord, Mr. Diggs are you all right?" Reverend Loring sat at the top of the stairs holding Mr. Diggs in his arms waving frantically at Schmidt, "Go, go, there are too many of them. Look for…" A third shot rang out and Reverend Loring fell across the entrance his feet dangling down the first three steps.

Schmidt started back up the steps and was grabbed by Anwar who pulled him back thrusting his Uzi out in front of him and stepping in front of Schmidt. He looked up the steps and could see Reverend Loring's body being pulled out of the way. He could see someone dressed in black starting down the steps with an M-16 rifle protruding out in front of him. Anwar let go with a salvo from his Uzi that sent bullets ricocheting wildly off the chapel walls and ceiling. Two legs from the knees down stood, as though unattached, on the second step down emitting a groan from an unknown source. The M-16 clattered down the steps landing at Ian's feet, who had stepped up behind Schmidt and Anwar and was tugging at both of them.

"Come on, let's see what's behind that door you found, maybe it's the tunnel the Reverend spoke of between here and Roslyn Castle."

Anwar held fast until a spray of bullets whistling down the steps and ricocheting wildly around the vault scrambled the trio in all different directions. Ian who had bent down to pick up the M-16 fell backwards, then leaped to his feet, "Anyone hit?" he hollered.

Anwar answered, "I'm okay, but we need to get out of here. Those ricochets are dangerous. Where's that door?" He finished his sentence with another round to the top of the steps. Satisfied with the noise of ricochets above him and the scurrying and shouts of men running and ducking, he turned and ran behind the others who had exited into a tunnel. He slammed a huge metal door behind him that clanged sending echoes up and down the tunnel, "Go, go, keep moving, they're probably right behind us." He walked backwards through the tunnel, the Uzi out in front of him ready to fire at anyone, who stepped through the door.

He heard Schmidt's voice ring out behind him, "Another door." The creaking and shuddering of something very old, opening for the first time in century's sent soft billows of light fluttering into the tunnel which had turned dark as the first door closed. Anwar ran for the daylight that was fast becoming a hazy dusk and kneeled just past the door to catch his breath as Schmidt and Ian put their shoulders together to close the heavy door.

"I didn't hear anyone behind me, but we better move. Where are we Ian?" He gasped slightly more from the pressure of the event then the exertion.

Ian looked around as he answered, "This is Rosslyn Castle that the Reverend told you about. It was built by Henry Sinclair many, many years ago for whatever difference that may make. It looks like we're in a service area which is the bottom floor, which puts us at ground level." He grinned, "This thing may be old, but it's five stories tall. We're lucky we didn't end up on the roof. There should be a path that leads back down to the Chapel. We need to get outside."

They followed Ian through an open doorway that had lost everything but a sturdy old wooden frame caressing the stone of the Castle as it had for centuries. An old stone roadway led them across a bridge with intact stone walls on either side. Indefinable remnants of old brick structures lined the road with stories to be told that would never be heard.

Schmidt sensed the intrigue with this old Castle that also caught up both Sadie and Anwar as they kept spinning around for one more look from a different perspective, "Come on, keep moving, we still have people chasing us and they have guns. Anwar you should know better."

The admonition was like a shot to the heart of Anwar who flushed red and shouted back as he grabbed Sadie and pulled her along, "I was just checking behind us." He turned more crimson as Sadie brushed off his grip and shot one of her glares in his direction.

"Sorry, Dr. Haddad, just trying to help," was all that he could muster up.

Ian who had run ahead saved him from Sadie's wrath shouting, "Hurry, there's a path over here."

Rosslyn Castle is surrounded on three sides by the North Esk River with a bridge that looks like a miniature of those that carry trains across a trellis like structure. They scurried quickly across the bridge and were on a path leading back to the Chapel. Schmidt who had taken the lead back from Ian said in a hushed voice, "Hold it, I can see the Chapel and oops, at least one guy standing next to the Hum Bee." You could see the wheels spinning in his head when Anwar moved past him and said in a whisper, "I'll get him."

Schmidt hissed at him, "Hold it, hold it, my special ops training has to be good for something. I'll get him. You follow behind me in case there's more than one."

Anwar nodded assent and held back.

Sadie grabbed Schmidt by the arm, "Don't kill him Smitty, he looks like a child from here."

Schmidt took a deep breath, patted her on the arm and winked, "Only if I have to." He moved towards the vehicle crouched down as far as he could get with Anwar just a few steps behind him. As he approached the lone guard he stopped short at the ring of a cell phone, which the young man switched on and started to listen then answered in a language Schmidt didn't understand.

Anwar scooted up next to him, "He said he would stay here until they got back. Apparently they're camped out in there figuring out how to flush us out without getting shot. Can you take him out? I still have the keys." He dangled the Hum Bee keys in front of Schmidt's nose.

Anwar threw a stone in front of the Hum Bee and the young man threw his gun, which he had dangling loosely at his side, up into a firing position, "Stop!" He shouted in English.

Schmidt stepped up without a sound from the rear of the truck and put a strangle hold on the man, who appeared to be half Schmidt's size, until he slumped in his arms. He laid him gently on the ground and motioned to Anwar, "Wave them down, he won't be out long and I don't want Sadie upset with me if I have to put him down permanently. Come on, let's go."

He jumped in on the passenger side while Anwar slipped the keys into the ignition about the same time that Ian and Sadie jumped into the back seat. The engine roared, tires squealed on the gravel road, the young guard woke up, spun around with his M-16 pointing to the sky and fired. Schmidt leaned out of his window as the Bee sped away and fired at the young man's feet sending him tripping into the wall that surrounded the Chapel.

Sadie grabbed Schmidt by the shoulders from the back seat and screamed at him, "Did you kill him?"

Schmidt shrugged her off and began firing in the direction of the Chapel where five men came running out firing M-16's at the Hum Bee. His return fire sent three of them sprawling on the ground and the other two back into the Chapel for cover. Only the roar of the Hum Bee could be heard, no more shots, when Schmidt turned to Sadie and said, "Missed them all, nobody died," and after turning back facing forward muttered to Anwar who was grinning at him said, "Some of them were old enough to die and might the next time."

It's only a ten minute ride to the airport from the Chapel and the only conversation was by Schmidt to Ian, "You still have the Tables after all that, right?"

"Right Smitty, I still have the Tables."

*

Anwar pulled the Hum Bee up in front of a beautiful plane which Schmidt recognized as an AJC, which he explained to Sadie before she asked, was an Airbus 319 Private Business Jet, and finished with an explanation, "Looks like the boss is here."

Anwar didn't wait for questions or discussion, but volunteered, "This is your ride, I'm taking mine back to Israel. We need to keep moving before the bad guys find their way here, although they might find a little more resistance," he pointed to a group of armed men in uniforms standing about fifty yards away, "It's been great. I haven't had so much fun in a long time. I hope to see you soon." He stepped forward and gave each one an embrace.

When he got to Sadie he smiled and said softly, "I audited one of your classes at Hebrew University. It was great," he paused and continued shyly, "and that young woman with the child at the airport, that was my wife and little Sadie. We were both so impressed with you we choose Sadie as her name." He saw tears whelm up in Sadie eyes and stepped back, "We tried Haddad, but it just didn't work."

He motioned them into the waiting plane which sat with the engines running and ran towards the group of uniformed men waving over his head, but not looking back, with one last shout, "Just another day at the office mates."

Schmidt watched him, shaking his head, and called back to him, "Just another day at the office you crazy bastard."

Anwar stopped and spun around one more time and with his right hand held in the air as if to salute shouted to them, "Oh yeah, I forgot, say hello to my cousin David." He disappeared into the group of armed men waiting in the distance.

Schmidt smiled, took a deep breath and uttered softly again, "You crazy bastard," then guided Ian and Sadie into the open door of the waiting jet, "Come on, the Senator's waiting."

Ian held him by the arm before he could move away from him and Sadie and asked quizzically, "Rosenthal?" and then asked quizzically again, "Cousin?"

Schmidt wrinkled his brow, looked back at him and said, "I'm afraid so on both counts. Could be good news you know."

Ian shot back at him, "That's a big plane for just one man."

Schmidt smiled and started up the stairway in front of them, "Maybe he's got company, come on, let's go."

CHAPTER 14: POEM FROM THE PAST

The AJC is a VIP corporate jet equipped to easily carry as many as twenty nine passengers across the Atlantic, with a huge lounge in the front of the cabin that can be split into three separate cabins as required. There are either or both, large comfortable leather seats or eleven beds for long distance flights.

There was a sense of uneasiness between Ian and Sadie as they mounted the steps leading into the plane. Their trip over from the states had been anything but luxurious and it didn't seem right to be returning on a plane that seemed at best ostentatious. Ian kept running the names of members of the Commission through his head wondering how many, if not all, of them might be on the plane. His musing brought him to a mild collision with Sadie who was walking ahead of him and came to an abrupt stop. She was startled, but not surprised, to see Senators Rosenthal, Berger and Tarnowski sitting in the lounge in the front of the cabin. All three rose in unison from their seats to greet her.

Senator Rosenthal surprised her by embracing her in a hug as though she were an old friend, shook his head in a negative fashion as though trying to display his discomfort with something and then in an apologetic tone said, "I am so sorry you had to endure such an arduous trip, but we are elated with your success."

Senators Tarnowski and Berger each graciously took her hand, ignoring any embrace, seemingly uncomfortable with the prospect because of their limited friendship with her, "We are indeed very glad to see you."

Ian who had held slightly back to better survey the situation stepped up and as he shook Rosenthal's hand asked with a wry grin, "Where's the rest of the Commission?"

Senator Berger thrust his hand forward, "They are each on separate missions attempting to address the various different aspects of a very difficult problem to be solved," he grinned at Ian as he spoke, "we have like you had some interesting problems to deal with."

Then with a hint of impatience said, "We'll explain, please sit."

Senator Tarnowski shook Ian's hand, and the three Senators shouted emphatically in unison to Schmidt who stood in the entrance to the cabin, "Good job Bob, good job."

Schmidt smiled graciously, "Thanks, but we need to take our seats, we're ready for takeoff." He nodded to the Captain and fell into a seat next to the group.

The roar of the AJC's jets silenced any conversation until they leveled out at which time it became apparent to all that they had F-16 fighter jets escorting them on both sides of the plane.

Ian was becoming more uncomfortable with what seemed to him like overkill from a class B movie. Rosenthal broke the awkward silence that had enveloped them glancing out of the window as he spoke, "They will be with us all the way to be certain we get home safely."

Ian responded with a grin to the Senator, "In that regard Senator, one of safety, we need to thank you for enlisting your cousin Major Glicktstein to help us, he certainly proved effective in tight moments, and sends his regards. I should add there was some wonderful chemistry between him and our guardian Mr. Schmidt."

Schmidt snickered at the reference to his role in the adventure hurling back at Ian what had now become their code reference, "Just another day at the office mate."

Rosenthal sat back and smiled, "They are both indeed two of the most interesting men I've ever had the pleasure of working with, Major Glickstien and I really are cousins. Our grandparents were both involved in the Zionist movement back in the forty's."

He paused and smiled again ready to get back on track, "May we see the Tables of Destiny which you labored so hard to obtain?"

Ian smiled at how easily Rosenthal shifted gears and then gave a knowing wink to Schmidt, "If Rosenthal knew enough to refer to them as the Tables of Destiny he had to have learned it from Schmidt."

Schmidt grinned, wrinkled his brow and mouthed the words without speaking, "Just another day at the office."

Ian turned his attention back to the Senator and said, "Of course." He passed the scrolls to Rosenthal who simply passed them in turn to Berger, who had taken the seat next to him. Berger quickly, but carefully, opened the scrolls on the table in front of him and began to scan the Tables.

"These look promising particularly if Dr. Haddad will decipher them for me," He looked up and smiled at Sadie, "you will help, wont you?"

Sadie sat uncomfortably looking from Ian and Rosenthal back to Berger. She still considered Berger an enemy of sorts, not expecting him to be the one who they turned the Tables over to, and was taken back at his request for her help. He certainly didn't help Ian at the Commission hearing.

Rosenthal sensed her discomfort and interjected, "When you entered the plane we said we would explain, this seems like an appropriate time to do just that. It's going to be a long trip, so let me fill you in. You certainly deserve to know as much as we do."

He paused before continuing and Ian shuffled in his seat thinking it was like they were all back in the senate building in another senate investigation.

Rosenthal continued, "When this Commission was established each member was picked for some particular expertise in anticipation of the difficult situation in front of us." He looked gravely at Ian and gave Sadie a slight smile, "For example, we knew we would need the help of both of you. Senator Blessing whose role was to recommend and recruit the expertise we needed to help define our situation knew both of you by reputation. His contact with The Oriental Institute in Chicago and the work you had done with them, Dr. Haddad, was the key we needed since you both were associated with the Institute in some manner. My fortuitous association with Bob Schmidt and his past friendship with you, Dr. MacGown, completed the picture."

Ian looked again at his old friend and before Schmidt could respond said out loud laughing as he did, "Just another day at the office mate."

Rosenthal smiling with one eyebrow raised said knowingly, "I do recognize my cousin's call letters." He sat up straight and in a manner befitting the head of the Commission said, "Let me continue."

"Senator Hyatt represented our interface with the media, and although it may have seemed like she was leaking information inappropriately, she was by design trying to draw the public into the circle without causing anymore unrest then absolutely necessary. As you probably realize by now we may have caused more alarm then we expected. We anticipated there would be consequences we didn't like, but realized that those consequences were inevitable, and were best dealt with earlier than later. In hindsight we were not too far off the mark considering how dire a situation we're facing."

He then skipped along like a good scribe dotting his I's and crossing his T's leaning into the task he had assigned himself, "Senator Brown is renowned for his work in all aspects of science and ancient history. Senator Ligget as you may have recognized is well known in the community of

Egyptologists and was important in assessing the potential correctness of what you or others presented to the Commission."

He paused, caught his breath and continued, "Senator Holland spent many years working with a variety of religious councils around the world, and will be extremely important in interfacing with those religious communities in gaining their support to allow us to complete our task. We felt this was extremely important recognizing that many people, including you Dr. MacGown, refer to those people of Nibiru as Gods."

He didn't wait for a response from Ian, but continued unabated, "Senator Hoesel before joining the senate had a business empire that took him to almost every major country in the world. He will have the task of helping us to generate both the funds and manufacturing resources we will undoubtedly need in the very near future."

"Senator Malick is our coordinator. When we are apart in our separate duties he maintains notes of progress at all levels and disseminates it to all the Commission members."

He looked from Ian and back to Sadie as if uncertain they were listening and buying into the team that he had assembled, and of which they had become a part. He made a final sweeping gesture to Berger and Tarnowski by his side, "Although we're not precisely sure at this time what our special needs may be in venturing out into space to meet up with Nibiru at some level, Senator Tarnowski has been heading up a task force to develop those space vehicles we know we will undoubtly require to deliver some payload into space."

Sadie's immediate discomfort with this line of thought became apparent to all in the plane and her quietness rose noisily above the drone of the jets.

Senator Rosenthal stopped and acknowledged with a smile that resembled a grimace, directed to nowhere in particular, that this young woman in front of him may hold the destiny of all of mankind in her hands; and yet knowing that continued almost offhandedly, "Senator Berger who is one of the world's leading astral-physicists and cosmologists, has done extensive work with NASA in space exploration, but," he paused, smiled again and looked back to Sadie, "he probably can't read those Tables without your help."

Sadie sat quietly looking back first at Rosenthal then at Tarnowski and Berger, then turned and looked at Ian who smiled and winked with a slight nod to her. She turned back to Rosenthal and speaking softly and methodically said, "I can't help you blow up a planet that may have people like us on it. I can't stop you, but I can't help you. I would like to think that we as a society have learned something more since the time of the ancients than how to blow things up."

Berger who had sat in a tight containment of silence throughout Rosenthal's discourse erupted in rage, "That's absurd, why would you bring us these Tables and then tell us you can't help us?" He slapped his hands loudly together as if some sort of violent noise might re-establish his control.

Rosenthal reached over and held Berger by the arm, "hold on, hold on," He looked at Tarnowski calling him by his first name, "Bob tell them."

Tarnowski's response was controlled and reassuring, "We're not going to blow up Nibiru. We never intended to. To be honest if we assembled all the nuclear material we have of weapons grade in the whole world and attacked Nibiru with it it's unlikely we would even make a dent in it."

He shifted his gaze to Berger, who had never mentioned blowing up Nibiru, but continued sitting red faced next to him, and addressed him in an accusatory manner, "Senator Berger is enough of a scientist to know that."

Ian reflected inwardly at the unusual exchange between them, "These are the guys who are going to save us?" Then broke though the heavy silence that fell on them following Berger's enraged outburst and Tarnowski's response, "Then what are you going to do?"

Senator Rosenthal took the lead back, but looking obviously uncertain since the first time Ian and Sadie had met him said, "This is awkward," he paused, looking back and forth from Berger to Tarnowski not sure of what his next thrust should be, then threw his hands up and said, "we're stuck, we need your help."

Ian looked astounded, "To do what? We found the Tables for you," he paused and gave Sadie a grave look, "and Sadie will help you with them within boundaries, but with what?"

Berger after a moment of silence in which Rosenthal, Tarnowski, and he Berger, seemed to be silently tossing a hot potato around, spoke up confidently and directly, "Remember that poem that you introduced at the hearing about Nibiru tripping over the moon, we think it may have value, particularly if we can determine exactly when Nibiru will arrive." He continued a little more sheepishly before either Ian or Sadie could answer, "Ridiculous as it may sound it may be the only lead we have right now."

Ian looked at Sadie with concern, "Sadie, I know we were pushing you in the Hall of Records looking at a lot of different things, but did you manage to get the complete poem into memory?"

Sadie without acknowledging Ian grinned at Berger, "You have your computer, can you type? This is your chance to help me." She started to recite and Berger without a word started to fill the computer screen with the poem as Sadie recited in an unusual cadence.

> The skies were ablaze
> Man was uneasy
> Great Nibiru was coming
> To embrace Mother Earth
>
> An embrace that would maim
> An embrace that would kill
>
> The Gods knew best
> The path He would take
> Decided poor Moon
> A sacrifice would make

> Trip over the Moon
> Was the cry and great hue
> Trip over the Moon
> Great Nibiru be gone
>
> But the Gods who knew best
> Left Earth in despair
> For eons of suffering
> Poor Earth paid
> For a miscalculation

Berger spun the computer screen around for all to read. Rosenthal after carefully reading the poem spoke first shaking his head incredulously, "Is that it? Is that all we get?"

He continued on the verge of hyper-ventilating, "The whole world is waiting for us to bring them a solution and we're here reading a poem that's barely understandable."

Ian sat back looking chagrined, "Hey, when we got into this we were hopeful you had solutions in hand if we could just convince you of the reality of the situation."

He continued more soberly, "You have to realize this poem was a simple attempt to relate thousands of years later how someone else, probably smarter than we are today, tried to handle the same situation. And we have to be realistic in assessing its value; they failed in their attempt ala the 9577BC event."

Tarnowski looked like a man mesmerized and stared intently at the poem then at Rosenthal, "Hang on David, that last line looks intriguing." Then he seemed to be asking himself more than the group, "What miscalculation? If they tried and failed, and we can figure out why they failed, we might have our own solution"

Ian looked at Sadie eager to get back on more positive footing, "Was there anything else you saw that might help us?"

Sadie showed a bit of pique at the question, "Well I started to tell you, but you were in a hurry to leave."

Ian grinned and shook his head, "Okay Sadie, I'm sorry. What else did you see?"

Sadie straightened up in her chair and addressed the group. "Actually there were two things. If you recall from Dr. MacGown's presentation at the Senate the gods after the 9577BC event returned and re-colonized the Earth. What I read at the Hall of Records, you have to realize, is that the poem was written sometime around 4000BC, long after the cataclysm had occurred. According to the Record it was written as a satire by a disgruntled demigod, who had been rebuked by the gods at that time in 4000BC since he was by their measure not of royal blood. He was in writing the poem saying they, the gods, were not that smart. His intent in writing the poem was to make fun of their past inadequacies in dealing with Nibiru and causing the destruction of the Earth back in 9577BC. He was telling a story according to history that he understood at that time."

Tarnowski looked astonished, "Wow, that certainly puts a different spin on things. You're saying the writer of the poem was doing so significantly after the time of the Event. He was also relying on historical knowledge."

Rosenthal was alternately looking at Tarnowski as he spoke and at the same time leaning forward intently studying the poem, "Okay, than what are we're saying? Does the idea to use the Moon to deflect Nibiru have merit or not."

Sadie responded sheepishly, "One of the steles in the Hall of Records said that, that was the intention of the ancients," She tipped over the word ancients trying to avoid saying Gods, "to in someway use the Moon to deflect Nibiru."

Ian looked puzzled, "What was that the second thing Sadie?" You said there were two things."

Sadie ignored Ian, "I'll come back to that," she said as she regained the lead in the questioning and looked away from the screen to the group, "There is something else that's strange, but may be important. Remember in your school days you learned about Iambic pentameter as a meter used in poetry to describe a particular rhythm. Iambic pentameter derived from Dactylic pentameter which is a form of meter that goes back to the Greeks, which in all probability reaches back even farther in antiquity."

Ian frowned at her, "Sadie please, what's the point?"

She hesitated, unsure, because of his interruption, "Well, although it's totally lost in translation the poet referred to the meter of his poem as Ionic not Iambic pentameter. He apparently meant it as some sort of a pun. Does that mean anything? As a linguist I must admit I have never heard of Ionic pentameter in literature."

Berger was vigorously shaking his head in disbelief, "My God, does this fantasy never end, we're looking at the end of the world if we don't get our heads together soon; and that means by starting to think clearly."

Tarnowski, however, sat grinning quietly as if he were filling up with ideas, and then exploded before Berger could continue, filling the cabin with his shouting, "Oh yeah, oh yeah, it means something. It means they used Ionic thrusters. It's a great lead, just great. Did they say anything else in your Hall of Records?" Tarnowski now brisling, eager for more, sat edgy in demeanor for fear that was all they had.

Ian sensed Tarnowski's tension that followed Sadie's comment about Ionic pentameter and answered almost defensively, "Yes they did, they said something about the path of the Moon. Sadie, help us, there was something about nudging the Moon."

Sadie began reciting without any reluctance like the brightest little girl in the fifth grade, "Each hour for the course of one full Moon nudge the Moon to a path calculated by the Tables of Destiny away from its normal path to meet great Nibiru to deflect to another path."

Tarnowski now totally animated was shouting, "That's it, that's it. They must have been using Ionic thrusters to try and move the Moon into

Nibiru's path." He pushed his hand out in front of him to deflect anyone from stopping him from continuing and began explaining.

"Back at the beginning of this century NASA was working with Ion propulsion systems that were capable of propelling a spacecraft at speeds of 200,000 miles per hour. To fully appreciate that speed, remember the space shuttle runs at a top speed of 18,000 mph. That's the good news. The bad news is that those systems applied very low thrust to the spacecraft involved. In other words they could go like hell, but could hardly push a cart in front of them. The intent was to use them for deep space exploration. Their other limitation was that it took a long time for them to reach those high speeds."

"NASA followed that by developing a method of ionization called electron cyclotron resonance which used high frequency radiation, which is basically microwaves," he paused for the first time in his diatribe to look if the group was following his discourse then added, "you know like the microwaves that were left over from the Big Bang that fill space throughout the universe."

Everyone including Berger looked slightly stunned and Rosenthal and Ian were chuckling at the fervor of this lesson on Ionic thrusters. Rosenthal reached up and pulled down Tarnowski's hand that had been extended, "Bob, slow down you've completely lost us."

Tarnowski pulled back with a slight grin on his face, "Sorry, but here's the deal, the Russians took NASA's work and in turn developed an Ionic thruster," He repeated for emphasis, "an Ionic thruster that rather than speed could develop an enormous, I mean enormous, amount of power," he paused reflectively and dramatically, "Maybe the kind of power that could nudge the moon to a different path."

He paused again and held his hand up again to deflect any detractors from his discourse, "Here's the coup, the Russians did it by exploding small nuclear devices that were limited in their destructive power in the area of an operating Ionic Thruster. Nuclear explosions result in charged particles, which when discharged in the area of the thruster became the basic fuel of the thruster. They were able in essence to supersaturate the Ionic Thruster with fuel to allow it to generate a massive amount of power in a relatively small package."

The small group listening intently was more stunned then responsive. He looked back at them, "Don't you get it. Your ancient friends probably had a similar Ionic Thruster, but by your admission may not have had enough nuclear fuel to make it work."

Schmidt spoke up, "I remember Sadie saying when we were in the Hall of Records that their lack of nuclear devices was their undoing."

Rosenthal sat up excitedly and took charge, "Okay, hang on, hang on, here's what we have."

"First of all we have the Tables that will let us know when Nibiru arrives, right Jim," He looked at Berger, who just kept shaking his head in disbelief.

"Secondly, we know we're going to have to nudge the Moon, whatever, nudge means, every hour for 27.3 days." He paused, "The Moon has a 27.3 day rotational cycle, right?" Several heads nodded in agreement.

"Okay, next, we suspect some sort of Ionic Thruster may be involved probably to nudge the Moon. How am I doing?" He glanced from Berger to Tarnowski.

"And last, since they didn't have enough or perhaps any nuclear fuel available we're going to have to scrape the bottom of the barrel for all the nuclear fuel we can find and hope it's enough to satisfy whatever calculations we end up with." He paused again and surveyed the group, "Did I leave anything out?"

This simplistic summary was too much for Berger who leaned forward across the round table in front of him facing Rosenthal, "And if we manage to nudge the moon," nudge rang out sarcastically throughout the cabin of the plane, "What will we have accomplished?"

He redirected his stare from Rosenthal to Ian and demanded, "What?"

Ian's eyes darted from Rosenthal, as if he expected him to answer, back to Berger, "You're probably a much better scientist than I am in that area Senator Berger. You must understand that Nibiru's mere presence in any proximity to Earth is going to cause some damage including at the least earthquakes and tsunami's. You must also understand that the farther away it is from us the less damage that will occur. The Ancient's undoubtedly understood that and must have attempted to simply move Nibiru farther away from us."

He sounded apologetically, "To nudge it somewhere else."

Berger sat rubbing the back of his neck as he listened, "You're right, I know. It just sounds so totally ridiculous, insane in fact."

Tarnowski grinned sheepishly, "We could go back to trying to blow it up, if that's alright with Dr. Haddad."

Sadie who understood Tarnowski's attempt at comic relief simply shook a finger at him and muttered softly, "Stop it."

Rosenthal was lost trying to absorb the facts of what he had just heard, "You're saying that there would be some damage even if we were successful in our mission." He looked to Berger for an answer, "How much damage Jim?"

"Enough to significantly, disrupt if not destroy civilization as we know it depending on how close it gets." He looked to Ian for agreement who nodded his head quietly.

Mule deer have been known when encountering an adversary too big to deal with, to rattle their antlers on a tree rather than face the adversary, Rosenthal had nowhere to go and resorted to an entirely innocuous action.

Without any idea where to direct the next line of conversation and unable to digest that which he had just heard, he turned back to Ian and Sadie, and as a distraction began to include them as the final step in his summary, "You guys did a great job. Now it's our turn to make things happen. We will need your help and advice right up to the end, however, so I've made arrangements for you to stay in the Washington area when we get back. Let me know whatever you may need."

He continued almost breathlessly as though he was running to a finish line that he knew was there but couldn't see, "We've been in touch with your children and ex-wife as well as your parents Dr. MacGown and whoever else you would like to be aware of your situation."

Ian was a little taken back by this sudden, seeming denial by Rosenthal, and his irrelevant interjection about his and Sadie's role, that sounded like something between a dismissal and a confinement. He too was unwilling for the moment to confront an adversary too unwieldy to deal with, so he responded by simply shaking his head up and down, "I will be allowed to talk to them directly, I presume."

He glanced over to Berger looking for some silent action or nod that might explain Rosenthal's unorthodox handling of the situation. Berger answered verbally what Rosenthal had on his mind but was reluctant to say, "We have to give the President a viable plan of action, this isn't viable."

Ian thought to himself, "And moving the Moon out of its normal course doesn't cut it," he continued his silent mind game, "you should have told us, we would have thought of something else."

Rosenthal flushed red answering Ian's last verbal communication, "Of course, of course, but there could be an initial difficult time, that because of a variety of dissident groups, that may require your temporary sequestering. I apologize. I did not mean to be so presumptuous."

Schmidt sensed a kind of artificial tension building in what sounded to him like a dismissal of Ian and Sadie and called out, "Those names for him to call are fine David, nobody else likes him."

Then Rosenthal who was thankful, for the comic relief smiled, sat back, looked at Sadie and asked, "How about you Dr. Haddad? Who should we put on your contact list?"

Sadie smiled grimly, "I've got Ian, Dr. MacGown." She immediately read what she perceived as concern on Rosenthal's face for her lack of response and punctuated her list.

"My parents died back in 2010 in the riots that took place in Iran. They were both journalists. My father was Iranian, of course, ala Haddad and my mother an Israeli. They were lovers out of touch with their environment and paid the price for trying to bring truth to the world." She stopped suddenly aware of how intently all were listening to her and ended with, "Just Ian, he's all I've got."

Berger attempted to break the awkward silence that followed, and with his first indication of agreement to the undefined plan waved his hand to Sadie and looked over to Rosenthal, "It's too early to let these guys go David, we still need more answers."

He smiled again at Sadie, "If you please Dr. Haddad, let's use one of the tables in the back and work the Tables of Destiny to find out when this sucker is going to hit us."

He then looked at Ian and said, "The only problem with Tables like these is they tell you how all the planets move in relation to each other, but you need a starting date. Have you got any ideas?"

Ian, who was still trying to figure out how the conversation had shifted so radically after Rosenthal's summary went with the flow, laughed and shouted back at Berger as he headed to the back of the plane, "Try 9577BC you know exactly where Nibiru was at that time. That's the best starting point anyone could ask for."

Berger turned and shouted back over his shoulder, "Exactly, exactly."

Sadie put her hand on Ian's shoulder as she moved past him to join Berger, bent down and gave him a kiss on the neck and said, "Thanks, I love you."

With Sadie out of earshot Rosenthal turned to Ian with eyebrows raised, gently shaking his head up and down and said, "She is a very unusual woman, talented and passionate."

Ian shook his head in agreement, "She is all that and more. I guess it's no secret how close we are."

"No, it's no secret anymore. I'm not sure it ever was. You have no reason to hide it. We accept you as a package. I'll tell you what to sweeten the deal I'll stop calling you Dr. MacGown and Dr. Haddad if you'll stop calling me Senator. My name is David, deal?"

Ian extended his hand smiling, thinking to himself, "This guy turns faster than anything I've ever encountered," answered, "Deal David." He then reached over to Tarnowski who sat with a hundred different solutions to their problems circling through his head and grabbed his hand, "Deal Bob?"

Tarnowski grinned, "Of course Ian."

Tarnowski turned immediately to Rosenthal, "I've got a problem with your summary. You forgot that they apparently made a miscalculation. What miscalculation?"

Before Rosenthal could respond Ian spoke up, "I've been thinking about that too. On the positive side it indicates that they did have a plan that included the Moon that may represent legitimate direction for us. They were a very technically advanced society probably more so than we are today. They may not, however, have had as sophisticated an infrastructure as we have today to deal with the problem at that time."

Tarnowski began to shake his head, "We still have a lot to figure out and to get accomplished. Timing could be very critical depending on what Jim and Dr. Haddad figure out about when this thing is going to hit us. We may get lucky in applying Ionic Thrusters to nudge the Moon. I've been in touch in the past with engineers in China who have been working on a program to establish stations on the Moon. Apparently back a few years ago when scarcity of resources was becoming a big deal in the world the Chinese decided they may want to establish Squatters Rights on the Moon. Hopefully we can use their technology to build some stations that will allow us to build and station Ionic Thrusters there."

He shook his head in a kind of desperation, "It's a lot to figure out. We're going to need a lot of help from people all over the world."

Rosenthal patted him gently on the arm, "We'll get it done Bob. We have no choice, and all those things that have been tearing this world apart are the things that will bring us together in a common effort."

Rosenthal pulled up short in his brief reverie, "If we do all make it, however, you can imagine the scramble that will take place to pick up the pieces when it's all over."

Ian, who had been quiet, looked at the two somewhat desperate men, taken with how each in their own way were so totally dedicated to the task at hand, "It's been the same for thousands of years. Even those ancients who initially colonized us spent as much time fighting over territory as they did working on the task they were assigned. As a species we are hard wired for many different activities." He stopped and grinned at them, "We're all hard wired for sex, but that's not the only thing. We have also been known to go to war in the face of imminent peril."

Their conversation was interrupted by Berger, who shouted from the rear of the plane, "Hold on to your hats, we may have a date."

Berger and Sadie moved back with the group with Berger holding his computer on his lap, "This thing is as high powered as they get. With Dr. Haddad's help I was able to run through calculations that showed us the path of Nibiru back over fifty thousand years and then forward another fifty thousand years, if anyone lasts that long."

Berger focused squarely on Ian, "Dr. MacGown, remember when you gave your pitch on Nibiru's cycle and pointed out that you felt initially it may have operated on a combination of segments of 923 years and 877 years. Well with the help of Dr. Haddad and the Tables you provided us I was able to determine that actually Nibiru's normal cycle was in segments of 936 years and 864 years respectively not 923 and 877.

That means that the 923 year cycle was really an anomaly when Nibiru deviated from its normal cycle. If we believe that, and if I've done my calculations correctly, an anomaly of sorts occurs every 11,602 years. That anomaly represents a thirteen year aberration in Nibiru's cycle. What all this means to us today is that one of your initial suggestions, in fact your very first guess of 2038 had merit."

He grinned at Ian like someone who had just won a big argument, "It was off, however by thirteen years, the difference between the 936 and the 923. If you subtract the thirteen years from 2038 you arrive at 2025. That's when we can expect to see Nibiru," He slammed the computer cover close as if to say end of discussion.

No one spoke for at least a minute trying to digest this very poignant piece of information. Then Tarnowski volunteered with a sense of disbelief in his response, "That's only a little over five years. We have an awful lot of work to do if we expect to survive." He asked Berger almost pleading, "Can you give me a month?"

Berger offered what assurance he could, "Yes, when we get back I can. I did a macro calculation here with this computer to determine the year. Putting a month on it is going to require a much more difficult, extensive calculation, particularly with a thirteen year anomaly thrown in. You had best presume its January and move as fast as you can."

Ian who like the others had not spoken mused out loud, "That was their miscalculation, the thirteen years. How could they have missed it? Maybe that's where unlucky thirteen really originated. How could they have missed it?"

There was a sense of relief, awe and fear that settled over the plane for all but the pilots, who like the general population were still unaware.

Sadie didn't respond at all, but simply stood up and walked to the rear of the plane where she pulled two seats together to form a bed, flopped down on it and was soon fast asleep.

Berger who had sat down wearily next to Rosenthal asked, "Do we dare release this to the public David?"

Rosenthal sat back, scratched his head, looked at Ian and directed the question to him, "What did they do ten thousand years ago Ian?"

Ian tapped his index finger repeatedly against his nose. Then grinning sheepishly at the ridiculousness of this conversation he was about to enter into shook his head and said, "I haven't a clue. The record shows they told Noah to build an ark. There must be something comparable we should do, but I am without any suggestions." He then put it back to Rosenthal with more than a grain of sarcasm, "What do you think David?"

"I've been so focused on avoiding the situation I haven't given any thought to the possible aftermath." He turned to Tarnowski and Berger, "What do you guys think?"

Tarnowski got up from his seat and started to walk to one of the tables in the rear of the plane, "I've got work to do, that's what I think. Come on Jim I can use your help." Berger obediently got up and followed to the rear of the plane moving as quietly as he could to avoid the sleeping Sadie.

Rosenthal pushed his seat back as far as it would go, closed his eyes and said, "We'll figure something out when we get there," Then added sarcastically, "we have five years."

Ian, however, wasn't quite ready to end all conversation and probed again on all that had just happened, "David, I don't get it. In the last hour we arrived at conclusions and solutions to things that just a few weeks ago were complete mysteries? What happened? It had to be more than just finding the Tables."

Without sitting up in his seat Rosenthal opened his eyes and grinned at Ian, "It's reasonable that you would ask." He paused obviously not sure where he wanted to start. "We didn't exactly lie to you, but we have been deceptive. When we invited you to the Commission we had already been working on the problem of Nibiru for several years. There were several prominent scientists of different countries around the world who had produced some, and I emphasize only some, evidence that Nibiru existed. It wasn't until about fifteen years ago that governments began to look at it as a potential problem."

He sat up in his seat more attentively, "I sure you must have read Sitchen's book, "The 12th Planet," which was written about the time you and I were born. That book put the public on notice that there was a Nibiru. You even mentioned it in your presentation."

Ian nodded in agreement, "Yes that's when they stared to get results from deciphering the old Sumerian texts they found back in the 1800's."

"Well somewhere along the line it was recognized at some high levels of government that Nibiru may have been the problem you described in your presentation."

Ian sounded let down, "Then why did we go through that whole charade with the Commission?"

Rosenthal scratched the side of his face as he answered, "It's complicated. At some point and I can't tell you exactly when, several of the major powers in the world sketched out a rough plan that would address the probability of the Earth being hit by a full sized planet. At that time they even began preliminary plans with assignments given on a variety of projects. The whole thing, however, was maintained at a very high level with directions being given for projects that didn't really exist, but would move developments along in a just in case situation."

He paused as if he didn't want to continue or wasn't sure how to, "That's why Tarnowski said he was aware that the Chinese were working on stations for the Moon. The people who are working that project really believe it is so their government can establish Squatters Rights like Tarnowski said. In fact none of the people on the Commission were aware of all this until relatively recently."

He paused again and with a kind of wonderment said, "I seriously doubt that when they were asked to address stations on the Moon, that anyone had any real idea that that might be one of the most important actions we could take."

Ian looked at Rosenthal like he thought he was being told another lie, "Then why bring me and Sadie into the whole thing?"

Rosenthal became more assertive in his answer, "Very simply, because for all we thought we knew, we still had no idea when. Then there you were on "Sixty Minutes" indicating you were pretty sure you knew we were going to be hit by another planet. If you were that sure we thought you may have some idea when it might hit us. We were out of options. We had nothing to lose."

Ian held his hand up out in front of him, "Hey, hang on I still don't get it. You knew there was a planet out there that was coming our way, but didn't know when, that doesn't make sense. Our telescopes look light years into the sky every day, how could we miss a planet?"

Rosenthal leaned forward, "Okay, this is like a science fiction novel. Some of our leading scientists have gone so far as to suggest that Nibiru could be using a cloaking device that would shield them from detection, because of what you called the 9577BC event," He blurted out one more thing before Ian could interrupt, "maybe they were hurt more in that first encounter then we realized."

Ian sat back shaking his head, "Then you knew, why did you let me go on like that?"

"We didn't want to coach you in any way. We wanted to let you speak, to see if you were real. That's why Berger was so aggressive."

"Okay, I get it, but why do you need me or Sadie anymore?"

"To help us convince our allies and supporters in this effort that the whole thing isn't a fantasy, that you really did find the Tables, that they are not some forgery. We don't have time for some major, protracted investigation on the validity of the Tables. And if we think our allies may have reservations on the Tables you can imagine their reserve when we tell them our best plan hinges on Sadie's interpretation of that poem."

Rosenthal took a deep breath and took one more shot at explaining, "To me personally this whole thing has been something like a house of cards, but when I sit back and look at what else we have I don't see any other viable option, do you?"

Ian slumped back in his seat, "All right, I understand. I guess I hoped the governments of the world might have more ideas on how to handle this than relying on two people with Doctorates in History that were earned on events that happened thousands of years ago."

Ian's posture indicated he was ready to surrender to whatever Rosenthal may require of him and Sadie and he threw his hands up in surrender, "What specifically do you need from Sadie and me?"

Rosenthal looked like the proverbial kid with his hand in the cookie jar, "Only to be present when we're meeting with those important players like China and Russia, who will undoubtedly challenge what we're proposing."

Ian clenched his fists and shook them out in front of him like a fighter ready for a tough encounter, "We'll be there to help however we can." He continued in a sort of reverie like he was releasing thoughts that had been bottled up too long, "When I was writing books and giving interviews on this sort of thing I guess I couldn't actually see or understand the reality of it all. I thought if I could just help define the situation someone else would take care of it."

Rosenthal nodded in agreement, "We understand Ian we all carry a little bit of that burden." He looked at the weariness that had settled over Ian and said, "Perhaps we should try to rest a bit, we'll be back in the states soon with a lot of people waiting to talk to us."

Ian sat back as far as his seat would allow him and closed his eyes without further comment.

Chapter 15: Family in Crisis

The AJC corporate jet circled easily over Ronald Reagan International Airport waiting as any other commercial or private carrier would for their place in line. Rosenthal had decided to maintain as low a profile as possible in their entry back into the States after this very important retrieval exercise. The F-16 fighters were gone.

The group had reassembled around the seats in the front cabin at Rosenthal's request for a quick briefing, "Here's how this is going to work when we land. Berger, Tarnowski and Schmidt can all head for home to spend time with their families. There will be cars waiting for each of you. I'll expect to see both Berger and tarnowski tomorrow ready to get back to work."

He looked at Ian and Sadie and continued like a Sergeant assigning a work detail, "The U.S. government has taken over the Hyatt Regency Hotel for an indefinite time to accommodate whatever visitors are required in Washington to complete whatever planning is required to handle this very difficult task in front of us."

He paused, looked again to Ian and Sadie without saying their names, "I've taken the liberty of putting you up in one of the Hyatt Regency's best suites with the expectation that you will remain with us in Washington for as long as required. We will meet your needs including clothing or whatever else you may need for as long as you are a part of this or…" He stopped abruptly taken back himself at what he had been about to say.

He continued more cautiously, "We have already advised your family and Dr. Haddad's employer of your situation. We have established an appropriate high level pay grade for both of you for the time you spend as U.S. employees, any comments?"

Ian grinned back at Rosenthal, who was afraid the grin was a sign of defiance, then Ian answered as if he were ashamed at what he had to say, "First of all, not even the U.S. government can afford Sadie's wardrobe. And secondly, you didn't tell my ex-wife where I'll be, did you?"

Rosenthal sat back laughing and shaking his head, "No, we would never divulge that kind of sensitive information. And as far as dealing with Sadie's," he was back to Sadie, not Dr. Haddad, "wardrobe we're negotiating a loan from the Chinese to cover the cost, alright with you Sadie?"

Sadie smirked at one then the other, "I don't care who buys my clothes as long as they're there when I need them."

Rosenthal accepted a nod from Ian and turned again to the other three men as the AJC made a final bank heading for the runway, "There are rooms assigned to each of you at the Hyatt for as long as you may need them for those days you may choose to remain in Washington. I will leave it to your discretion as to how you use them and how much time may be required with your families."

A soft bump as the AJC's wheels took hold of the runway put a temporary end to conversation and a mild tension in the air took over as each member of the group braced themselves for the landing and the task ahead.

*

Sadie snuggled up close to Ian in what appeared to be the same black limousine and driver that brought them to the Hyatt on their first trip. Sadie grinned at Ian, "Do you think it's him?"

Ian smiled back, "Ask him if he knows where the Hyatt is?"

"No way, I had to deal with him the last time. Maybe we are being kidnapped this time."

"Are you kidding, Rosenthal wouldn't allow it. I've never met anyone as organized as he is. Did you notice he never mentioned where he would be staying. We don't even know if he has a family other than cousin Anwar back in Israel."

Sadie gave Ian a knowing smile, "I'll bet you we see him at dinner tonight."

Ian shook his head, "No, more likely he'll be with the President and the Chiefs of Staffs'. Okay, pay attention we're coming up to the Hyatt. We don't know what kind of crowd there may be."

The driver without giving any signal made a quick turn which seemed to be away from the Hyatt, but ended up with the limo parked at the entrance at the back of the Hyatt House. He ran around, opened the door on Ian's side and signaled them to follow him. They obeyed as directed and after a short sprint, up one flight of stairs and then on to the elevator, found themselves at the door of one of the hotels suites. The driver unlocked the door, ushered them in, handed Ian a key and exited to the hallway all without a word. He quickly disappeared then was back standing at the door with and their bags in hand. The bags were plopped down in the entrance to the suite, and as he pulled the door closed he leaned back into the room and with broken English that Sadie immediately recognized, said, "Thank you, thank you."

Both Ian and Sadie were a little taken back in the simple realization that their bags for the moment represented the total of their possessions that were usable, and they were essentially mid-eastern garb. Sadie kicked the nearest bag and chuckled as she spoke, "I was through with all that other stuff anyway."

Ian said grimly, "It'll probably all be out of style in the next five years."

Sadie's retort was said without humor, "I hope that's not all that goes out of style." She broke back into a grin and spun around looking from wall to wall in the suite, "Wow, look at this place Ian it's bigger then our condo. We even have a dining room. Will we be eating in tonight sir?"

Then she seemed to go sour again, "Ian I can't get that five year figure out of my head. It's like a death sentence."

He walked over and pulled her up tightly against him, "I know, I know, it's a tough hand to play. I keep thinking of the blissfulness in ignorance. Just stay close. Don't get too far away from me no matter what happens. If there's only one chapter left for us we'll read it together."

She was shuddering as she held him more tightly and kissed him softly on the lips, "I don't want it to ever end, not ever. I lived too many years without you."

The enormity of their situation filled the room, and they held on in an embrace that they hoped was filled with endless tomorrows and a future that promised more than disaster.

It was a poignant moment and when the phone blared out ringing loudly Ian would have ignored it if Sadie hadn't gently let go and urged him to check and see what "they" wanted.

Ian picked up and was immediately confronted by his mother's angry, anxious voice, "Ian where have you been? Why are you in Washington staying at that big hotel? Why…?"

Ian still caught up in the moment with Sadie was unprepared for the onslaught and interrupted firmly, "Mom, Mom, slow down. There's a lot to talk about. I'm working with our government on an important project…"

She in turn interrupted him, "The television says you're crazy. That you're saying the world is coming to an end. That you don't believe in God. That you're some sort of crazy atheist."

Her tone was insistent and pleading, "Ian what's going on. What are you doing? What are you involved in?"

He tried to deflect her attack, "Mom is Dad there? Can I say hello to him?"

"I'm here Ian," the soft reply was from his father, "We're on the speaker phone?"

She wanted answers and barged right through their short greeting to each other, "Ian, do you believe in God or not?" Her tone was authoritative and demanding.

Ian sighed, he knew she was not to be denied and fell into a conversation he hoped would never happen, "I believe in a Creator of All Things that…"

"But do you believe in God Ian? The television says you believe there is more than one God. Do you believe that Ian? Answer me!"

Ian loved his parents and had never tried to push them beyond the boundaries of their personal beliefs, but this unbridled aggression was too much and he was ready to fire back when Sadie intuitively touched him softly on the arm and shook her head, "no". He softened at her touch and leveled his tone to one responsive and calm, laced with understanding, "I believe God is perceived by each of us individually in our own way…"

She was not calm and virtually screamed into the phone almost in a sense of panic, "Do you believe in the Bible Ian like we taught you?"

He tried again to answer as he had with friends, who believed differently than he did, "In Genesis, God in the plural is used repeatedly…" He pulled up short realizing that he was just lighting another fuse.

In an awkward way she saved him from jumping into a pit from which there was no return with her continual interruptions, "Ian I am so, so disappointed in you, so disappointed. Your father and I never thought you would ever treat us like this."

"Mom, there is so much more to this than what our individual beliefs in God are. There's a world of people at stake. Try to understand."

"I don't understand Ian. I doubt if I ever will." He could hear the despondency in her voice, "I've got to hang up now. I've said all I need to say. Call me when you think you might have more to say that makes more sense, and maybe than you can also explain why you're living with a woman who isn't your wife."

There was a soft click at the other end of the line and Ian was filled with dread that he may never again have the opportunity to explain to two people he loved dearly how he had ended up on this unusual journey.

He gently set the phone in its cradle and it in turn responded loudly before he could let go. He placed it back to his ear and after an initial pause began shaking his head, "I see, I understand. Is there a number where I can call you back? Yes, I will. Thank you."

He set the phone back in the cradle, looked at Sadie quizzically and said, "It's "Sixty Minutes" they want us, not just me on their show next week for an interview. I'm not sure I want to do it and I doubt if Rosenthal would be very happy about it. How do you feel about it?"

Sadie pulled him back to her embrace, "You get a lot of interesting phone calls. You're an interesting man. I can see why they would want to interview you."

"Two, two phone calls, that's all and they weren't that interesting. I'll be very happy if I never get another."

She gave him a soft kiss on the neck and patted him south of his waist line, "Then why is that little red light flashing?" She giggled and pushed him towards the phone.

Ian's posture slumped, "I'm not sure if I'm ready for anymore right now, maybe it's for you."

Sadie snickered at the suggestion, "Yeah, maybe it's my dead parents or the long, lost aunt I never met. You're it Ian for me, and you're right here with me Lover. You may as well get it all over with then maybe we can have a peaceful dinner."

Ian picked the phone up once again and dialed the operator. His tone was aggressive to an operator who had spent her day taking messages and explaining why people didn't return messages. Her response was curt and to the point, "You have two messages sir, do you want the numbers?"

Ian was more conciliatory, "Can you tell me who called?"

"Scotty and Julie, do you want the numbers sir?"

"Yes, yes of course, I don't see a pencil here. I'll pick them up when I come down for dinner. Thank you."

Sadie pulled him towards the door, "Come on it's a little early for dinner, but we can both use a drink. Do you have the key? Let's case the joint, see who is here and all that. You can call your kids after dinner. You'll be in a better mood. Okay?"

Ian nodded agreement and two minutes later they were sitting at the bar listening to muffled conversations in a variety of dialects throughout the room.

Ian sat only long enough to order a drink than slid back from the bar stool and gently patted Sadie on the knee, "I'll be right back, I forgot to get those numbers from the operator."

He walked quickly towards the desk at the front of the hotel and was back almost immediately. He was taken aback to see Rosenthal sitting next to Sadie. "How did he get there so quickly and what was he up to?" He thought to himself.

Rosenthal spun around on the barstool and extended his hand towards Ian, "Ah, there you are. I saw this beautiful young lady sitting here alone, and came to offer her protection in your absence."

Both Ian and Sadie smiled broadly at this new Rosenthal with a drink in his hand, who they had never seen behave this way. Ian grasped the extended hand and confirmed from the strong smell of alcohol that Rosenthal had indeed been drinking, "David, what's going on? What are you doing protecting my lady?"

Rosenthal answered without any apparent guile, open and to the point, "What I always do, get people to do what the government wants them to do even if they don't want to do it."

His comment rang home as he abruptly looked directly at Ian and asked, "Has Sixty Minutes contacted you yet? They've been all over my office and the President's Office. They want you on their program this week."

Ian started to answer, but Rosenthal wasn't through yet and added emphatically, "Neither the President or I think it would be a good idea."

Rosenthal lifted his drink for another sip and Ian took the opportunity to answer, "I talked to them just a few minutes ago. I told them I would call them back and let them know."

Rosenthal suddenly seemed totally sober, "Ian, I don't think it's a good idea. We need to control how we feed what's happening to the public and "Sixty Minutes" doesn't seem like the right vehicle to us. I think you should pass on it."

"To be honest I never really intended to after my last go around with them. Besides what could I tell them? That we broke into the Great Pyramid and then followed up by virtually destroying Rosslyn Chapel leaving two men dead on the Chapel floor."

Rosenthal remained in his sober countenance, "Don't worry everyone already knows you were at the Chapel. That's why "Sixty Minutes" wants to interview you even though they may not know how or why you got there; and don't worry both the Minister and his helper survived. The Scottish police arrived in time to get them to the hospital."

It was the top of the hour and before Rosenthal could continue a television that had been showing sports information blared out on a new subject, the lead news story for the evening. A picture of Ian looking like Indiana Jones brandishing an M-16 flashed on the screen. Rosenthal and Sadie seeing the wonder in Ian's eyes turned to face the screen.

"That's what I mean. How do we deal with that and maintain order?" Rosenthal sputtered. He spun back around to face Ian who spoke with astonishment and aggravation, "I have never even held a rifle. How do they do they do that?"

Sadie, who had sat quietly said, "If you don't mind the cliché', I think you look rather dashing."

Their repartee was punctuated by the sound of shots coming out of the TV as they watched some unidentified men run around firing shots into the air with intermittent pictures of Rosslyn Chapel and Ian with his M-16 thrown on the screen.

Ian stood shaking his head, "No wonder my own mother thinks I'm a mad man." He continued shaking his head looking squarely at Rosenthal, "Tell the President not to worry, we," he glanced in Sadie's direction, "will not be giving any interviews."

Rosenthal sat his half empty glass on the bar, "Okay, that's good news. We need to control what we feed to the media. They're going to keep probing and we need to dance away from them for now."

He sat back and took a deep breath continuing to sit next to Sadie while Ian stood facing them, "What we have told them is simply that you and Sadie led a team that found and retained the Holy Grail from underneath the Rosslyn Chapel."

Rosenthal was now back to his old style giving information in a directive manner, "We've told them that a terrorist group attempted to steal the Grail and it was only as a result of the heroic efforts of the two Scotchmen that they were stopped. For now we've indicated that the mysteries of the Grail are being explored and there will be reports coming later."

He looked from Ian to Sadie, "You both okay with that?"

He didn't wait for an answer, but looked at Sadie, "Berger is going to need your help tomorrow morning working with the Tables. Ian I think you should be there also."

Appearing completely sober now he slid off the barstool, started to walk away then turned and said, "I'm staying here so I'll see you at breakfast at 7:30 and get you over to be with Berger."

Ian shook his head, "That's good, we'll be there, we were going to get something to eat now if you would like to join us."

Rosenthal smiled, "Thanks that's nice, but the President asked me to join him and his staff."

Ian put his hand out to Sadie, "Then it's just you and me babe. Let's get some prime ribs then I have some phone calls to make."

Sadie slid gracefully off the barstool, than tripping into Ian ended her brief journey with a hug around his neck. She took advantage of her position to look over his shoulder at the departing Rosenthal and whispered into his ear, "I hope he sobers up before he gets there." Then she stepped back and took Ian by the shoulders as if she were straightening him up, gave him a quick kiss and said, "Okay, I can't seem to shake you or the prime ribs. I may as well go for it."

*

Sadie flopped down on the king size bed of their suite before the door had clicked solidly shut, "I'm exhausted. I was never cut out to be a spy or adventurer or whatever else we've been doing. Are you going to make your calls? I'm just going to rest for a minute or two."

Ian grinned as he reached for the phone, he knew she would be purring softly before he finished dialing.

"Hello, Scotty it's me, Dad, how goes the battle?"

A somewhat weary sounding Scotty replied, "Not necessarily good, but probably better than the media suggests about you. I never realized my father was such a kook until I read the papers, and what the TV offers is even worse. What's up Dad? If you've done half of what they're saying about you then you are my hero more than ever."

Ian grinned into the phone, "As a matter of fact I just witnessed myself wielding an M-16 rifle, although I'm not sure I would have any idea on how to even load it, so I have to admit that part about slaying one hundred

Philistines with one shot was a little exaggerated. There was probably no more than ten or eleven and I used an Uzi not a sling."

There was silence on the other end then, "Did you really kill someone?"

Ian laughed, "No Scotty, you know me better than that. I'm more of a poet than a gun slinger, although I have to admit I've been running with some pretty heavy company and there were times when bullets were flying."

"Did you really find the Holy Grail? Is it a silver chalice like they've said?"

"We did find something but it wasn't a cup of any sort. It was more like a map of the heavens that could represent salvation for all of mankind just like the old writings suggest."

"What happened in Scotland Dad? Who were the people that were with you and who was the woman the press is saying is like a mystical shaman?"

Ian paused to collect his thoughts, he had anticipated a question like this and smiled at the image of Sadie as a shaman, "One man you know is Bob Schmidt, a very old friend who works for the government and the woman is someone, who since the time your mother and I parted ways, has become very important to me. She also is a very important player in a huge government project."

"Her name is Sadie."

Sadie stirred briefly on the bed at the sound of her name, "What?" then fell back to sleep.

"If she's important to you I'd like to meet her someday and," he paused, "I know about the government project. NASA is putting me and a lot of other young guys on a program to learn to fly a new type of space vehicle that's only in the development phase. It's supposed to be a one man space vehicle capable of making it to the moon and back to deliver some kind of payload without landing. That's all they'll tell us, but so far all the training has either been simulation exercises or flying standard jets at supersonic speeds. They describe this thing as something that will ultimately exceed speeds of 25000 MPH, but will also be capable of hovering like a humming bird then take off at lightning speed again, kind of like the old UFO's. It's really mind boggling, but very demanding and a little tedious. I don't mind saying I'm already whipped and we're just getting started."

Ian listened quietly as his son expanded on something he was already aware of, "The ridiculous part about it is that they don't even have this "Spacejet" developed yet."

Scotty stopped abruptly, "Dad, are you involved in this somehow?"

The silence that followed Scotty's question made it clear what the situation was before Ian could answer, "Maybe a little bit."

"A little bit, how?" Scotty came back more quizzically than his first inquiry.

"A little bit," Ian was obviously holding back, "I'm not really sure at this point. I'm not sure if Sadie and I are the foil or the point of the sword. As I writer I have done the unthinkable in my participation, I've written chapter after chapter without knowing the ending. It's as bad as not having a plot."

Scotty sounded hesitant and concerned, "I don't get it Dad, what's up?"

"I owe it to you as my son Scotty to tell you we are all facing a very uncertain future; and you and I both seem to be into it up to our necks. I can't really tell you anything more, but I think you may be in a position to find out more very soon."

"Dad, I understand, there have been inferences made, that on one hand make me glad that I may be a part of it and on the other hand make me wish I was back in high school playing soccer."

"Dad, you need to call Julie, she's really upset and needs to clear the air with you. I think Grandma has been talking to her. I know she's been on my case and it hasn't been very complimentary to you, don't worry I just listened, I didn't argue back, call Julie, please."

"Dad, I've got to go, we have a tutorial session scheduled tonight and I beginning to run a little late. They are as you might imagine totally unforgivable. I love you. Please call me again first chance you get, bye, Dad."

"Bye Scotty, I love you."

Scotty's abrupt signing off left Ian a little shaken with that same feeling of dread he felt when his mother hung up on him. The unsubstantiated worry that he may never talk to him again. He knew he should call Julie, but having set the phone down couldn't pick it up again, stood there frozen, looking over his shoulder at Sadie lying on the bed, wondering if she might waken if he dialed the phone again. "That's ridiculous," He thought, pulled the phone up in front of him, and started dialing. It seemed to ring endlessly without a response and it was not until he was about to set it back in the cradle that he heard Julie's soft voice, "Hello, hello I'm here, who is it please?"

"Julie, it's me, your father," Ian was shocked at how stilted his voice sounded, "How are you doing sweetheart?"

Julie at the sound of his voice started sobbing like an injured child who had run over two blocks before breaking into tears at her mother's door, "Awful, just awful, that's how I am. Where have you been? Why haven't you called? I've left so many messages."

"I've......," His response was going to have to wait until she had vented her spleen.

"Grandma is saying some awful things about you. That you are the head of some cult that doesn't believe in God, and that we're all descended from aliens. She says that some awful woman has taken hold of you and, and......," The sobs broke into a wail, "Daddy, I'm pregnant. I need you to hold me, to tell me everything is going to be alright and Grandma says you don't care. She says......."

"Hush sweetheart, hush I'm right here, I love you, I always have and always will through any situation. Your Grandmother means well. She's just frightened by some of the things she hears from strangers."

"But she says we are all going to die and it's your fault. That you've made God angry."

"Julie, stop sweetheart you must realize how silly that sounds. Have you talked to your Mom? She can tell you how hormones when you're pregnant can be very upsetting."

The predictable but unanticipated response for that comment by Ian hit him between the eyes, as Julie began wailing louder than ever, "I don't want my child to die, I want him to live. I don't want this awful thing that's happening to be your fault. I don't......."

The wailing subsided again into a soft sob and Ian could hear his ex-wife comforting her, "Ian, this is Sarah, I'm sorry but she's having a lot of trouble right now. I'll have her call you when she's more settled. Are you alright? From what I read you must need a break about now." She didn't wait for an answer but said, "We've got to hang up right now." A soft click left Ian standing once more with the phone in his hand, the dial tone ringing in his ears like the flat line on a heart monitor.

Sadie was sitting up on the side of the bed awakened by the wailing that filled the room, "Is everything okay Ian, Are you alright?"

Ian looked back at her, a sardonic grin on his face, "I think the end is coming faster than I thought. My last conversation with her she told me she was engaged ready to get married and now she's pregnant."

Chapter 16: Nibiru Deciphered

Ian and Sadie walked into the Article One Grille and were waved to a table where Rosenthal sat sipping a large mug of coffee. "Come, sit, coffee cures more ills than alcohol," He grinned, "Sometimes."

It was clear Rosenthal was back on his game as he helped Sadie with her chair, "I've got a car coming by in about forty minutes. He'll take you over to the Pentagon where you'll hook up with Berger and I think Tarnowski is going to sit in. No need to hurry your breakfast they have probably already begun, and may need some prep time."

He continued briskly wolfing down different parts of his breakfast as he spoke, "You both look like jet lag has not yet sunk in, sometimes it takes a day or two for it to hit you. I've always been somewhat impervious to it since I never seem to stay more than a day or two overseas."

He paused collecting his thoughts for just a second before continuing almost like a stream of consciousness, "This project is being taken very seriously at all levels of government here and around the world. The Chinese and Russians, both of whom have important roles have responded as we hoped they would. At the level of top governments there is an understanding that we're all dependent on each other," he paused, "to survive."

He glanced towards the entrance of the hotel where you could already hear people mingling about beginning their daily protest, "Maintaining order in the streets may require a different effort."

He looked back at Ian and Sadie, "Like I told you on the plane, a lot things were already in motion while you were still involved in your search. There is momentum in many different directions and we, you, have to be careful you don't get swept away in the wrong direction."

Ian sounded unsure when he asked, "Should we order now, if they're going to be here soon to pick us up?"

Rosenthal wasn't sharp or impolite, but said simply, "They'll wait."

Ian took the lead back, "I'm not sure what you're concerned about David. We've agreed positively not to appear on "Sixty Minutes or any similar show for that case."

Rosenthal sat back a little more at ease, "There was that as a concern." He shifted his gaze to Sadie, "And," he paused again than let it all hang out, "You're going to be working with Berger today on what could be the most important part of this total effort. If we are not properly directed any attempt we make to divert this thing coming at us is bound to fail."

He was emphatic and continued his strong focus on Sadie, "He needs your help Sadie to establish the proper coordinates to attack and redirect this thing. We, including the President and her staff are accepting your premise that Nibiru must trip over the moon." He grinned and snickered, "It seems to be all we've got. The President wasn't exactly elated at what we presented, but she listened carefully and seemed to understand our situation."

Then as if he had a crick in his neck he broke his gaze on Sadie and looked off to a corner of the room as if totally distracted, "If she, we, can't rely on you, if you are in any way concerned about life on Nibiru and the impact this effort may have them, we are bound to fail."

Sadie wasn't sure if Rosenthal meant the President or Berger. She sighed and Ian saw tears whelm up in her eyes as she reached over and touched Rosenthal lightly on the arm, "I will do my best to help in whatever way I can. I understand life here is very important. I can come to terms with trying to divert their planet. I just didn't want to be a part of raining bombs on them, and expressed my discomfort with that prospect. Trust me David, we'll find a way to make it work."

Rosenthal pushed his plate away and stood up, "The Eggs Benedict are delicious here. You better order. I'll tell the driver to wait for you that you'll be there." He walked towards the entrance waving in a kind of salute without another word.

Sadie looked up at the waiter who had moved to their table in sync with Rosenthal's departure and said to the waiter, smiling with tears in her eyes, "I'll have the Eggs Benedict I hear they're very good."

*

The crowd outside the hotel hardly noticed them, in spite of their growing notoriety, as they slipped into the limo with their favorite driver, who grinned and spoke once more in his broken English, "I thought you would be at the back door."

Both grinned, but didn't respond, than Ian said soberly to Sadie, "Maybe David wanted us to see the crowd."

The drive to the Pentagon with two people reflective on their respective roles in a growing drama, and a driver worried that his thrust at humor had silenced two people who had always seemed to be laughing, was a quiet one.

Surprisingly, Tarnowski was standing at the curb as they pulled up and hastened to open the limo door before the driver could make his move. Ian was out first and Tarnowski slapped him on the shoulder like an old buddy and squeezed his hand in a firm grip. He let go to help Sadie out of the limo and took her hand like he was going to kiss it, than thought better of it and gave her a hug, "Come on, Jim's waiting, we have a lot to do."

Both followed obediently, not sure of what seemed to be an excessively warm greeting, wondering what was coming next. Tarnowski led them to a large room that Ian was sure must be one of the fabled War Rooms that our armed forces used to design winning strategies on the battlefield. There were charts of what appeared to be the solar system in a variety of configurations spread around the room.

At their entrance Berger hugged Sadie as Tarnowski had and embraced Ian holding him by the shoulders, which looked awkward because of the apparent size difference in Ian's favor. He offered no verbal greeting, but waved his hand around the room at the various charts, "They're all computer generated, but I think they are all wrong. Remember on the plane I said I needed a month with which to start my query and you said to presume it was January. I did that and it doesn't really work. If you remember I did macro calculations going backwards and forward to establish a thirteen year anomaly each 11602 years. I was excited because that put me close to your 2038 date which you had proposed in your initial presentation."

He stopped and raised his hands as though pleading, "Dr. MacGown, Ian, how did you arrive at that date?"

He didn't wait for an answer but turned to Sadie, "Dr. Haddad, when you initially got me set up on my computer on the plane, you were reading off positions of planets relative to each other, without a starting date, which Ian suggested might be 9577BC. Was there any other indication of a specific starting date written anywhere in the Tables? I'm okay with all that and the 2025 date we established," He stuttered, "but, but now I need a specific month, a specific month that I can home in on as a starting date."

He stopped his discourse abruptly, looking at them like one gone completely blank, waiting for the reset button to be pushed.

Sadie sat down at a table, neatly arranged with four chairs, and looked across at Berger, "I've read everything in the Tables, I didn't have any difficulty understanding them and don't believe I left anything out. I'll be glad to go over them again if you would like me to."

Berger quickly produced the Tables, which had been lying on an adjacent table that also held a keyboard that appeared to be without a computer.

Berger saw Ian's quizzical look, "I'm tied into one of the main frames in the Pentagon that can tell me almost anything but the month I need."

Sadie took the Tables and pulled aside to a third smaller table, and began quietly reading through them.

Berger turned back to Ian, "Do you have any ideas Ian as to time, specifically the month of the year that the initial cataclysm happened?"

Ian rubbed his hands together as you would on a cold winter day, "Maybe we can do some deductive reasoning. Let's list what we have so far, I'm game if you are."

Berger nodded, "Sure, go ahead."

Ian's wrinkled brow said he wasn't sure where to start, but he began to write on a pad Berger had pushed in front of him, "Well, we know from the Bible and the Sumerian Texts that the ancient's knew at that time Nibiru was coming at them. That's why they asked Noah to build the Ark."

Berger typed into his computer recording Ian's remarks as he spoke ignoring the fact that he had given him a pad to write on. He stopped as though he had just comprehended what had been said and snickered loudly before Ian could continue, "If that's all you've got, we're in bigger trouble than I thought, that's old hat."

Ian nodded slightly chagrined for having been cut off so early in his effort, but shrugged his shoulders and said, "Hey, I was just warming up, were you able to put anything more current or relevant together?"

Berger, who loved the podium, pushed his chair back to begin his oration, "Well I did learn something useful from the Tables. I was able to create an algorithm based on the changing position of Nibiru as it moved into and through our solar system that told me the speed at which it was traveling as it passed through and approached Earth."

He nodded in Ian's direction, "I give credit to you however, going back to your pitch on Napta Playa. You indicated at that time that your ancient friends were among other things tracking the speed of various stars. It made me think."

He became suddenly very expansive in his speech, not guarded as he was in his initial comments. "I made a supposition that Nibiru's orbit was much like that of Pluto, our most distant planet, whose orbit is elongated more than any other planet and is tipped at a greater angle than the others."

He raised his finger in the air carving a large arc in front of him and held it there for emphasis, "Pluto's orbit, which although it is more distant than all the others, is so elongated, that when it approaches it's perigee, that part of the orbit which is closest to the Sun, it is actually closer to the Sun for twenty years or so than Neptune, our second most distant planet."

He picked up the pace of his diatribe speaking rapidly, afraid he might be interrupted, "Orbital velocity of our Solar System planets is much slower the further out from the Sun you get with Pluto traveling at much slower speeds than Earth or Mars who are closer to the Sun."

The extended finger was shaking for additional emphasis, "Picture this if you can. Using my algorithm to calculate Nibiru's speed as it moved into and through our known Solar System, I than calculated it would actually take almost twelve years for it to move from the orbit of Pluto to the orbit of Neptune. It would take another, almost ten years, to move from Neptune's orbit to that of Uranus and almost eight more years before reaching Saturn."

Sadie had turned to listen to Berger's discourse and Ian had his hand out in front of him saying, "Whoa, just a minute."

Berger kept the forward finger shaking, "Hang on, let me finish. It's important."

He pulled up straight and clasped his hands together shaking them in unison as he spoke, "It would take another two years and eight months to reach Mars."

His pause at that juncture was especially dramatic and he mouthed each word distinctly, "When it got there we would see it as the brightest star in the sky."

He let the punch line flow verbally caressing it to make his point, "Remember the Magi following the star?"

Ian pulled his hand down and sat back trying to absorb what Berger was saying. Sadie got up from her chair and moved back to the table with the others. Tarnowski had not said a word, but sat listening intently.

With no response from his small audience Berger continued more softly and controlled, "That star would appear to get closer and closer for about a year at which time it would seem to be hovering just above or around the Moon. It may at times appear to be larger than the moon and would remain there for a little over a month, maybe thirty five days, although I can't tell you at this point, if it would sweep past the Moon and move even closer to the Earth; or we might actually get it to trip over the moon and bounce away from us." He couldn't help adding sarcastically, "And while it's hovering for those 35 days or more it might rain day and night."

Ian could no longer restrain himself and he interrupted, his tone was demanding, "Do you realize what you're saying? How did you establish those figures, because if you're right and our 2025 figure is right Nibiru has been grinding through our solar system for thirty or more years and is currently half way between Saturn and Jupiter, how could all of our high powdered telescopes and astronomers miss it?"

He threw his hands up in the air, "For over thirty years, and I'm a bad guy for saying it might actually be there. How could we miss it?"

Ian after sitting slumped surrounded in silence in his chair, after his outburst, regained his composure, "Okay tell us. How did you get to these figures?"

Berger waited for Ian to get back in step with him and was ready to continue his pitch, which he went on with without any additional provocation, "It wasn't that complicated. I used Bode's law to establish what I believed should be Nibiru's orbital position and speed at that distance. With that as a starting point and knowing the distance from the Sun for each of our planets I was able to use the Tables showing relative changes in positions with Nibiru along with my algorithm to calculate varying speeds and consequent changes in position of Nibiru. It only works if you have the Tables to define Nibiru's shifting positions."

Ian grinned sardonically at Berger, "You did say that at the beginning of all this that you could only do it if you had the tables, but why aren't our astronomers screaming from the roof tops if you're right? Why do you think we're going to see it as a bright star in the sky if we haven't been able to find it for over thirty years? Maybe it isn't even there and we're all wrong."

Tarnowski who had sat totally silent made a stuttering sound as if he had a question and pointed at Ian, "When you were in front of the Commission you said the ancients came here to mine gold and that they were going to make gold flakes to create an artificial atmosphere to save their planet."

He stopped abruptly as though he wasn't sure he remembered correctly what he had been told and stuttered to a conclusion, "You know, you, you said they were losing their atmosphere and had no alternative, remember."

Ian, who was still stinging from learning the thirty year figure, sat up straight to listen and responded more aggressively than necessary, "Yeah, you're right. That's essentially what I said. What's your point?"

Tarnowski's demeanor was now more self assured, "What if, and this is only a wild guess on my part, what if the reflective quality of the gold flakes somehow functioned as a cloaking device?"

Both Ian and Berger looked stunned both because of the unreasonable audacity of the suggestion, and the possibility that resonated through the room that it may have merit.

Ian spoke first, "That would bring us back to the reality that 2025 is a legitimate date and we're on the right track."

Berger said almost in a whisper, "I still need a month to start my calculations especially if Bob is right."

Sadie said almost like a whimper, "Then you think it really is out there. I keep hoping we're wrong."

Berger smiled at her and said, "It's okay, we're working on it," He seemed more interested in solving the puzzle in front of him than the fate that may come with the solution.

He turned back to Ian, "Okay, we have no alternative but to assume it really is out there whether it's being cloaked by gold flakes or not."

Sadie who had begun to feel uncomfortable as she let a growing despair take hold of her regained her composure, straightened her shoulders and spoke with authority, "I think I may be able to help in identifying the month you're looking for." All three men turned to listen, "I remember in reading different publications about the great cataclysm or flood, whichever you prefer to call it, one of the articles described a great wooly mammoth that appeared to be frozen instantaneously."

Berger chimed in, "Yes, Ian mentioned that in his presentation to us and most of us read about them in our early studies. How does it apply here Dr. Haddad?"

"Scientists were able, because it had been frozen almost instantaneously, to describe the food content of the animal's stomach. What they found was a plant known as a Fig Buttercup which grows in Siberia. That particular plant, which is basically a ground plant, begins to flower from March through May with about fifty percent of the plants in bloom around April 1st and essentially all gone by the end of May. That would mean that in the month of April they would come to full bloom and begin to disappear in May. This animal had a full and extensive amount of Fig Buttercups in his stomach when they found him all those years later."

Sadie brightened up as she completed her discourse doing what she did best, providing important information at critical times. She smiled broadly at Berger, "If I had to bet Dr. Berger I would say April is your month."

Berger rubbed his hand across his forehead lost in thought as though he hadn't heard a word she said then shouted, "Sadie, you are a genius, a genius."

He rushed over to the keyboard sitting on the adjacent table pushing a chair out of the way and mumbling audibly, "I think I've got it." He started vigorously and rapidly punching the keyboard turning his head slightly to the others, speaking as he typed, "I think I've got it now. I can plug in at April, 9577BC and work my way forward using the Tables as my guide. Thank you Sadie, I knew I could count on you and Ian."

He threw an anxious glance over to Tarnowski, "This is going to take me a while. Bob, why don't you take our guests to the cafeteria and get them something to eat." He paused and looked at Ian and Sadie, "I know it's a little early for lunch, but it'll give me the time I need."

Ian looked concerned, "Are you sure, it doesn't sound right. We're betting our future on an ancient poem, Ionic pentameter, gold flakes and now Buttercups in a mammoth's stomach. To be honest we're getting a little thin in our reasoning even for me to stay with it, and we're using ideas that I introduced."

Tarnowski, who had remained quiet after the gold flakes discussion spoke up, "To be honest Ian until you and Sadie came along we were making all sorts of preparations around the world and had no idea what we were actually going to do."

He looked at Sadie, "We weren't going to bomb them," and continued, "I personally think everything we're doing right now boarders on the outer edge of the most fantastic science fiction you can imagine, but it's a plan."

He stopped for a moment and then grinned broadly, "And it's exciting. It's like running into battle firing with everything you've got. I think our chances may be slim, but I don't want to be standing on the sidelines at the end of this thinking I should've......." His voice trailed off then picked up again, "Let's get some lunch."

Berger smiled reassuringly, "Don't worry I'm sure with the Tables, the algorithms I've developed and this computer at my beck and call I should be able to do at least as well as someone trying to follow the movement of Orion's belt through the sky."

Every one was smiling now but Tarnowski, who had his hands cupped in front of his mouth blowing into them to relieve tension, "Yeah, maybe now we can go to work on how we're going to nudge the moon every hour for 27.3 days and where we're supposed to nudge it to; and what we're supposed to nudge it with."

He recovered from his short funk, took them both by the arm and said, "Come on, let's get that lunch we talked about."

*

Ian's eating habits recently had been anything but disciplined or regular, and although it was early for lunch he felt unusually hungry. He leaned forward reading the posted menu in the cafeteria when he felt someone clutching his shoulders, "Hey, you can't eat here, this is my restaurant." Smitty's familiar voice was comforting to him in the fact that he was okay."

"Smitty, how the hell are you? I thought they probably threw you in jail."

Schmidt grinned sheepishly, "As a matter of fact I'm here for a debriefing. It's good though, I get a chance to tell my story about what happened at Rosslyn."

Ian was taken back a bit, "I don't get it Smitty who's after you?"

Schmidt snickered, "Just about everybody in one way or another, listen to this Ian," Schmidt stood poised with both hands out in front of him like a policeman trying to hold back a crowd, "one of the bad guys, who got shot was from India probably part of Patel's group, so the government of India is filing a complaint against the Scots for not giving him adequate protection while he was in their country. The Scots in turn have him in custody and are charging him with felony assault because of the injuries to Reverend Loring and his assistant. I assume you knew they both survived."

"Yeah, that was great news and……," Ian wanted to say more but was interrupted by Schmidt. "Hold on, there's a lot more. They're all fighting over the Holy Grail. Scotland is saying we had no right to take it out of the country and we should return it immediately."

Ian glanced over to Sadie, "That must be what's troubling Rosenthal and why he keeps meeting with the President."

He looked back to Schmidt, "We still have it you know, the Grail or Tables. We were just looking at them with Berger."

Schmidt was wound up, "Well they're probably also meeting with Israel who feel the Holy Grail, whatever it is, belongs to them because of its religious significance and want it returned to their country."

"On that particular score Scotland is claiming Anwar was a spy and that removal of the Grail amounts to espionage. They're asking for his extradition and want to try him as a spy."

He gave Ian a mock shove, "See what you guys started and I'm the one standing here to be debriefed." He stopped short and grinned broadly, "Wait a minute, are you also here to be debriefed?"

Ian returned the mock shove, "No such luck on your part, Rosenthal sent us over to help Berger. We came down to get some early lunch to give him some time to finish up on something."

Tarnowski who had stood silently by extended his hand to Schmidt, "How are you Bob, everyone at the Senate thinks you did a great job. I doubt if you have anything to worry about in the debriefing. Would you like to join us, I'm buying."

"No I'm……" Before Schmidt could finish Ian jumped in, "He's not joining anyone they're going to put him on a fast plane back to Scotland."

Schmidt grinned, waved at each of them, "I've got to go. Don't let him get you into anymore trouble Sadie." Then as he left did his Swartzenegger impression, "I'll be back."

Sadie called after him, "Whatever happened to Bogart and 007?"

The reply was hardly audible as he turned a corner, "They're in deep cover."

*

When they returned to Berger's war room they found him leaning back on a chair with his hands clasped in front of him. He called out to Tarnowski the second Tarnowski's frame filled the doorway, "Okay Bob, I'm ready. It was much easier than I thought. I can tell you where," he emphasized, "where", you need to nudge the moon each hour for 27.3 days and "when", emphasis again on "when," "you need to nudge it. I just don't have any fucking idea how you're going to get it done."

The bottle of scotch sitting on the table next to him and his unusual, for him, use of language, explained he had used the Tables well and then came to a dead end in his effort.

Tarnowski with a huge grin on his face walked over, picked up the Scotch and gave Berger a pat on his shoulder, "I didn't know you had any fucking scotch, pour me a drink and we'll see if we can figure this fucking thing out together."

Berger looked sheepishly over at Sadie, "I'm sorry, I apologize Sadie, but you heard him, he's much worse than I am."

Sadie led Ian over next to the two cussing scientists, took the bottle of Scotch and said mouthing the offensive word without saying it, "Why don't we all have a drink and help Jim figure it out."

Everyone exploded with laughter, tee-he, giggling laughter of the kind that relieves tension. Ian thought as the laughter subsided, "I wonder if the ancients were cussing and laughing when they got to this point."

Berger went into his explanation, holding Tarnowski by the arm as he did so he couldn't get away, describing coordinates that had to be met to lead the Moon into the path of Nibiru.

When Berger was through, Tarnowski gently removed the clutching hand, rolled back in his chair and said with an air of confidence, "I've got it from here Jim. Now I need to meet with our Chinese and Russian friends and see what they've got to help work the problem."

He looked from Ian to Sadie, I'm not sure you need to be there except to offer support as to why we're taking this tack. They're bound to be skeptical even when we tell them what we've got. I'm sure they'll acquiesce when they realize they probably don't have anything better."

He looked to Berger, "You'll definitely have to be there to explain your part to them and you better bring some vodka with your scotch."

Berger looked again at Sadie, "I'm sorry, I......."

Sadie cut him off with a hug, "Its okay, what you've done is very, very important. We all have a lot to thank you for and Ian and I will be there with the Chinese and Russians to tell them this whole hair brained scheme was our idea."

Tarnowski raised his hand, "Its tomorrow. They're already both here waiting for us to come to a conclusion. They're staying at the Hyatt with the rest of us."

An awkward silence followed then Ian said, "We'll be there."

Berger said, "Of course I will, and I'll bring the scotch and vodka to help things along. I'm not sure of the normal protocols, but as the old saying goes, "Desperate times call for desperate measures."

Ian gave Berger a quizzical look, "I not sure that expression fits here, but bring your scotch and vodka anyway."

Tarnowski signaled towards the doorway, "Come on, I'll get your limo and get you back to the Hyatt."

Sadie slid once more into the waiting limo and flopped down on the seat with Ian right behind her after a short exchange with Tarnowski.

Their ever present driver turned with his huge smile and in his broken English said, "To the Hyatt, please," and then laughed at his own silliness. Ian grinned at Sadie, "I didn't know he could laugh."

Sadie reached forward and tapped on the window which separated them from the driver. Without turning around, the driver slid the window open with his right hand over his head and asked again in a language that only Sadie seemed to understand, "Am I in trouble?"

Sadie laughed, "No, no I just want to know your name if you're going to be driving us all the time, no trouble."

"Jose, my name is Jose," he spit the words out in a ringing, lilting fashion.

Sadie countered, "No, no, that's not right. Jose would be from Mexico or South America. I can tell you're from the middle-east."

"Other drivers call me Jose, my name is Jose."

"Okay, Jose, thank you for driving us." Sadie grinning broadly slid the glass panel closed and then like an afterthought turned to Ian, "What was that all about with Tarnowski just now?"

Ian yawned as he answered, "Nothing serious, he was just reminding me one more time we're going to do this tomorrow and that," he paused and grinned, "Jose will be picking us up at the Hyatt as usual."

Sadie slid over closer to him, "Are you tired?"

The grin returned, "No, I just need a f...... drink." Drink came out alright, but Sadie clasped her hand across his lips before he could say all of it. "Ian, stop it, you're not funny." She clarified her position, "Berger was exhausted and frustrated from all the effort he had to put into this."

Ian put his arm around her, "He is a pretty intense guy, but I think it's going to pay off for us; if we're going to get this done right."

Sadie was quiet, lost in thought for a moment, then asked not sure of the answer she wanted, "Do you think they're going to keep us involved?"

"At least for a while, probably all day tomorrow as a minimum," he rubbed his tired eyes.

"That's not an answer, what do you think," she insisted.

"I think we're arriving at the Hyatt and that crowd is twice as big as it was this morning," he leaned forward trying to get a better view, "and they look mean."

Chapter 17: United Nations Assembly

Ian flipped the only remaining light in their suite to an off position and slipped into the king size bed next to a purring Sadie. As he shuffled his pillow back and forth looking for a comfortable position he was jarred awake by the phone. He reached for the flashing red light and grasped the phone franticly hoping not to waken Sadie, who immediately rolled over asking wearily "Who is it?"

"It's okay Bob we're still awake, what's up?" Ian's phone demeanor disguised his real situation. He listened attentively then said, "I see, that's no problem, we'll be there."

Sadie sat up and flicked on the lamp next to her side of the bed, "What's going on Ian?"

"It sounds like something big. After our meeting today Jim and Bob met with Rosenthal, who apparently was impressed with the meetings results. So," Ian took a deep breath, "he decided to cancel our meeting tomorrow. And, if I understood Tarnowski correctly we will be attending a, much, larger meeting two days from now in New York that will include a lot more people than just the Chinese and the Russians. In fact they're going to hold it in the United Nations General Assembly Hall as an Emergency Special Session."

Ian slid his legs from his sitting position over the side of the bed then turned back to face Sadie as he picked up the phone to dial, "And get this, Rosenthal will chair the session after the President speaks."

"President of the General Assembly or our U.S. president Ian," Sadie asked quizzically, "which one?"

Ian didn't immediately answer, but seemed focused on dialing the phone. "What are you doing Ian? Who are you calling," Sadie looked even more puzzled at what Ian was doing than what he had said.

"We're going to need plane and hotel reservations, and apparently we're on our own this time."

"What about all those people out in front Ian, are they going to be a problem if we leave without some sort of escort?" Sadie could not get the mob in front of the Hyatt out of her head.

"To be honest, I have no idea, but if I had to guess I would bet that just about everyone in this Hotel will be leaving to go to New York, and I doubt if anyone will pay any particular attention to us."

Sadie satisfied for the moment with his answer, got up from the bed and absentmindedly turned on the television, while Ian launched into negotiations on the phone for their travel to New York.

Big bold letters rippled across the screen in front of her, NEWS ALERT.

Sadie watched incredulously at the report, "Ian, look quickly they're talking about Rosslyn Chapel."

Ian finished with his negotiation, sat the phone down and moved over next to Sadie on the couch facing the TV.

"Look Ian, that's Reverend Loring and he's holding one of those big goblets that were in one of those trunks in the Chapel."

"Holy Grail" flashed across the kneecaps of Reverend Loring as he stood with one arm dangling from a sling and the other bravely holding the goblet from the trunk out in front of him. Mr. Diggs stood by his side with an ominous looking bandage wrapped around his head.

There was no mention of Ian, Sadie, Schmidt, or the Tables of Destiny. The report extolled the Reverend and Mr. Digg's bravery in overpowering a ruffian looking Israelite, who attempted to steal the "Holy Grail" from them after they had retrieved it from the vault underneath Rosslyn Chapel. Attempts were underway between the Scottish and Israeli governments to extradite the assailant involved in the attempted robbery back to Scotland to face charges of holding the Reverend and Diggs at gun point before shooting both of them. Mr. Diggs, who was only slightly wounded, was able to strike down the assailant with a large crowbar that had been used in the retrieval of the "Holy Grail." Although the assailant was injured from Mr. Diggs action, he was able to escape in a van that sped away from the scene. The men were able to identify the assailant as Israeli by a hat he was wearing that appeared to be one of an Israeli army soldier.

Israel denied any culpability in the alleged theft of the "Grail", but insisted it be returned to them now that the existence of it was known.

Ian sat back grinning, "They never mentioned the guy from India that Smitty said got shot and that they had captured; and you and I were never there. Apparently their first news reports were in error. My second guess, from what I said before is that, if we went out and danced in front of the Hotel, no one at this juncture of events would pay any attention to us."

He gave Sadie, who was now snuggled up next to him, a hug, flipped off the TV and said, "Come on, let's go to bed, I've got us an early flight tomorrow into Newark. We can get the train from the airport to Manhattan and decide what our next step is when we get there. There are hotels and motels either at the airport or Manhattan, whichever makes sense to us."

*

Their departure from the hotel was uneventful, although there was still a small smattering of people milling about out in front, who seemed more interested in the early morning coffee they were sipping and their intense conversation that seemed to be directed to anywhere than what might be going on inside the hotel.

Ian and Sadie elected to walk to a nearby Redline train station that would take them to Ronald Reagan International and on to Newark Airport via Continental Airlines.

Sadie quipped as they walked unencumbered by any crowds or suspicious looking men, "I think I enjoyed our brief moment of fame, but I'm glad that it's probably over."

Ian stopped and smiled at her, "I'm not sure it's over or that we ever enjoyed any real fame; infamous, maybe but not really famous."

"Who cares really? I think we accomplished something important. Don't you think, Ian?" She looked to him for assurance.

Ian smiled again, "I'll tell you what I think after this meeting, and we'll have a whole day in New York to think about it before the meeting."

The trip via the Redline, Continental Air and the New Jersey Transit system left them standing in the middle of Penn Station amid a throng of people, still undeterred by the recent reports about the existence of Nibiru, hustling about on their way to thousands of different jobs and activities.

As they headed to an exit from the station Ian felt a tug at his right elbow.

He turned to face his old nemesis, "Dr. Patel, what the hell are you doing here? You're going to get that bad penny reputation if you're not careful," Ian smiled and extended his hand to meet Patel's which was extended like a symbol of peace.

Patel eagerly grasped Ian's hand between his than turned and attempted to hug Sadie, who drew back and thrust her hand out in front of her showing a bit of reluctance in greeting this old adversary.

"Sadie, Ian," He looked from one to the other, "I have a lot of "I nevers" to share with you. Yes, I have never stopped following you, and I never stopped trying to impede your progress. But also, I never shot at you and never meant you any harm."

"What have you been trying to do?" Sadie asked incredulously at what she considered an audacious approach by Patel.

"Trying to save lives, trying to meet my end of the bargain not only to Protect; but to also try to Preserve. I was afraid that you like Rosenthal's Commission were intent on attempting to blow Nibiru to smithereens with nuclear weapons."

He continued just short of ranting afraid that he could lose his audience at any moment, "I wasn't comfortable with that idea and believe in not only Protection of life and civilization, but beyond that, it's Preservation. I realize now that your motives always were and remain much the same as mine."

Ian started to speak and pulled back when he saw Patel wasn't through, "I don't think it matters at this point if I tell you there are sources in the Pentagon who agreed with my point of view and that were privy to your meeting with Dr. Berger. They told me how you as a team were able to develop an alternative to blowing up Nibiru."

He suddenly paused as though he wanted to be sure both Ian and Sadie were listening, "I applaud you and what you have done, but I hope that you, as I do, realize there is still much more to be done."

"Dr. Patel......" Ian tried again to say something. Patel threw his hand up to hold him back, "I would never support blowing anything up and I never, never shot at you or attempted to harm you."

Sadie, who had listened intently to all that Patel had to say, stepped over, as you would to calm a hysterical child, and put her hand on Patel's wrist, "Dr. Patel, why don't we find a place to get some lunch, it's almost time for that, and see if we can't talk this out." She grinned at him, "Right now you seem like you might be more interesting than the museum Ian and I were going to visit."

Patel grabbed her and gave her the hug he had intended earlier, "Thank you Sadie, you have always been a gracious woman."

Sadie endured the overly aggressive hug and took the hand of both men leading them out of Penn station to a café she knew was just around the corner.

Patel sat in the booth across from Ian and Sadie elbows on the table, leaning forward eager to talk. With apologies completed his demeanor seemed more confident and secure, more like the man they had both dealt with for so many years gone past.

He flinched again, however, when both Ian and Sadie ordered hamburgers instead of the vegetable plate Patel had identified in the bottom corner of the menu. He was able to grin as he tapped on the large print on the menu describing different kinds of hamburgers, "You people just don't care about the poor cow, do you?"

Ian expecting something more somber for openers to a difficult conversation grinned, "Sorry, I guess we both forgot. We were being insensitive. We can change our order if you are uncomfortable with two beef eaters sitting across from you."

Patel laughed, "No that's not necessary. It's just a reminder how each of us gets stamped on the forehead as we exit the untainted world inside a mother's womb, whether or not we will be eating beef; will we be Muslim or Christian, believe in God or the Devil."

Ian picked up the cadence, "Don't forget Democrat or Republican if you live in the states or Shiite or Sunni if you were born with a name like Haddad."

"Is race or ethnic orientation what you consider a stamp on the forehead?" Sadie entered the jousting.

"Those aren't options. They're simply something you're probably going to have to deal with at some young age before you're ready to," Ian countered.

Patel drew back from the table with his arms crossed in front of him, "I know I started this line of conversation, but does any of it matter given the situation we have in front of us."

Patel sat up, now absolutely straight, and words began to flow in a cascade as if they came from a top down storage bin, "Nibiru doesn't have to make a direct hit on us to be a problem. Even if it bounces off the moon as you've planned it will have come close enough to Earth to end civilization as we know it this moment. We'll either suffer in darkness with no light from the sun from the cloud of volcanic ash around the world, or be drowned in the greatest tsunami the world has seen for over ten thousand years. We may be able to mitigate against it somewhat with the work you've started and Rosenthal intends to carry out, but there is no stopping Nibiru completely."

"No stopping it!" He raised his voice causing others in the café to turn and look.

Sadie listened intently wondering where he was going, "Dr. Patel, I don't understand. If you feel that way about us as a civilization, don't you think the same applies to Nibiru's civilization?"

"Wont they also be destroyed by the encounter?" Sadie seemed very unsure of her ground but continued, "I personally found the idea of bombing Nibiru totally abhorrent, but I'm not sure I understand why you were so adamant against bombing Nibiru if you know and understand that contact with us will likely destroy us all."

"Sadie, I don't have a good answer for you. I've known about the Commission for some time and my inside source told me that at least one of their proposals was to blow up Nibiru if they could, and I believed my source. I was ultimately told that wasn't the case, but couldn't get the possibility out of my head."

He obviously was dodging the gist of her query and looked back despairingly at her, "Haven't you ever felt that way?"

Ian recognized the awkwardness of the conversation for Patel and moved in to cut it short, "Dr. Patel, where are you now in your thinking? What are your specific plans?"

Without hesitation Patel skipped from his exchange with Sadie back to Ian, "Don't' you see Ian? Don't you see? The adventure is over for you, for Sadie, for me. Rosenthal has the reins for the whole world in his hands. He and hundreds, probably thousands, of his recruits are going to take the information you've presented to him and work to that fatal day when Nibiru appears in our skies. They will do their best to change what fate has decreed, but their success or failure will not be defined until that day."

He continued like a man setting down a heavy burden that he had carried for too long a time, "They will live the adventure until that climatic day, working against odds, giving it their all, not knowing if all of us will live or die."

He stopped, leaned back across the table and in a low solemn voice repeated, "But for you and for me the adventure is over."

"It's over."

Ian sat back from him and sighed, "I get where you are, where you're going, but I'm not sure I agree with your insinuation that Rosenthal may not need us anymore; not that it makes any difference."

Ian felt a twinge inside as he answered Patel and thought back to his conversation with Sadie on the walk to the Redline, "Why are you pursuing this with me and Sadie at this time. I don't get it."

"Because I was a member of your Think Tank, remember, Protect and Preserve. We were talking about civilization, remember?" Patel's response was aggressive not allowing much wiggle room for Ian.

He waited allowing time for Ian to respond, sensed Ian wasn't ready, and fell back into his diatribe, "You and Sadie have done more than anyone has or will to protect us, but the job is only half done. There is a need to look now to the preservation of civilization here on Earth. Barring a miracle it's almost certain that Rosenthal and his group cannot protect us to the point of avoiding all contact with Nibiru and the resultant chaos that will follow."

Ian now leaned forward ready to speak, but Patel having started again was ready to continue, "I am developing an organization that looks to the tasks, that need to be done now, to prepare for the preservation of civilization, after this pending cataclysm."

"You must have thought about this at sometime once you went on the "Sixty Minutes" to talk about a planet about to hit us. You would have to realize all the things we would need after such an impact." Patel paused and then started to innumerate what he thought would be high on a list of such needs.

"Technology held in the minds of scientists and professors would be paramount. We will need tools to make tools of production and manufacture, albeit at the lowest level of technology. We certainly will not need to concern ourselves with nuclear in any form, but agriculture and husbandry will be absolute requirements. We will need young people and though you may not want to thrust them into a harsh environment, children."

He realized he was reciting what you could probably find in a children's text book to a college professor and ratcheted up a notch. "Ian consider this, the English back around 2000 began a Frozen Ark Project where they collected frozen DNA from thousands of species. Their contribution to an effort like this would be invaluable, but I can't imagine them simply turning such a project over to us. I need someone like you with your current reputation and eloquent negotiating skills to bring people like them to our side in a cooperative effort." He paused again to measure his progress in selling Ian.

"This sort of thing has been done before Ian, you know that as an historian. Any school boy who has read the story of Noah and the ark knows that. And any historian worth his salt knows Noah didn't build the only ark. There must be dozens of projects similar in nature to the Frozen Ark Project that would benefit from a unified approach that would be extremely important to a survival effort. There is an opportunity here to do for the preservation of mankind and civilization equal to and as important, to that which, your fabled Commission is attempting to do at the protection level."

"And we've all read about Quetzalcoatl and Viracocha, who arrived in Central America to bring civilization back to mankind after the great flood, to teach men the rudiments of husbandry, architecture, science and astronomy. They were there to bring law and order back to a people who had lapsed into a savage way of life after that first great cataclysm."

"Osiris the Egyptian god like Quetzalcoatl and Viracocha was believed to have saved the Egyptians, who had slipped into cannibalism, bringing them back to agriculture and husbandry while teaching them the refinements of civilization."

He stopped and shook his head, "Why am I telling you this, Ian, you're a better historian than I am, but I'm sure you get the gist of what I'm saying. There is a need as great as that which Rosenthal is attempting to address, following the aftermath of the encounter with Nibiru. I'm attempting to take the lead in meeting that need, but I need help. I need help from people like you and Sadie, who understand all that's involved. It's only a very short step from your recent exploits to a task as profound as anything you've ever done. It's no less in importance then attempting to thrust the moon into the path of Nibiru."

Ian slumped back seemingly exhausted from Patel's insistent conversation, "Why me Dr. Patel? Why Sadie? We've just finished what you call an adventure that's left me in shambles with some important relationships in what's left of my life." He stopped as though he was accusing Patel and asked insistently, "Why me?"

Patel drew his left hand across the base of his jaw and looked absentmindedly into the table in front of him like a man studying a Ouija board looking for answers.

The response to Ian came not from Patel but from Sadie, "The greater the perception the greater the responsibility." She turned to make eye contact with Ian before repeating the second tenant of responsibility, "The greater the perception the greater the sin."

"You are blessed with perceptions others may not have Ian, but with that perception comes the burden of responsibility. You taught me that Ian, that's why Dr. Patel needs your, our help."

Three people sat together in silence trying to find a comfortable position under the yoke of an unusual heavy responsibility.

Dr. Patel abruptly banged his hands on the table, stood up and smiled at his two companions, "I call you after you've had a chance to attend the session tomorrow. I've enjoyed the conversation with you and hope you'll give it some thought." He stepped out away from the booth and with a flourish waved good bye, "I'll call you."

He leaned back into the booth one more time, "The adventure is over, this is a pilgrimage of a different sort, Preservation," he repeated, "Preservation."

Then with an always leave them laughing attitude turned, tapped on the menu still laying on the table, and grinned at them, "You can box my hamburger and take it with you, save it, we may need it."

He was gone.

Sadie put her hand on Ian's shoulder and shook him gently, "Maybe that museum might be more interesting than we thought."

Ian, who was sitting in a kind of undefined funk, smiled grimly, "We need to finish our lunch and find a hotel, then I'll go to a museum with you, but that's all I'm committing to for now."

*

Ian elected not to call, but to walk to The Mansfield Hotel on 44th street between 5th and 6th avenues. He was sure they would have rooms available and it would be an easy walk to the United Nations in the morning. It was an old favorite of his where he had stayed many times in his visits to New York. The Mansfield Hotel had a storied past reaching back into the 1920's that exuded a certain kind of mystery for a hard core historian like him. They walked in through an elegant entryway with a pretty young clerk standing at the desk at the end of the hallway leading into the hotel. She smiled graciously welcoming them, "How can I help you today?"

"Room for two, tonight and tomorrow night please," Ian's manner was easy and sing song in pitch.

The clerk coyly began to shake her head "no" as she shuffled through her reservations then suddenly looked up, "Oops, one left, you're lucky we had a cancellation just about an hour ago."

She eyed Sadie's mid-eastern complexion and smiled, "I'll bet you're here for that United Nations meeting. You really were lucky most of the better hotels filled up immediately yesterday by noon including us."

Sadie couldn't resist and in Arabic yielding a free translation squeezed Ian's arm and said, "You are one lucky Son of a Bitch, you've got me."

Ian didn't understand the words but got the meaning. As the young attractive clerk slipped back into a side room to get something for their check in, Sadie still squeezing his arm whispered in English, "She certainly is pretty, isn't she."

As they moved towards the elevator Ian in turn squeezed Sadie's arm, "But not as foxy as the lady I'm with."

Sadie grinned and said, "Sorry, just normal female hormones taking their toll. I know you love me, even through all of this nonsense we've had to endure."

Ian shook his head as they entered their room, "It's not over Sadie, it's not over."

*

After a quiet evening with dinner at a local restaurant, another of Ian's favorites, they were up early and one of the first to arrive at the hotel's complimentary breakfast in the M Bar just off the main lobby.

Just as they were about to sit down they saw Berger and Tarnowski, with a small entourage about them, rushing out of the hotel. Tarnowski spotted them and stopped just long enough to turn and shout, "Ian, glad you made it, we'll see you later." He turned a second time and shouted, "You're all set at the U.N." and was gone.

Berger either didn't see them or didn't have time to stop. Ian quipped to Sadie who looked askance at Berger's departing figure, "It doesn't matter."

*

The walk to the U.N. building was easy and relaxed with most conversation between them directed away from what they felt was in the day ahead. Their entry into the General Assembly Hall was as Tarnowski said, "All set." They were quickly seated in the section reserved for Observer nations and watched as the seats around them and throughout the Hall filled up with a thousand different dialects flowing all about them. Sadie with her language skills grinned as she picked up the many irrelevant and irreverent remarks about a myriad of topics including lodging accommodations the night before and all the good food served in New York restaurants.

Neither Ian nor Sadie had ever been inside this unusual dome like structure and Sadie sat somewhat in awe of the beautiful architecture surrounding them.

A call to order from the Secretary General came without any other remarks, "The normal protocols of this assembly will not be observed today but instead will focus on a serious problem facing all of us in this fragile world we live in. The President of the United States will lead us in this discussion."

A murmur swept across the members as the President stepped forward and stood silently waiting for quiet.

Sadie nudged Ian, "This may be as close as we ever get to actually meeting her. She looks a little drawn, don't you think?"

Ian didn't immediately answer, but studied what seemed like a frail figure standing far removed from him at the front of the vast hall, then with concern answered, "Yes, she does."

The President's speech was calm and confident as she began to outline what she described as an improbable, unexpected and unanticipated situation that was threatening all of civilization. It was a situation that would require all of mankind's resources and dedication to effectively meet this threat. There could be no dissention, no quarreling, and there must be an immediate, unequivocal end to all conflicts, without sanctions or reservations. This must be a joint effort whose only two options are survival or death for all of mankind. There will be no winners, no losers only survivors.

She was eloquent and an unusual calm settled on the room as she spoke. All were both awed and mesmerized at what they were hearing. When she was finished she asked them to listen now to the hope of the future and to what plans must be developed to affect their salvation.

After a long pause, which had the effect of a moment of prayer, she introduced Senator Rosenthal, who in turn introduced all of the members of his Commission, carefully describing their individual functions and responsibilities as he had with Ian on the plane on their return from Scotland.

There was no mention of Ian or Sadie.

He saved his last introduction for Senator Berger, and extolled his broad, extensive background and experience in the astral-physics discipline.

Senator Berger stepped to the podium with an air of confidence and esteem. He easily took control of the meeting and began to describe the various algorithms he had developed to initially discover and then track the movement of Nibiru. His algorithms and knowledge of the movement of all the planets in the solar system allowed him to define with pin point accuracy when Nibiru would arrive, even though other scientists were not yet ready at this time to even effectively state that Nibiru was indeed the tenth plant of our solar system. His manner was solemn as he outlined how the world would suffer without an immediate and cooperative effort from the worldwide community to rebuff this Beowulf in the skies.

He accented the need and urgency of the situation when he referred back to the cataclysm that had occurred over ten thousand years ago, and how people in those times had no effective method to either identify or deal with the problem; and consequently suffered their ultimate fate in the great flood.

He dotted his "I's" and crossed his "T's" in each sentence describing again and again his own extraordinary effort in arriving at this juncture in giving final, complete definition to the time of the arrival of Nibiru.

"April 2025," the words shot across the auditorium sweeping by all like a soaring jet plane and rattling the senses of all in that huddled mass.

A gasp, defining the world's reaction in the unified voice of the United Nations members, hung on like an awkward caveat to the April, 2025 announcement.

Thunderous voices rang out in dissent, each one lost in the din of hundreds of others screaming, wailing, demanding answers.

Rosenthal literally pushed Berger out of way waving his arms almost hysterically, pounding on the podium in front of him, demanding, ultimately, pleading, for quiet.

The din like a wild animal wandered around the assembly room uncontrolled, inciting fear in people now wandering from their seats, mingling with others in hysterical, frightened voices. Others pushed towards the podium causing Rosenthal and Berger to take a momentary retreat. Kill the messenger was attaining a prominent status in the thinking of what could now only be described as a mob.

The call for world unity had not quite taken hold, and Ian and Sadie sat huddled together in their seats in the shadow of this new, very present threat.

The raucous melee continued out of control for over an hour. Police who were called in to bridle the wild beast were only effective in containing the quasi riot to the confines of the building. A bloc of religious leaders adamantly opposed to any thought of life on other planets persistently pushed at doorways being blocked by the police in an attempt to leave the UN Assembly.

Finally totally spent and exhausted people slumped back in their seats resigned to the fact they must look for a new direction.

With some semblance of order established Rosenthal regained his composure and stood once again in front of the petulant mob, and began anew hammering away on the podium calling again and again for order until his was the only voice to be heard. He took a deep breath, cleared his throat and leaned forward staring into remnants of the disturbance that he and Berger had created.

"There is hope, you must not despair. If you will stay a little longer and listen Senator Tarnowski of my staff will outline plans that have been developed that will make us safe." His offer sounded more like a plea for help than a possible solution to all their concerns that now loomed in front of him like a black hole ready to envelop him if he got too close to the edge.

Tarnowski is not a particularly large imposing man being just under, six feet tall and slight of build, but he can on occasion present a confident, commanding appearance. He didn't shout as Rosenthal had, but raised his hands over his head and held them there until there was absolute quiet in the auditorium.

"There are solutions to every problem in life. Some problems are assuredly more difficult to deal with than others. This is an extremely difficult one to wrestle with, but we can bring it to its knees," He paused and looked around for what seemed like the proverbial lifetime. Perhaps he didn't have answers, "With your help."

"We know what to do to meet and deal with this intruder," That last phrase shot through Sadie's raw nerve endings as she remembered the threat to bomb Nibiru with nuclear weapons. She clutched Ian's arm ready for the verbal bomb to drop. Everything inside her was sure the commission was going to renege on their promise. They were going to use nuclear bomb's to destroy Nibiru.

She turned pale as Tarnowski continued, "We have discovered a method that if properly implemented will divert this threat away from Earth and keep us safe. We will in accomplishing that, require the resources and support of all the nations represented in this room today," he paused measuring their collective response in terms of nods or lack thereof, "that's why we asked you here today."

He launched into an evangelistic shout, "Not to scare you, but to save you."

He immediately settled back to a demeanor of that like a businessman about to outline a deal you couldn't say "no" to. "To accomplish what we must, we will need to build several stations on our moon. The Chinese government already has plans on the drawing board that will allow us to do that."

Without any additional eloquent speeches or explanations Tarnowski described how those stations would support a battery of newly designed Ionic Thrusters more powerful than any jet engine ever invented. These Ionic Thrusters would gain their incredible thrust by the infusion of nuclear particles deposited in the intake of the Thrusters by pilots flying Spacejets cable of delivering a nuclear payload safely and returning to Earth after their mission. The nuclear explosions created for the required nuclear particles would be time delayed and the newly developed Spacejets would have acceleration characteristics sufficient to attain an escape velocity away from the detonation of the nuclear explosion. The infusion of nuclear particles into the inlets of the battery of Thrusters would be managed in such a way that there was no damage to the Thrusters themselves.

Tarnowski sounded lackadaisical like someone describing a new toy that was absolutely safe for use by children of all ages.

He flashed images up on a large screen mounted above his podium as he spoke. Images first of the Moon's surface with sketches of powerful looking rockets mounted horizontally, followed by an extremely sleek looking jet that had elements of both a rocket and an aero plane. He followed with images of nuclear explosions side by side on the screen, one erupting violently and the other slowly puffing up to the configuration they all recognized as a mushroom cloud.

Although he couldn't see the screen above him he pointed his right hand upward, "These Ionic Thrusters will be capable of rotating three hundred and sixty degrees on their bases to follow the rotation of the moon, and place a continual forward thrust on the moon over an extended period of time of 27.3 days. The times and direction of that effort had all been carefully calculated by Senator Berger and when successfully employed will direct the moon into the path of this renegade planet, bouncing it off into outer space away from the Earth."

All within the room sat silently trying to absorb this tale told to them by either an idiot or one of the greatest minds of their time. They weren't sure which description was apropos.

Tarnowski was satisfied that silence construed consent and continued with the second half of his presentation, "We're going to need manufacturing facilities to build those stations on the moon. We're going to need spacecraft to deliver building material to the moon to erect those stations and brave teams of men to erect them in a hostile environment."

"We will need to build the Spacejets I've described and train pilots to complete the most important part of the mission of delivering nuclear power to the Ionic thrusters."

"Those pilots will be the finest from every country in the world and," he hesitated again, "to allow them to be effective in this bold effort those countries who still retain nuclear warheads must surrender them and all the nuclear material they may have in their possession over to us in this new effort for our use and command."

Initially the crowd remained still until the import of what he was saying sunk in and then an increasing loud murmur swept over the Hall reverberating off the back wall and thundering back to the podium.

Tarnowski raised both hands out in front of him ready to deflect any objections to a request that in a world that had languished in conflict for eons could only be seen as audacious at best and more probably a threat to their ultimate security.

The response was so intense that it brought both Rosenthal and the President of the United States back to his side. The President stepped forward solemn in her demeanor, asking for calm, asking to be heard. Her eloquence in taking them back through her initial remarks and reminding them of the severity of the situation brought them back to sitting upright in their seats as willing listeners. Finally, she asked them only to listen and consider what was at risk and what must be done.

With this new support and no apparent immediate opposition to his proposal Tarnowski steadfastly began to read off the names of those countries believed to have nuclear capability and a description of what their arsenal contained. He knew in his heart that all those nations who ultimately had signed the Nuclear Non-Proliferation Treaty had retained a nuclear capability. When he was through he had named seventeen different nations with arsenals ranging from fifteen thousand warheads to as small as five warheads.

Five of the seventeen named nations stood up in unison to be on record to state their objections to the request, but agreed to work with the Commission through negotiations. Tarnowski recognized the five as nations who had never come to peaceful terms with the rest of the world and all of whom were suffering economically.

Tarnowski stepped away from the podium with a slurred statement, "That's all I've got." and waved Rosenthal back to the podium.

Rosenthal's summing up was emphatic that this was an emergency meeting to alert the world of a great danger and that each country would be contacted in some way to learn what participation would be required by them to meet this challenge.

If something this important and threatening could possibly be anti-climatic that's how the meeting ended, quietly, with some talking in small groups together and others simply filing out of the building like they had just finished their lunch break and were ready to go back to work.

Ian and Sadie walked back to the Mansfield without a word spoken until Ian stopped at the entrance, pulled his hands over the back of his neck as if to relieve a crick in his neck and with wrinkled brow grinned at Sadie, "Patel was right Sadie, for us the adventure is over, theirs has just begun."

Sadie simply looked back at him and said, "It seems so eerily quiet Ian, so eerily quiet."

"It'll be different tomorrow Sadie, I promise you."

Chapter 18: U.N. Aftermath

Of course Ian was right and within the next twenty-four hours after the meeting's end people were in the streets around the world, some peacefully demonstrating, some protesting, others in full scale rioting. It was difficult to discern if there were any real differences, other than method, as to why either the protestors or the rioters were in the streets. The issues, that were presented by the activists, as far as anyone could figure out revolved around either race, religion, gender or a cry for freedom. There was no mention of Nibiru or the announcements that were made at the United Nations.

In the pit of their stomachs people were all frightened out of their wits in the face of this pending disaster, which had now been acknowledged at the U.N. as being inevitable. Many who had been hungry for years, and whose only purpose in life had been to relieve those pangs of continual hunger, were now convinced they would die hungry probably more because of the forecasted shortages then the cataclysm about to envelop them. They had nothing to lose and followed the tried and true tradition of looting whenever any new world problem provided the anarchy needed to cover their insurrection.

The media was there with cameras, of course, long before the ubiquitous tanks, that for what seemed like eons always attended insurrections around the world. It would be weeks before people returned to their homes to tend to their children and chores left undone. They had accomplished no more with their disparate protests than those in the United Nations Assembly Hall had. Ultimately they had no choice but to sit back and listen to whatever direction was given to them. What else could they do then put themselves back in the hands of their respective governments, who had now coalesced into one unit directing all their combined efforts and resources behind the direction of Rosenthal's Commission.

Each member and unit of Rosenthal's Commission hit the streets, so to speak, ready to take action with immediate notoriety going to Senator Holland, who formed a universal church that was open to all religions and used the power of the pulpit of many beliefs to stand fast together to prepare for the future whatever it may bring. His success was marked by his particular ability in working with those religious groups, who objected to aliens even being mentioned, in their religious activities. Holland was able to cull them out into small prayer groups, that existed within the boundaries of the larger unit that he had created, but with enough independence to maintain the basic tenants of their respective belief systems. In this manner he was able to control a variety of dissimilar belief systems and keep them focused on Commission objectives. This singular effort literally kept millions of potential protesters and demonstrators off the streets, and consequently provided no opposition but rather tacit acceptance to actions directed by the Commission.

He was remarkable in his ultimate achievements and in less than one year's time would be recognized as one of the greatest teachers the world had ever known.

Senator Hoesel, still unrecognized and unheralded, miraculously produced manufacturing and production facilities to meet all the needs of the Commission outlined, so briefly, by Tarnowski. There would be Spacejets and pilots to fly them, Ionic Thrusters, and enough nuclear fuel to feed them with the power they needed to carry out this arduous task.

Senators Brown and Ligget would work as a team spending the next five years of their lives trying to retrace the steps of our three heroes, trying to find their way into the Hall of Records, where they hoped to find some undisclosed bit of information left by the ancients, that would turn the tide in the coming battle with Nibiru. The government of Egypt initially offered support, working with Brown and Ligget at all levels, and then ultimately turning to devices of their own making.

Unfortunately, the trust that had once existed between Ian and Sadie and Commission members had become badly frayed around the edges with a consequent loss of communication in this effort. Ligget and Brown gave it their all, but without the support of our Sadie, the Oracle of Knowledge, they ultimately embraced bitterness as their final ally.

Senator Hyatt's career as a news analyst and anchor for a major broadcasting station soared, and she was soon being recognized as a top runner for the office of President of the United States. Her insights into the workings of government and world affairs were heralded as profound in their judgments, and she became a candidate for the Nobel Peace Prize in addition to the many other accolades afforded her.

Senator Blessing who had been responsible for identifying Ian and Sadie, as being instrumental to the success of the Commission, finished his term in the Senate then retired back to private life in a role as a Professor at the University of Chicago, and was never really heard of again.

Senator Malick, the unsung hero in the back room, continued coordinating the respective activities of Commission members carefully working to draw in whatever additional support was required by each of them, and working as Rosenthal's right hand man to be certain all worked in synchronization with each other.

Rosenthal because of his Jewish heritage was viewed by many around the world as the new messiah, who would lead them away from the tyranny of this new threat that was holding them captive; while others for no particular reason dubbed him as other great leaders had been in the past, as the Anti-Christ.

Ian ultimately gave a positive response to Dr. Patel's call to work with him for the future preservation of civilization, but with some caveats. He wanted to include his mother and father along with Julie and her child in one of the sanctuaries being created.

Dr. Patel respectfully declined to include Ian's parents as being too old and as being of doubtful value in any role they might play in preserving even the immediate future. In fact he was adamant that anyone over forty-five years of age would not be included without unusual credentials that would be meaningful in their survival effort.

Ian grinned sardonically at Sadie and pointed out that in the year 2025 he would have exceeded the forty-five years of age, and wondered if Patel would then drop him as unnecessary like the Commission had dropped him. He was laughing to the point of spilling his drink when he begged her to take him with her, because her language skills would be an absolute necessity to Patel's scheme. She assured him that if he would give her a week to think about it she would, "let him know," and poured him another drink.

Patel unaware of Ian and Sadie's drinking and laughing was significantly more receptive to Julie and her child and recommended that the father also be included to project a strong family unit. His only reserve was in the fact that they brought no additional skills or knowledge with them that might be important to a future civilization.

Patel's plan was to build sanctuaries in the underground labyrinths under cities such as Istanbul, Turkey and Rome, particularly those that didn't exist over, or in the vicinity of a fault line. He was quick to point out to Ian that both, Cincinnati, where his parents lived and San Francisco, where Julie lived were above recognized, established fault lines.

Ian suggested retrofitting retired cruise liners, or freighters, to play the role of an ark, presuming flooding would be an even greater threat than volcanic activity or earthquakes. This was only the beginning of many long, difficult conversations, that in the frightened, audacious approaches that followed had a greater sense of lunacy to them than simply standing pat and letting the proverbial chips fall.

In the course of it all Ian ultimately went back to Cincinnati to make peace with his mother as one would visiting someone on their deathbed. He asked Sadie to go with him and she respectfully declined emphasizing this was an area of their relationship that had to stand on its own. Ultimately she realized how important it was to him and allowed him to buy tickets for two.

The visit with his mother, as you might expect, was unusual. She realized for the first time that she had only known the child, and to a lesser extent the young man, who had lived with them intermittently throughout his college years; who drew farther away at the end of each of his visits to return home. She admitted, more even temperedly, that she didn't really know the man she had so vigorously attacked on the phone. She asked innocently and correctly, "whose fault is it when parent and child grow so far apart?"

Ian remembered again what he had said to Rosenthal and what Sadie had whispered softly to remind him in his conversation with Patel, "The greater the perception the greater the responsibility, the greater the perception the greater the sin."

His mother caught him off guard with her own insights when she smiled and said softly, "I realize after a great deal of thought that you don't have to be wrong in what you believe for me to be secure in what I believe. I was wrong in the way I acted on the phone for fear that you may be right about what's going to happen. Please forgive me."

Ian realized how guilty he had been for many years in not reaching back and trying to understand more about a woman he loved dearly, that he had only seen through one singular prism that reflected a boy's mother and no one else. He smiled and hugged her close to him, "I'm the more, sorry of the two of us, when I realize how fragile and inconsequential those pious judgments we both cling to, are in the face of honest responsibility. It was so easy for both of us not to ask more questions, not to try and understand."

Her eyes were pleading with him in response, "Ian, forgive me again for what I've done, I called Bob Schmidt and asked him about your friend Sadie, I should have called you. He said she is everything you need in a friend and companion. That she understands your needs and is always there for you. I wish I hadn't been so judgmental, I wish I had met her."

Ian stood up smiling, "She's waiting in the car, I'll ask her to come in."

The meeting between Sadie and Ian's mom was very cordial both realizing that there was no competition, but a shared love for a guy who wanted them to be friends. It was a fitting parting given the circumstance looming in their future. There would be trouble enough for everyone without petty differences pricking the sensitivities laid on them by this tumultuous situation. They parted as friends ready for an uncertain future that would be theirs to share one way or the other.

The trip to San Francisco was more traumatic with hormones once again dictating the course of the conversation between Ian and Julie. The time and situation was not of the sort for parent and child to share perceptions that could make them whole as a family unit.

The whole thing in San Francisco was complicated by Sarah's presence, whose reluctance to leave the side of a child in constant tears, in concert with the history she and Ian shared, filled the room like a lubricant for more salty tears. Ian left hurriedly, to rejoin Sadie who had remained in the Hyatt Regency Hotel at the airport using her time to wander along the bay area, which seemed unusually quiet, almost eerie.

It would take some coaxing and understanding, but Julie would ultimately join one of Patel's sanctuaries with her newly acquired child and husband, leaving her mother alone, who had no particular credentials and was fast approaching the age of forty-five.

A world in turmoil, possibly on the edge of extinction, limped along, some like Ian, trying to put things in order the best they could, others pretending a kind of ignorance continued on from day to day ignoring the affront they would ultimately have to deal with.

The uneven, disconnected events that followed throughout 2019 as Nibiru, lolly-gagged, between Uranus and Saturn took one ugly turn after the other, and had the guise of being a three ring circus.

UFO sightings immediately increased around the world with one unconfirmed landing in the middle-east near the holy city of Jerusalem.

A manned space probe was launched by the Chinese to attempt a "sighting" of Nibiru and confirm its existence utilizing a vehicle originally intended for a probe of one of Jupiter's moons. Human rights groups in China objected to the probe since it was to be a one way mission for the pilots involved.

The space probe by the Chinese caused an additional group worldwide stir because they refused to surrender some of their best astronauts that the Commission required to man the French Space Bus built to carry Thruster components to the moon, in favor of the suicide mission they had designed.

Stock markets around the world plummeted initially then soared upward, repeating this saw tooth pattern again and again, until ultimately setting off the largest government investigation ever in the United States regarding insider trading.

Conflicts beyond the reach of Senator Holland over the Holy city of Jerusalem between Christians and Muslims including so many disparate groups it was impossible to begin to address a possible solution, even by someone with the clout Senator Holland had attained.

The Vatican released statements almost daily on the Jerusalem situation as well as the overall pending doom. It wasn't clear exactly where they stood on either situation, and many of their constituents remained in a kind of neutrality waiting before taking action on anything.

A mob of several hundred people stormed Area 54 in the United States believing that "Escape Vehicles" were being manufactured there for the exclusive use the United States top brass. Sixty-six people were killed in the attempt as the government worked to maintain control of this important installation. The world looked at the number sixty-six and gasped at its unusual connotation, certain that it was the devil himself responsible for the murder of innocent people.

Senator Blessing was asked to return to lead an investigation of this outrageous act by the Army, but declined, deferring to a junior senator from New Mexico.

An obscure cult of only twenty-five people, who had learned of Dr. Haddad's existence and her role in the Commission's activity planned to kidnap her to become their leader. Because of the sensitivity of Dr. Haddad's knowledge of the important mission ahead, all of the cult members were captured and held indefinitely in a federal prison for interrogation, at the specific direction of Senator Rosenthal.

That's not all that happened, but it's the gist of it, and by the time all that had unfurled we had seen the end of 2019 and most of 2020. Nibiru had completed almost eighty percent of its journey between Uranus and Saturn in the year 2019. The journey between Uranus and Saturn continued for about four more months into 2020 before continuing on to Jupiter from Saturn picking up speed as it moved closer to the Sun. Because it had not yet been spotted by astronomers, some doubt remained about its existence.

The year 2021 did not look any more promising.

CHAPTER 19: NIBIRU ARRIVES

Dateline 2021

It can be an extremely difficult task to get eight billion plus people to behave in an orderly fashion no matter what's at stake, and our world as it existed in the year 2021 didn't disappoint us in that regard. Here's more of what happened.

Food shortages were beginning to be felt in grocery stores as hoarding of food began around the world. This fearful situation caused would be hoarders to raid the fields of farmers, who had anticipated excessively nice profits, since government controls on prices had been eased, and consequently had crops growing in every field, that was available, making easy targets for the raiders.

In an effort to take action against the raids in the fields many farmers began to use armed guards to protect their crops, while others simply gave up and deserted the fields, leaving them unattended and unsowed for the future. As would be expected food shortages more severe than before developed causing many governments to step in and attempt to grow crops.

Dismal does not accurately describe the clumsy, untrained efforts and results that ensued in this particular calamity. The net result was more protesting and riots around the world. In the midst of all this turmoil the railroad and trucking industries cut back on services with some railways running only every other day restricting the distribution of food more than ever.

Many countries with infrastructures that were more developed did not feel the immediate pinch on their lifestyle, and with normal excesses of food in the past, still a part of their memories and within their immediate grasp, stumbled but didn't fall. In fact Qatar won the world Soccer Cup, and the Hawaii Turtles won the World Series with players imported from Japan and Cuba representing the main stay of their teams.

Football play continued strongly in the United States with both the BCS College and Super Bowl championships successfully being played with record breaking attendance at both.

Some people in the Western world were beginning to get a little edgy, but still felt, however, as they always had, that programs proposed by the government would probably take care of them. And they had a worldwide syndicated anchor woman named Hyatt keeping them abreast of everything that happened each evening on the six o'clock news to assure them over and over that everything was alright.

On the bright side Julie had an eight and one half pound baby boy and named him Ian after his grand dad. She and her fiancé were married a week before the baby arrived, and both were extremely enthusiastic about the role they were destined to play in one of Patel's sanctuaries, although that role had not as yet been clearly defined to them.

Telescope and computer sales soared with people certain that they personally would figure out where the mysterious planet was lingering and would bring it into "sight," even though the Chinese had come away empty-handed in their more sophisticated probe.

Ian's father became ill very suddenly, and passed away before Ian could return to Cincinnati in time to be with him. Both Ian and his mother had a shared regretted for not having included Ian's father, more than they had, in the several conversations that had ensued after Ian and Sadie's poignant visit.

Birthrates around the world took a dramatic decline with scientists insisting it had nothing to do with this precarious situation, and agreed with the Mayan community that it was probably the result of an inordinate number of sun spots.

Rosenthal realized his error in releasing the amount of information in the manner in which it was done, and took a verbal chastising from the President in the Press as a result. He retracted much of the information that had been released, but continued leading the world charge to confront Nibiru. Rosenthal in turn, then chastised the Press for making too much of the Rosslyn Chapel incident, and emphasized that any ongoing discussion about the Holy Grail existed only between Scotland and Israel. As an additional disclaimer he let it be known, that he personally believed that the Holy Grail belonged in Israel and that his Jewish heritage has nothing to do with his feelings.

Dateline 2022

Nibiru moved through the second leg of its journey from Saturn to Jupiter for the next twelve months still undetected by the body of astronomers searching the skies diligently every day, and sending reports to the world through Cynthia Hyatt's evening newscast.

A dissident group kidnapped Senator Hoesel and held him for ransom for two weeks, before the American government paid three million dollars considering it pocket change in lieu of the circumstance and Hoesel's importance to the success of the mission. Security was dramatically increased around this important asset and two men were killed one month later in a subsequent attempt to abduct the Senator. Their bodies were disposed of almost ruthlessly without any investigation by any governing body. The remains of the two perpetrators in turn were callously displayed in all the Media for over two weeks, and no additional attempts at kidnapping Senator Hoesel were made.

United States sports fans are undaunted by the presumed growing presence of Nibiru, and break attendance records as the Boise Dodgers win the World Series and the San Diageo Bengals triumph in the Super

Bowl. A controversy rages before and after the Dodgers win regarding the inordinate number of both Cuban and Japanese players on the team, which constitutes nearly eighty percent of the total number of players.

The sale of prefabricated underground tornado shelters soar and are in such demand that in an effort to meet the demand kits are offered to those who feel they have the required property and equipment to complete building shelters of their own. Restrictive zoning laws, where they exist, are ignored recognizing the urgency of the situation.

The stockpiling of medicines by the infirmed, who are fearful they will be unable to obtain them, ignites a battle in Congress over the rights of Medicare D patients.

Hoarding that remained in its infancy in 2021 begins to escalate out of control requiring the need for stringent controls by the government in the commodities markets.

Dateline 2023

Nibiru continues on the long journey between Saturn and Jupiter for twelve more months. There are many unconfirmed reports that it has finally been spotted. The most significant precursor of its probable presence occurs in disruptive weather patterns around the world.

A significant increase in earthquakes and volcanic activity is noted. Rain that goes on sometimes for weeks at a time, followed by uncontrolled flooding in areas that are usually considered dry areas, is also noted. People are initially excited about the increase in the rain in normally arid regions believing that important crop growth will result; than ultimately become dismayed when they realize the consequences of the change.

A planned annual summit meeting on global warming is cancelled at the last minute by scientists who are busy with other activities.

The sale of alcohol and cigarette sales soar and actually become black market items because of restrictions imposed on growing the crops required for their manufacture.

Dateline 2024

Nibiu passes Jupiter and begins its journey en route to Mars and ultimately appears like a huge star larger than Mars in the night sky. Activist religious groups perceive it is being equivalent to the star that led the Magi to Jerusalem and begin pilgrimages heading to hundreds of different sacred places in the world to make ready for a new messiah, who they believe has yet to be born.

In celebration of the now visible Nibiru Senator Holland is carried through the streets of Jerusalem on the back of an ass wearing a long white gown and sandals. The Vatican initially denies that Holland has any religious significance, than ultimately embrace him as a great prophet.

Conflicts become intense particularly in the middle-east and the Western Press publishes article after article about the long term effect of the Crusades that happened almost a thousand years ago.

Many Jews from countries around the world riot at airports which, following government orders, deny them passage to fly to the Holy City of Jerusalem.

Food hoarding and riots again become the order of the day. Riots related to food are so rampant in underdeveloped countries in the context of so many different subjects and events, that they are essentially ignored. What food is available in those ravaged areas is closely guarded by the elite and government of the countries for their personal consumption.

The number of earthquakes and volcanoes increases every day as Nibiru begins more and more to make its presence known. Tsunamis following earthquake activity have now become a major factor in world events, particularly in the middle-east. Relief efforts have by this time been drained from a plethora of other disasters and thousands of people are left to deal with nature's wrath.

The news analyst Cynthia Hyatt reports each new occurrence and lists a daily tally on both earthquakes and new volcanoes erupting.

Bob Schmidt is injured while working with local police trying to quell the activities of overly aggressive protesters. The injury isn't serious but sends him home for a week of recovery.

Governments begin to hoard fuel for their Spacebus activity moving Ionic Thruster parts to the Moon to be erected there. Governments, also in anticipation of the need to fly Spacejets to deliver their nuclear payloads for the 27.3 days required to effectively move the Moon into the path of Nibiru begin strict regulations on the distribution and use of gasoline. All but limited commercial use of gasoline is prohibited and pleasure cars begin to sit idle in garages. Ultimately the masses are forced to rely on public transportation or just plain hoofing it.

Horses and other draft animals regain a new stature in communities around the world, although in some countries they're slaughtered to meet an immediate need for food.

Patel's Preservation shelter in India is discovered and ransacked by a group dedicated to "survival today". He does his best to relocate those people with the highest and most important skill levels to other sanctuaries. Remarkably no one is killed in the intrusion which is both forced and aggressive.

Stock markets around the world nose dive as people begin to trade stocks for hard assets such as gold, silver and precious stones.

Another major government investigation on "short selling" in the United States stops all market activity for over a week creating yet another riot, this time on Wall Street as clients attempt a run on the Market akin to that like the run on the Banks in the early 1900's.

The Vatican issues another statement, reversing an earlier stand, asking that Nibiru and its people be embraced as a positive entity.

The Egyptians reveal they have completed work in building a time capsule from huge granite blocks similar to the Great Pyramid. They insist, but refuse to validate that they have also successfully located the Hall of Records, and have included all of its information in this new venture to enlighten future civilizations about all of mankind's accomplishments.

The United States government allows enough resources to be diverted from the Moon project to launch a rocket into space with updated information on our DNA, history and current unwieldy situation.

The Commission and its members maintain their focus, and construction of the Thrusters is completed far ahead of schedule. They become operational at a low level on a test basis and are not yet affecting the movement of the moon, but run essentially in an idle position.

The best pilots from countries around the world have completed training that will allow them to fly the newly designed Spacejets to the moon and back to feed the Thrusters with their nuclear payloads. Unfortunately, because of Scotty's role in the program, conversation between Scotty and Ian is greatly restricted and Ian essentially loses contact with his son, uncertain of his whereabouts or progression in the special program.

Dateline 2025

Nibiru grows brighter and brighter in the evening sky outshining Venus. For the next three months it continues to become larger and even brighter in the morning and evening skies until it appears like a huge sun looming behind the Moon. In the morning when the Moon appears as a faint grey ball in the sky it is particularly ominous to see Nibiru behind it, seemingly beginning to envelop it.

Spacejets have been running daily sorties to the Thrusters on the Moon depositing their nuclear payloads before jetting back to the safety of Earth, putting unreasonable strain on the bodies of the pilots as they accelerate away from the explosions at speeds of over Mach three following their deliveries.

The Thrusters easily suck in and absorb the nuclear particles left in their wake seeming to grunt as they push the Moon ahead of them for its encounter with Nibiru.

The effects of Nibiru's presence this close to Earth are already being felt with ever increasingly violent, volcanic activity, excessive winds around the world, and a growing number of reported earth quakes with consequent devastating tsunamis. The world remains intact however, holding its breath waiting for this growing torment to end.

Ian and Sadie have returned to their Chicago Condo after hanging out at the Hyatt in Washington until boredom and gloom in the face of the coming disaster completely overtook them. Patel's continual insistence that they be a part of his plan finally convinced them there was a place and opportunity for them to lead an effort in the Chicago area to develop a sanctuary. Their contacts at the University of Chicago make it a natural for the success of the sanctuary. The exact location of the sanctuary is known by a relatively few, after the incident in India regarding Patel's sanctuary, and is believed by some to actually be located in northern Iowa, rather than the Chicago area, utilizing local tornado shelter technology.

Another rumor persists for some time that it may have been established on a collection old barges floating on Lake Michigan.

Dateline April 25, 2025

Ian rushed into the bedroom of their condo and shook Sadie, who had suffered from mild exhaustion in the never ending work involved in their new vocation and was fast asleep, "Wake up Babe, we've got to go to O'Hare and there's a car waiting for us. Tarnowski sent one of the government limos over to get us."

Sadie sat up and rubbed the sleep out of her eyes, "Are we going to the shelter, its time you know. This is it Ian."

"I know, but Tarnowski, our old buddy, called and this is something else. According to him, Scotty apparently placed second in his class out of the total number of pilot's in the program, and because of that placement is flying one of the last two Spacejets for the final payloads to be delivered to the Thrusters; and its happening out of O'Hare airport. Apparently Rosenthal remembered us and sent Tarnowski to get us. There's going to be a lot of people there, but they've made room for us," he grinned at Sadie, who was on her feet, dressed and already putting her makeup on, "take a wild guess who the only other pilot involved is, the guy who scored first ahead of Scotty."

Sadie looked reflectively and posed her answer more like a question than a statement, "Anwar?" She shook her head in a kind of disbelief, "Major Glickstien is back."

Ian corrected her, "Colonel Glickstien, come on they're waiting for us.

The infrastructure of society was beginning to break down around the world as Nibiru made its presence known more and more each day that passed, and Chicago was no exception. Ian led the way as they darted down six flights of stairs to the waiting limo. Elevators had stopped running almost two months ago when large turbine generators, which supplied power to cities like Chicago, began to shut down one by one; failing either from economic shortfalls of fuel or a battering from the ravages of the now present Nibiru.

Where reliable power was an absolute necessity, such as the current event at O'Hare Airport the government utilized large portable power units

Refrigerated foods were fast becoming a thing of the past and both Ian and Sadie munched on an energy bar en route to the limo in their descent down the stairs.

Many of the high rise luxury apartments had become deserted because of the lack of power available, and many of the lower storied units were being shared by people who until recently were strangers to each other. The world had already changed dramatically, but was still not ready for what probably lay ahead.

The limo was waiting at the curb with two handsome young army lieutenants standing at attention, guns holstered on their sides, waiting with doors open for their entry. The lieutenants looked like no nonsense guys on a mission, and had a sense of urgency to them. They ushered Sadie and then Ian into the limo with a minimum of polite conversation and took off without another word racing through streets empty of all but military vehicles.

Sadie sat back and sighed, "What about the sanctuary, shouldn't we be there?"

"Tarnowski said he would take care of transportation for us, which may actually make it easier to get there than what we had planned."

"What is he doing when this thing hits us? Do he and Berger and the others have a place to go?"

"They have made their own accommodations which he declined to share with me, but suggested we might be able to join them in a pinch."

"What about our sanctuary, don't they need us?" She was growing more concerned as the conversation went on about what Ian considered an imponderable. He came back a little snippy, more worried that the sanctuary might actually fail without his and Sadie's constant support, than he was with Sadie's concern.

The rest of the ride to the airport was quiet and uneasy with more going on that particular day at O'Hare Airport than most people have to deal with in a life time, and everyone including Ian and Sadie mulling it over and over in their heads.

Upon arrival they were escorted to the control tower where many high level people were bustling around. Rosenthal stood up from a seat and waved to them, and then immediately sat back down to attend to some important task in front of him. Ian saw Scotty and Anwar being led over to where Rosenthal was sitting. They didn't see him and he resigned himself to settle into the situation when a familiar voice standing beside him asked, "How are you Dr. MacGown?" Sadie, who heard the familiar voice, leaned across Ian from the other side and answered before Ian had a chance, "Senator Hyatt, how are you?" Sadie couldn't resist, even in a situation as dire as this one, "we've seen a lot of you on the news."

Hyatt undaunted came back, "Why thank you Dr. Haddad, may I call you Sadie?" She didn't wait for Ian to acknowledge her greeting but pointed in the direction of Scotty and Anwar, "They're the two who fly this last mission. The older guy is an Israeli Colonel and the tall black kid is American," She paused admiring Scotty, "He's really handsome."

Ian, who had stood studying Scotty trying to take his psychological pulse finally acknowledged Hyatt, "That's my son."

She in turn grinned back at him with a quizzical look and said, "Ah, I can see the resemblance."

Ian undaunted smiled back, "He looks like his mother."

Another voice entered the conversation from behind them, "Yeah, the kid got lucky and didn't get his father's looks." Once again Ian had to endure the bear hug from behind as he had many times throughout his adult life, "Smitty, why are you always sneaking up behind me, it's embarrassing."

Schmidt let go of Ian and gave Sadie one of his bear hugs looking over her shoulder as he did smiling at Ian, "Don't care, I'm here to take care of you guys, got to do my best to keep you out of trouble." He released Sadie and smiled sheepishly, "Actually, to be honest I've got my family here, Rosenthal set it up for us to be included in the refuge package that's been established for the Commission members. I thought you were also to be included, I know Scotty is when he gets back."

Ian took his friend Smitty by the shoulders and embraced him the best he could without hugging him back, "Thank you Smitty, we're okay, but would not have been without you. Whatever happens, it's been a great friendship."

Schmidt a little awkward with the sincerity of the moment snarled back at Ian and put his arm around Sadie, "I only did it when you brought this lovely lady into the picture."

Sadie saved them from themselves, "Okay enough you guys, there's still a lot that has to be done."

A speaker system blared out interrupting them, and asking them to leave the control tower to find a place marked out for them on the tarmac below.

It was 7:30 AM and the group of observers including Ian, Sadie and Schmidt descended from the Control Tower to the tarmac to observe the take off of the two Spacejets. The Spacejets were designed similarly to Columbia and Challenger crafts but with the distinct difference of being able to take off at runway speeds before accelerating as a rocket to speeds of 18000 MPH on their way to the moon.

Upon arrival at the moon they would deliver their payload at speeds of Mach two and then accelerate away from the explosion at Mach three speeds before heading back to Earth for a runway landing. Only the very best, well conditioned and trained pilots were able to carry out this grueling task.

Round trip to complete their mission would take over twenty-seven hours requiring the pilot to be at full alert for most of the mission except for a short cat nap during his descent back to Earth. Mission control had installed an automatic alarm system as a kind of fail safe to go off after the Spacejet had been airborne for twenty-four hours to be certain pilots were awake for the final descent and landing. In addition they were in constant communication throughout the flight.

A loud speaker blared out to those on the tarmac telling them what to expect from minute to minute. They watched as two Spacejets taxied onto the runway, one of them painted to emulate peeling, white paint and a picture of the Great Pyramid on its side; a little hokey perhaps, but a small concession to someone who had scored highest in his class and was about to risk his life for all of mankind. Then with a burst of speed the Spacejets shot off the runway banking sharply, and then shooting straight upward, rapidly disappearing from view.

Sadie who stood at the edge of the crowd on the tarmac watching their ascent into the heavens began jumping up and down, clapping her hands, grabbing Ian by the arm, "Look, Ian look." Ian turned in the direction pointed to by Sadie to see three men in shinning white garments, faces aglow, standing, saluting the departing Spacejets, then turning and facing them on the tarmac, saluting two people who with wisdom and grit, and a little help from some friends, were able to give civilization one more chance to survive, and perhaps to ultimately flourish as never before, if they could just make it over this one last bump.

Sadie with tears rolling down her cheeks and still clutching Ian's arm asked, "Do you think it will work Ian?"

She could feel the tension in his body ease as the Spacejets disappeared and the "Shinning Ones" faded away holding their salute.

Ian's response was non-committal, "It didn't the last time," He paused not sure of what he wanted to say, "But it's got to this time."

*

It wasn't quite over and Ian and Sadie returned that evening, with the moon bright in the sky above, albeit against the backdrop of Nibiru. The crowd had reassembled on the tarmac listening to conversation, which blared out from speakers in the control tower, between the two valiant pilots and Rosenthal.

Ian winched as he heard Scotty shouting back from space, "We've got a problem Control, we've got a problem. Colonel Glickstien's jet looks like it took a hit from some flying debris. It looks like it came from one of the thrusters, which is starting to come apart. I've lost communication with him."

Anwar's voice suddenly blared over the speakers, "Sorry mates, I couldn't talk for a second, I've been busy with other things. I'm trying to keep this sucker flying."

The panic in Rosenthal's voice rang out for all to hear, "Are you all right Aaron, are you all right? Can you finish the mission?"

"I'm still flying, just not as well as I used to." The response seemed to silence all but the crackling noise of space.

"Can you……" Rosenthal's question, unfinished, left hanging was interrupted by Scotty's voice, calm, but demanding, "What do you want us to do Control?"

Anwar didn't wait for a response from the ground and took command, "Get in there kid, do your part, I'll finish the job. Go, there's not much time."

Scotty's voice rang out again, "I'm going in mate, get out of my way."

A thud was heard over the speakers then Scotty's voice again, "Bingo, I'm out, your turn mate."

Rosenthal shouted in his mike, "Good job Scotty, well done. Aaron, are you still there? Are you okay?"

There was an ominous pause, "Yep, I'm still here. I'm okay, but I'm afraid this buggy is shot. I can deliver the package, and I'll give it a shot to get out, but if……, let my wife and daughter know I was thinking of them and that I will love them forever."

Rosenthal's voice shouted frantically, "Aaron, don't……"

Anwar's response was understood by only a few of those watching and listening, "Just another day at the office, just a……"

Chapter 20: The Last Chapter

Anwar's last heroic thrust sent Nibiru careening away from the Earth, and although Nibiru did a little more damage before heading back into space, everyone agreed it was not as bad as it could have been. Actually the world was saved that day and civilization although, a little more tattered then when this story began was still intact.

The mystery as to why Nibiru was able to enter our known solar system undetected for most of its passage towards Earth was never solved or understood, and there was never a clear consensus regarding who the real bad guys were. I personally think that each of the people involved was trying to do what they thought was best for everyone, although it can be very difficult to find someone willing to take the hard lick necessary to save the rest of us. Thank God Anwar found his way into our story.

Patel's sanctuaries, established around the world, would provide much of what was needed to offset some of the shortages that would continue to cause problems for many years ahead until fallen infrastructures could be reestablished. He had correctly anticipated what it would take to keep civilization going. I don't have to spell it out for you. I'm sure you would have done the same thing given the chance.

I'm also sure there are many Rosenthal's, Berger's and Tarnowski's who will always search for answers and develop solutions to important problems. They in turn will always derive support from unsung heroes like Malick, Hoesel, Brown and Ligget, and of course Hyatt will always be there to keep us informed.

We salute them all. Ian for his bravery in standing tall when it was uncomfortable, Smitty for his loyalty and unending service, and most of all Sadie, who was tuned into knowledge from any source, mystical, ancient or a new idea from a friend. She offered us genuine humanity and spirit by offering wisdom and knowledge without boundaries.

The world and civilization are safe for the moment and as far as we know it will probably be another thousand years or so before we need another Oracle of Knowledge, or one brave man to come forward and save us. Who knows from whence they'll get their help next time.

Made in United States
Orlando, FL
10 February 2025

58362422R00166